# River's Child

# River's Child

MARK DANIEL SEILER

OWL HOUSE BOOKS

Published in 2018 by Owl House Books
Front Cover Image © By Tithi Luadthong | Shutterstock.com
Cover and Interior Designed by Leslie M. Browning
ISBN 978-1-947003-39-2
First Edition Trade Paperback

Owl House Books
An Imprint of Homebound Publications
WWW.HOMEBOUNDPUBLICATIONS.COM

10 9 8 7 6 5 4 3 2 1

Owl House Books, like all imprints of Homebound Publications, is committed to ecological stewardship. We greatly value the natural environment and invest in environmental conservation. Our books are printed on paper with chain of custody certification from the Forest Stewardship Council, Sustainable Forestry Initiative, and the Program for the Endorsement of Forest Certification.

# Longyearbyen Village, Spitsbergen

To see things in a seed, that is genius.
—Lao Tzu

"Hey, Chief, you gonna do a rain dance for us?"

Mavin ignored the insult and tried to get the barmaid's attention. The world's northernmost brewpub was packed to the gills.

Sebastian Volkov held court in his usual booth near the cocktail waitress station. "Chief, where is your bow and arrow?"

Mavin's mind ignored the slur, but his body turned and walked up to the table of six Russian fishermen.

The Svalbar went quiet.

Locals assumed by Mavin's dark hair, brown eyes and complexion that he was Inuit. When they caught wind he was American Indian, they seldom could fight the urge to play cowboys and Indians.

"Leave it, Mavin!" Lars knew that look in his best friend's eye; things were about to get ugly.

Mavin glared at Sebastian. "Comrades." He was outnumbered six to one. Locals knew better than to drink down at the Five Bells, the fisherman's pub at the harbor. The island's only ambulance was permanently parked across from the pier. Bloody brawls were common, and Sebastian was more often than not in the middle of things.

Mavin reached into his pocket and pulled out a wad of bills. His grandpa Latigo would say he was cowboy rich. "Any of you gentlemen care to make a small wager?"

"Fifty Kroner says the Injun can make it rain." Sebastian laughed and lit a cigarette. Maybe he wasn't a chuckcha, but was there much of a difference between an Eskimo and an Indian?

"I was thinking more along the lines of a dip in the harbor. First one out of the drink buys a round for the house. What do you say?" Mavin threw down the gauntlet.

A deafening roar erupted. Locals knew a win-win when they heard one.

Sebastian leaped to his feet, spit in his hand, and shook on it. "Evidently, Chief, you don't know my nickname."

The entire clientele of the Svalbar followed the two contenders down Main Street to the harbor.

Trish Fuller, who worked with Mavin at the seed vault, whistled as he unzipped and pulled down his wool pants. He looked her way, keeping his game face on as he pulled off his boxers. He swung them over his head three times before jumping in the icy slush.

An appreciative cheer broke out from the growing crowd.

Sebastian, embarrassed to still be standing on the dock, jumped in wearing his black socks.

Trish stood on the pier gripping the rail. The look on Mavin's face disturbed her. Was he relaxed or so angry that the ice-cold water wasn't bothering him?

Drunken fishermen poured out of The Five Bells and joined the Russian cheering section. "Da-vai! Go, Sea Bass!" They didn't care to drink with chuckchas. "Go, Sea Bass!"

Lars mingled with the fisherman and took bets on the side.

Sebastian flopped around in the slush directing a stream of obscenities at his adversary.

Mavin didn't understand a word of Russian, but he wanted to ask, "Can we leave my mother out of this?"

Sebastian's buddies pulled him out ten minutes later when he stopped flopping and began to sink. The fishermen booed and spat. Lars helped Mavin up on the dock and held on to his arm until he could stand on his own.

Trish held her hand over her mouth, giggling in delight. She couldn't help but notice the effect the icy water had on her champion's anatomy.

When they got back to the pub everyone switched from beer to vodka. After several rounds of shots, all was forgiven. Sebastian bear-hugged Mavin. "Chief, you must be part Inuit."

"Thanks, Sea Bass. I'll take that as a compliment," though, Mavin was pretty sure it wasn't meant as one. His jaw was still chattering.

An hour before his shift, the neighbor's three malamutes caught wind of a fox. Their staccato barking landed like bricks on Mavin's head. He rolled out of bed and staggered into the bathroom. "Beer and vodka is a terrible combination," he informed his reflection in the mirror. He bundled up and jumped in his trusty Toyota and turned her over. She always started, no matter how cold it got. He backed out of the drive until he heard a pop.

"Shit!"

He slammed on the brakes, remembering that he'd forgotten to unplug the engine heater. He got out to inspect the damage. "Nothing a little duct tape can't cure." He looked up and saw the Kittywake gull circling high overhead. "You ready to go to work?" He was amazed how regularly the bird followed him up the mountain.

The blast doors of the seed vault reflected the morning sun like a lighthouse beacon showing the way. He rubbed the ice off the driver's side window with his elbow and spotted the gull. His left front tire struck a chunk of ice causing the steering wheel to pop out of his gloved hand. He maneuvered back into the snowplow's wake. The BBC news faded in and out like a shortwave radio, "Americans living on the eastern seaboard are bracing themselves for superstorm Samantha. The category five hurricane is expected to make landfall at 2:30 GMT, bludgeoning the eastern coast with winds exceeding 250 kilometers per hour... flash flood warnings have been posted from New England to Northern Florida... FEMA estimates the death toll...."

Mavin had heard enough. "You like music?" He looked up at the gull and nudged the Gypsy Kings's CD in the slot.

*Un amor*
*Un amor viví*
*Llorando. Y me decía*
*Las palabras de Dios*

He belted out the lyrics in perfect unison and imagined the gull flying over the green hills of Catalonia, not the frozen island of Spitsbergen.

"Longyearbyen is right," he confessed to the gull. "The village founders knew their apples. Truth-in-advertizing, baby. This must be the longest year on record."

Einstein measured the universe using the constant speed of light. In a world of unpredictable weather, there remained one constant, it was going to be a cold shitty day on Spitsbergen. The endless midnight sun was currently producing a scorching two degrees above the donut, accompanied by a stiff northeasterly breeze gusting to 45 knots. He did the math; wind-chill 30 degrees below zero, the perfect summer day. When he emerged from the canyon of plowed snow, a gust of wind rocked the suspension of his rig.

He wasn't one of the longest running employees at the Svalbard seed vault for nothing. He knew his special gift was doing miserable better than other people; just ask Sea Bass or his own ex-girlfriend. "Who knew that not remembering to put the toilet seat down could cause a major international incident?"

If sleeping on the top of the world in endless daylight wasn't enough to make you crazy, then working underground all day finished the job. "It may not be Shangri-La, but at least it's not the frickin' desert." He kicked the defroster down a notch. He didn't miss the heat one bit.

"Gemini!" An arctic fox darted across the narrow track. Mavin pumped his brakes and swerved. He looked in the rearview mirror.

The white fox stood on the side of the road, its red eyes reflecting the brake lights. "You've all frickin' day! So yeah, why not wait for the only rig on the road before you decide to cross?" He remembered how coyotes would dart across the dirt road in front of his grandpa's pickup when he was a kid. He looked out across the windblown landscape and chuckled. This part of Svalbard was considered high arctic polar desert. He had traded a hot desert for a frozen one.

"Don't feel alone, Mrs. Fox. Everyone on Mysterious Island is bonkers," he mused. Either you arrived in said condition, or it was a short wait. Gunnarson, his boss was a cross between a cuckoo clock maker and a hatter. In a house full of wing nuts it was easy enough to bluff having your lid screwed down tight.

He parked in the lot at the end of the plowed road and climbed into the back of the rig. The sled seat was frozen and hard. He flipped on the choke, pulled the rope three times and gunned the Ski-Doo until it held an idle. The two cycle oil fumes tasted syrupy through his wool scarf. The aluminum ramp was hopelessly frozen to the bed of the truck, so he pulled his goggles over his Ray-Bans, and launched into the powder dry snow. It was a short ten-minute ride up the mountain to the vault.

He pulled his left glove off with his teeth, punched in the security code and looked into the iris scanner. "Come on, Kep." He glanced up at the security camera. "Get a wiggle on. It's frickin' freezing out here! And, I seriously need to take a leak." The wind reached under his parka. When the blast doors finally opened, he bounded in and hit Level Two.

When the elevator doors slid closed his eyes immediately relaxed, grateful to have a break from the endless daylight glaring off the snow. He propped his shades on top of his head. Despite the high-speed lift, it took five long minutes to travel the four hundred feet below the surface.

The solitary ride into the heart of the mountain provided a moment to reflect on what he was doing with his life. The vault had started out as a passive hole in the sandstone mountain where the permafrost would preserve the world's seeds, come hell or high water. And then the world changed.

Despite decades of warnings from the scientific community, rapid changes in the atmosphere caught the world by surprise. The four seasons were replaced by too hot, too cold, too wet, and too dry. Whether you believed in an angry god in the heavens or carbon dioxide in the atmosphere, the result was the same. Super storms were the new enemy of humankind.

In an ever-changing environment of droughts and floods, the Svalbard seed vault had become a symbol of human survival. The Global Crop Diversity Trust reached rock star status. Mavin showed up for work every day, but he was beginning to lose trust in the Trust. Rather than being the cure everyone claimed, maybe the vault was more of a symptom of just how precarious life on earth had become. It was a Hail Mary shot just before the buzzer.

Earlier in the year, the wall had been breached. Under intense political pressure, Norway reversed its policy and began allowing importation of genetically modified organisms into the country. Money flowed like milk and honey from the big agro-chemical companies. The facility was in the middle of yet another expansion. With little difference between day and night in the summer, double shifts were running through the end of September. Roughneck construction workers mixed with plant biologists and computer scientists.

Mavin missed being out in the field collecting seeds from their places of origin. Dr. Sinclair, his favorite professor, had taken Mavin under his wing while still in grad school. Dr. Sinclair was famous for finding the oldest variety of wheat on the planet. Nothing but a lowly looking weed, and completely inedible, a single tiny grain held a treasure trove of genetic information. From this humble plant, geneticists were able to produce drought-resistant strains of wheat to feed millions of people worldwide.

Just before Dr. Sinclair retired, he and his young assistant delivered their field collections from the Indian subcontinent to Svalbard. When they arrived at the seed vault there was rampant chaos due to a complete electrical system failure.

The director, Stine Gunnarson met Dr. Sinclair at the gate and explained the situation. The backup generators had kicked on and were running smoothly, but for some unknown reason, the entire facility remained without lights or power. "Our electrical foreman has two crews working around the clock to correct the problem."

"Sounds like a job for Mavin." Sinclair pointed out his young assistant. "That's him over there talking to the guy in the orange hardhat. I'll loan him to you, Gunnarson, under one condition; I get him back once the lights are back on."

"Is he an electrician?" Gunnarson looked the kid over.

"Ever wondered how they built the pyramids? I suspect it was a bunch of skinny kids like him. Problems and obstacles are his playthings." Dr. Sinclair knew where this was heading. Was there ever a more undisciplined student? He would sorely miss his protégé.

Once Mavin verified the main breakers were off, he borrowed a flashlight and followed an array of conduits from the main panel down the long dark tunnel. The conduits were strapped to the side of the round corrugated metal culvert lining the passageway. Three hundred feet inside the mountain, his flashlight flickered and died. No light from the entrance reached him. "Just like being in the bottom of a kiva," he said to the flashlight and pounded it on the heel of his palm. The bulb flickered. He walked slowly, aiming the weak beam on the conduit and noticed an icicle completely encasing a junction box. He chipped away with his Swiss Army knife until he could unscrew the j-box cover and carefully dig out the ice from around the wire connections. Forty-five minutes later the facility had power.

Gunnarson broke his promise to Sinclair. That afternoon he made Mavin a generous offer to stay on at the fledgling seed vault. "We could use a jack of all trades around here."

Mavin loved traveling the world with Dr. Sinclair, but his mentor was retiring. It was next to impossible to find work with a degree in biology. Later that evening, he met Sinclair at the Svalbar for a whiskey. They were both already feeling the loss.

Mavin raised his glass and offered a toast to his mentor and friend. "Mobilis in Mobili," quoting the motto of the *Nautilus*. "Changing amidst the changes."

"Here, here." Sinclair raised his glass. "Aside from the Latin, Nemo's motto certainly sounds Buddhist. One forgets the Captain of the *Nautilus* was from India."

Mavin loved Sinclair like the father he never knew. "So, Professor Aronnax, do you think I should take the job?" Keeping up the game helped Mavin from becoming overwhelmed with emotion and embarrassing them both. Stiff upper lip, he told himself.

Sinclair enjoyed hearing his protégé call him Professor Aronnax, Jules Verne's famous character and narrator of, *Twenty Thousand Leagues Under the Sea*. He played along, calling Mavin by Nemo's given name. "You know very well, Prince Dakkar, that opportunities present themselves for a reason."

"Spitsbergen is a Mysterious Island."

"Indeed."

* * * *

Mavin's full bladder felt the lift slow before the chime sounded. When the elevator doors opened he sprinted for the lavatory.

"Morning, Beard." Trish was just coming out of the bathroom.

"Hey, Trish." He hurried in and kicked the door closed. He reached down to lift the toilet lid forgetting about his Ray Bans. They slid off his head directly into the bowl. "What the—" He reached in and plucked them out with two fingers. "The toilet seat strikes back!" He emptied his bladder and washed his sunglasses and hands with the smelly foam soap from the wall dispenser. The paper towel dispenser was empty. "Talk about a Monday morning."

When he reached his small cubicle on Level Five, he logged on to Kep. "Only a hundred and fifty-nine unread emails. And a hundred and forty-eight of them junk. Kep, you're one of the most powerful computers in the world. How about a little help filtering my junk mail? Speaking of the gods of spam, why's Gunnarson writing me?" He clicked on the director's email.

U.S. Senator, Ted Collins from Texas and the directors of Syngenta, DowDuPont Pioneer, and Monsanto are scheduled to tour the facility at 9:00 am. Director Gunnarson's flight was delayed in Oslo, due to inclement weather. Mavin read the last paragraphs, "Mavin Cedarstrom is to act as docent. Under no circumstances is he to use the term, 'Doomsday Vault.'"

Director Gunnarson waged a losing battle against the seed vault's nickname.

"That's just frickin' great." Mavin's fingers flew over the keyboard as he responded to Gunnarson and then deleted the junk mail from his inbox. "The hits keep rolling in. So much for getting any actual work done." Mavin didn't mind leading tours.

Aside from having to wear a tie, he even enjoyed it, depending on the group. This was different. Mavin was not happy about the Norwegian government being coerced into allowing genetically modified seeds to be stored in the facility. The directors of Monsanto and Syngenta were coming, no doubt, to view one of the last castles of the enemy to fall.

He was painfully aware of where most of the construction budget and the money to run the facility came from. The big money was in designing and patenting genetically modified seeds. His mentor, professor Sinclair had a deep affinity for open-pollinated plants. Pollen flowing between individual plants allows them to adapt to local conditions because they are connected to their environment. The original purpose of the seed vault was to protect diversity. "Hello? What's the point?" he asked Kep, using a fake Southern drawl. "Jobs," he answered. "Darling, my paycheck's enough for a coupla cases of beer." He let the song write itself, "Sweetheart, it's Monday all frickin' week long till Friday is here."

\* \* \* \*

Mavin went to his locker on Level Two and put on a dress shirt, tie and blazer before meeting the group on Level One. The vips were in a sugar huddle by the lift entrance, all dressed in white lab coats and shiny blue hardhats. "My name is Mavin Cedarstrom, I'll be your guide today. Director Gunnerson's flight was delayed in Oslo. He regrets not being able to welcome you personally to the Svalbard Global Seed Vault."

It suddenly occurred to Mavin that Gunnerson had missed his flight on purpose. Perhaps he had misjudged "Old Stine" as he was affectionately known.

"You're standing three hundred and ninety feet inside of a sandstone mountain," Mavin continued. "To give you an idea of the scale, that's roughly the equivalent of a forty-story building, or the height of the tallest living thing, Sequoia sempervirens."

Their blank expressions told him he was in for a long morning. Should I have said, redwood tree? He wondered. "I'm sure you couldn't help but notice the titanium blast doors at the top of the lift. Svalbard is not a seed bank—but a seed vault. The facility is designed to survive a direct nuclear attack."

He scanned the group for brain activity and forged on. "Level One is the original passive vault, designed with minimum technology. The geography and the geology alone ensure the stability and security of these seeds for centuries."

Rows of metal shelving were crammed full of hundreds of black cases filled with vacuum packed four-ply bags of seeds. The sight of the planet's entire plant genome was doing precious little to spark the imagination of the special guests. Mavin closed his eyes before rolling them. He decided to skip to Level Five.

"Here on five we have the servers for our Linux-based supercomputer, Kepler 22b, Kep for short. If you're keeping track, Kep was named after the super-earth located 600 light years from earth. Kep's architecture is similar to the human brain. Like dendrites, Kep interconnects using a three-dimensional folded torus network. As we move through the facility, Kep is monitoring our location, our vital signs, as well as the air temperature, humidity, the current weather outside and around the globe. Kep is a storehouse of all human knowledge, the entire history of civilization, every book, song, poem, magazine, newspaper and film ever made. Kep is an up to the minute digital library containing everything from that funny YouTube of a puppy playing Beethoven, to how to split an atom. A colossal earth battery provides power for Kep, and the entire facility. Tens of thousands of copper and iron rods driven into the frozen tundra three feet apart covered half the island. The

rods produced an inexhaustible source of energy. In the event of
a global catastrophe, Kep is programmed to go into sleep mode
for centuries."

"Why spend the money for a supercomputer if the goal is to
simply store information?"

"That's an excellent question." It surprised Mavin that a brain
had been installed in one of the clones. "Kep considers millions
of options per second and is capable of basic decision making.
In the event of a global catastrophe, Kep is capable of managing
the facility."

The Monsanto CEO suggested to the Syngenta CFO that their
company might turn a profit if Kep were put in charge.

Mavin did his best to ignore their inane bantering.

Mavin noticed that the clones were talking rather than listening, so he herded them back into the lift. He decided to skip
Level Six, knowing the mechanical systems wouldn't be of much
interest. When the elevator doors opened on Level Seven, the
group went quiet.

"The moment you've all been waiting for—Level Seven. The
newest and final phase of the facility is home to our cryogenics
vault where select seeds are frozen in liquid nitrogen and helium.
This vault contains three hundred triple-walled stainless storage
tanks, which in turn hold 330 smaller metal containers. These
smaller containers hold up to as many as 27,000 samples depending on the size of the seed."

The group of VIPs, fanned out into the vestibule.

"For your continued safety, Kep is monitoring the oxygen
content in the air. In the event of an accidental gas leak, an array
of giant fans exchange the air on this entire level every 90 seconds." Mavin gave his best impersonation of a flight attendant,
signaling with his arms. "In the unlikely event of an emergency,
exit through the doors to your right. Follow the lit stairs to Level
Six and out the emergency evacuation tunnel."

Most of the group had long since become immune to the sound of Mavin's voice and were trying to find bars on their smartphones, or taking selfies.

Mavin sojourned on, "Behind the six-inch thick blast-proof glass, seeds are being prepared for deep-freeze. I regret that visitors are not permitted in the cryo lab. Aside from issues of contamination, our hardhats would not afford us much protection against minus 180 degrees Celsius. Don't feel slighted, I've worked here for years and I've never—"

"Son, do you expect me to believe that freezing a million packets of garden seeds is going to keep the world safe?" Senator Collins from Texas had heard enough.

"I wasn't suggesting…"

"Not a single word out of your mouth today has made a lick a sense. How can you justify spending seven billion dollars on a mountain filled with foil packets of sunflower seeds?"

The GMO executives chuckled to each other.

Mavin didn't want help from the clones. "Senator, do you believe god created all these seeds?"

"Well, of course he did."

"Well sir, we're making it our business to protect his creation." Mavin was an old hand at dealing with people who harbored a distrust of anything scientific.

"You're saying you're doing God's work?"

"Think of the mountain as a Noah's Ark for plants. No other structure in history has been constructed with this kind of time horizon in mind. This facility is engineered to last for tens of thousands of years."

"You're saying this is Mount Ararat?" The senator scoffed. A week ago he didn't know this tiny Norwegian island existed.

Mavin was tempted to inform the senator how the Taliban had destroyed Afghanistan's seed bank back in 2001, but he had no wish to prolong the discussion. Thankfully, he noticed Trish coming through the airlock and to the rescue. The remaining security seal opened with an impressive burst of frozen gas, like a steam locomotive pulling into the station.

Trish smiled and handed out thick blue rubber gloves.

"Thank you for your attention. I'm leaving you in the capable hands of Dr. Trish Fuller. Please enjoy the rest of your time in Svalbard." Mavin wasn't surprised when not one of the special guests acknowledged or thanked him for his time.

Senator Collins pulled on a pair of rubber gloves with help from his young female aide. Dr. Fuller handed him a sealed container of liquid nitrogen. "Young lady, why freeze frozen seeds? It doesn't make sense." Senator Collins admonished. "Throwing good money after bad."

"You may call me, Dr. Fuller." She gave the senator a stern look. She wasn't his girl Friday. "In 2012 a team of Russian scientist germinated a 32,000-year-old date palm seed. The seed was found in 124-foot deep layer of Siberian permafrost." When she saw the lack of reaction from the group, Trish shot a glance at Mavin, pleading with him not to abandon her.

Mavin responded by beating an immediate retreat to the heated cafeteria on Level Three. The cook, Mrs. Jenson, caught him leaving the serving spoon in the mashed potatoes, a transgression of the highest order. He could see Mrs. Jenson downloading her launch codes and decided to forgo the mushroom chicken and make a run for it. Lars Albjorn sat at their usual table.

"Hey, Mavin. How were the bigwigs? Did they have you by the short hairs?"

"Very funny." Although Lars was a gifted computer programmer, he never tired of prepubescent humor. "Uneventful, would be overselling the experience." Mavin pulled his tie off and stuffed it in his coat pocket. "You can't teach that kind of knuckle-dragging stupidity. It must be passed down generation to generation.

If it's necessary to explain the importance of safeguarding the world's plant genome to adults, then you probably should know better than to try."

"That bad?"

"Absolutely nothing to recommend the experience, other than every time I do a tour, I strengthen my bargaining position with Gunnarson. He knows we need more rack space for heirlooms."

"Good luck with that, heirlooms are old hat."

"Bite your tongue," Mavin barked. Most of the things he cherished were old hat. "You can't genetically improve a seed without information, information that exists only in the original seeds."

"Come on, Mavin you can't roll back the clock to the good old days. Norway reversed its position on genetically modified organisms, so man up." Lars reached over with his fork and took a shovel-full of Mavin's mashed potatoes, destroying the side of the gravy crater.

"Why do you even work here, Lars? Or do you work here? I've never actually seen you do anything. You don't even like plants. You certainly don't believe in anything, let alone the environment." Mavin moved his spuds out of Lars's boarding house reach.

"Programmers are like detectives. We follow the money."

"Exactly my point. Thank you." Mavin realized he was venting after touring around the Darth Vaders of the seed world. "The plants that make the most money are getting the most rack space."

"The world isn't black and white, Mavin. Just because there is money in GMO corn doesn't make it evil, or, for that matter, interesting." Lars ran on a binary system: computers interesting—corn not interesting.

Christian Bates, the Level Seven supervisor, walked past with a sardonic smile and a tray full of desserts. "Beard. Albjorn."

"Master." Lars gave Bates the finger under the table.

Most of the construction crew had thick Viking beards they'd cultivated for years. When they sighted Mavin, they'd yell, "Beard!" as if they'd spotted a whale's blow, and then roar with laughter. It was Mavin's Zuni blood. His father and grand-father never grew a beard. Every year his Norwegian co-workers gave him a pack of disposable razors for Christmas.

"Bates gives me the heebie-jeebies." Mavin shivered. "He's a cross between an undertaker and a carny."

"Where's your retinue of Neanderthal VIPs? Don't they want to sample our cuisine?" Lars asked.

"I left them with Trish."

"The carpet muncher?"

"Lars!"

"What? She is."

"Because she doesn't want to go out with you? That makes every woman on the planet a lesbian."

"Beard, when you enter puberty we'll talk about it."

"Speaking of growing up, when are you lazy-ass computer nerds going to have Kep filter our spam?" Mavin complained.

"Kep can beat a grandmaster at chess, but there's something you need to know, my young Padawan. Three things never go away: death, taxes and spam."

"What if I get you a date with Trish Fuller?"

"Deal."

# The Seer of Seattle

The seed of everything is in everything else.
—ANAXAGORAS

Saturday morning, Mavin met Trish for their weekly chess match at the Fruene Kaffe. After the morning rush, the cafe was quiet until lunchtime.

Trish moved her knight, staving off the inevitable. Her opponent lacked focus.

Despite four aspirins, Mavin's head was pounding. "Vodka and beer is a terrible combination," he reminded her.

"Yeah, that's why I never drink vodka with beer."

"Did you have fun with our visitors?" Mavin asked. "Senator Collins from the great state of Texas made me homesick for the Southwest. I hope he never runs for president."

"That reminds me, you sure disappeared in a hurry. Thanks a lot." She took his knight, knocking it off the board, pretending she was knocking him on the noggin as payback. "Are you even trying?"

"I saw the way you were staring at the tall blond Monsanto clone. His strong Aryan features."

"Don't even try, Mavin. I'm not biting the cheese. The government changed its policy. GMO seeds can legally enter Norway. Get over it. You're floating down that river in Egypt. At some point you're going to have to move from denial to acceptance."

"You know how much I hate that pop psych shit." Mavin rubbed his temples.

"Good to know," she said without remorse. "News flash. Cryopreservation is my passion. I'm not going to waste my energy arguing with my superiors over which seeds deserve more protection than others. I love my job, so stop making waves."

"Back in the seventies, Kissinger said, 'if you control the oil, you control the country. If you control food, you control the population.' Do you honestly believe that it's moral or right to patent life?" He tried staring her down, but realized it was futile. He looked down at the board and thought; I'm getting my ass handed to me, again.

"Sounds like you've been catching up on your conspiracy theory blogs." She shook her head as he moved his remaining knight into further danger.

"I think Old Stine missed his flight on purpose." Mavin ventured. "I don't think he could stomach having those mouth breathing agro-chemical execs slithering around the place he put so much of his heart into." He held his finger on top of his knight and looked around the board.

She tried to summon the outrage to tell Mavin he was full of it, but she suspected there was some truth to what he was saying about Director Gunnarson. Out of frustration, she changed the subject, "Come on, Mavin. You're a better player than this. Do you remember Botvinnik versus Reshevsky '38?"

"Yeah, the Dutch defense." He noticed his weakness on the diagonal. Even though he had lifted his finger a full three seconds, he moved his knight back, and castled instead. "So, you're saying my game is improving?"

She smiled. "Not as weak as truck stop coffee, but not as strong as ashram tea."

"Speaking of strong. Yesterday, I was replacing a sensor relay in the ventilation system and there was a distinct smell of animals," Mavin recalled.

"Maybe your buddy Lars walked by?"

"What are you really doing down there in the cryo lab?"

"You're hopeless, Mavin. You know the policy. You're not cleared for Level Seven. So, get off it."

"I thought you were freezing animal DNA, not whole animals."

"You know I only work with seeds." She took his remaining knight with a vengeance. "Don't quote me, but it's my understanding that Dr. Rayburn is working to save the DNA of the most critically endangered species, like the Arabian leopard."

"So, you're telling me you have a live leopard down there?"

"Shush! Damn it, Mavin! This is how rumors get started." She whispered and gave him a dirty look. "You're so immature sometimes."

"You make it sound like a bad thing."

"Concentrate on the board. You're toast in three moves." She knew Mavin was an extraordinary man. He had a natural intelligence, a kind of rational intuition. If it weren't for his hat size already being two sizes too big, she would tell him that Dr. Rayburn was using the numerical solution algorithm that Mavin had written. He had solved the problem that had flummoxed a whole team of engineers, how to keep the coolant flowing evenly despite the expansion and contraction due to constant temperature fluctuations. The techs called Mavin the Systems Whisperer. Thanks in part to Mavin's algorithm; Rayburn's project was ahead of schedule.

"If I win, will you get me a pass to the cryo lab?" Mavin gave her his best smile.

"Not going to happen."

"If I beat you at chess, will you go out with Lars?"

"And... we're done here."

\*   \*   \*   \*

The first of October signaled winter's willingness to stay, dropping 18 inches of snow. Mavin followed the flashing yellow lights of the snowplow winding up the mountain to the seed vault.

A white fox jutted across the road just behind the snowplow.

Mavin pumped his brakes. "Have you got a gambling disorder?" The fox stood on the side of the road, both eyes glowing from his brake lights. "Third time's a charm. Change your wicked ways, Miss Fox, before it's too late."

At lunch, Mavin held up the line waiting for the cook to refill the steamed lutefisk. Mrs. Jensen threatened him with her serving spoon to keep the line moving.

Lars bumped Mavin's tray and reached over, plucking two steaming brats from the vat, dripping grease on Mavin's plate. "Hey, Beard, did you hear? The Seer of Seattle is touring the cryo lab, as we speak. They say he's the one bank-rolling the frozen zoo project."

"No shit?" Mavin was impressed. "Michael Paul in the flesh. Almost as big a deal as when King Harald visited."

"You're from New Mexico right?"

"Yeah, Shiwinna, actually. The Zuni Pueblo, why?"

"When I was flying back from Nordaustlandet this morning with Scary Larry, we flew over a sub's conning tower sticking out of the ice. Eric Johansson, who works security, told me it's the, USS *New Mexico*." Lars lifted his eyebrows up until he was sure Mavin comprehended.

"Please tell me, you didn't drink coffee from Larry's thermos!"

"Hell no! Only a fool drinks from a bush pilot's thermos." A backcountry flight was often eight hours or more long and there was no bathroom onboard.

"Larry swears he washes it out with soap every time." Mavin made a face. "So, what's so special about this sub?"

"Evidently it dropped off Michael Paul."

Mavin dropped the tongs in the lutefisk.

"Pikansjos!" Mrs. Jenson barked. The sneeze guard was only thing protecting Mavin from the cook's wrath.

He picked up the tongs and set them beside the tray. "Klamme luderso," he cursed under his breath. It was not a good idea to get on the wrong side of Mrs. Jenson.

When they settled in to their table, Lars quickly dispatched his first brat and looked up from his food, "What's wrong, Beard? You're sweating like a whore in church."

"The USS New Mexico is a Virginia-class Nuclear sub."

"Yeah, Johansson told me." Lars was impressed. "Seriously, you keep up with your current submarine fleet? What the fuck? You Americans and your toys."

"My dad was a submariner. It's a sick hobby of mine." Mavin knew that people slept peacefully in their beds at night because brave men and women were doing their jobs around the world keeping everyone safe. He lost sleep worrying that the people who thought up Mutually Assured Destruction were busy thinking of something else.

Spitsbergen was Submarine Alley. It wasn't uncommon to hear of submarines punching through the ice. It was rumored that every Russian sub sailing out of the Barents Sea for the last forty years had been met and followed by a more silent American attack sub. This never-ending ballet of the doomsday machines was accepted as both normal and essential.

Mavin often wondered if his dad had died under the ice cap playing hide and seek with the Russians. "Not counting spooks, civilians haven't been allowed on nuclear subs for nearly thirty years."

"Spooks?" Lars didn't follow.

"CIA."

"So you're saying Michael Paul is a spy?" Lars giggled.

"I'm serious, Lars. "I'm telling you, there's some crazy shit going on down there on seven. They're not just freezing seeds and animal DNA. I think they're freezing live animals."

"Okay. So, you're saying Michael Paul wrote a billion dollar check so he can become the world's first billion-dollar popsicle? That doesn't make any sense."

"Maybe Paul has an incurable disease and is going to die anyway." Mavin speculated. "Maybe he plans to be unfrozen in the future when they find a cure."

"Cryogenically-frozen billionaire spies? It's only a matter of time before the seed asylum gets to us. You've finally cracked up my friend."

# The Underworld

They tried to bury us. They didn't know we were seeds.
—Dinos Christianopoulos

Mavin looked out the window at the lonesome gull following him up the mountain to work. It was late fall, the swing shifts that had been running all summer had ended. His headlights reached something darting across the road. "What?" He tapped his brakes. The red glow of his brake lights lit the eyes of the white fox in his rearview mirror. It unnerved him. "You are definitely kissing cousins with TwoBeers's coyote friends." He remembered waking up in the desert with a coyote staring right at him.

"Were you just gonna stand there and let him take a bite out of me?" Mavin yelled.

"He didn't want to eat you. He recognized you," his grandfather said with a straight face.

"From where?"

"From before."

Grandfather Two Feathers was known for chewing peyote. The old man would wake up miles from nowhere and not remember how he got there.

The parking area at the end of the plowed road was empty. Mavin was often the first to work and the last to leave. When he got to his desk he logged on to Kep. The screen lit up.

"Good morning, Beard," Kep's audio greeting sounded like a young Judy Dench.

"Ha ha! That's frickin hilarious! Way to burn through the budget, Lars." He was impressed by his friend's prank. "And good morning to you, Kep. Let's see if you filtered my spam? Now, that would be something." He checked his email to see if his dream had come true. Sure enough—no junk mail. "All right, Lars! Amazing. Now I've got to get you that date with Trish."

The lights dimmed and a recorded voice looped over the intercom. "The GCDC is in emergency lockdown. The GCDC is in emergency lockdown."

Mavin picked up the phone and pressed 5 for his supervisor. No answer. He tried Lars and then dialed out to the main office in Oslo.

"The number you have called cannot be completed as dialed."

He activated Kep's voice command feature. "Kep, what's going on?"

"Unknown." The automated female voice with a British accent answered.

"Is this a drill?"

"This is not a drill."

"Is there an emergency?"

"The GCDC is in emergency lockdown."

"No shit. Tell me something I don't know." The following silence unnerved him. "Are any other employees in the facility?"

"Negative."

"When is Gunnarson due in this morning?"

"The GCDC is in emergency lockdown."

"You mean the doors are locked?"

"Affirmative."

"Well, unlock them." Mavin clicked on the weather icon and waited. "Why is there no Internet or phone?"

"Unknown."

"Kep, dial Director Gunnarson's cell. Check that—use every available line, dial all the numbers at the administration office. I need to find out what the fuck just happened."

Mavin began to hyperventilate. "What's the temperature outside, Kep?"

"Unknown."

"Why is it unknown?"

Mavin tried every question he could think of, but Kep was unable to access any information from outside the facility. He walked to the lift, but it was in lockdown mode. "Kep, how many stairs to the upper exit doors?"

"Twelve hundred and seven."

"That's just peachy." It took Mavin until noon to climb the emergency stairs to the upper exit. He struggled with the manual release for the emergency exit. "Kep, open the door."

"The GCDC is in emergency lockdown."

"Open the fucking door, Kep!"

"The GCDC is in emergency lockdown."

"This is an emergency! Over-ride the emergency drill. Open the goddamn door!" He kicked the panic bar on the door and felt a twinge in his ankle. "Fuck!" He hobbled down to the cafeteria on Level Three and packed a bottle of water and a handful of energy bars. He took the stairs to Level Six and walked the long emergency evacuation tunnel to the exit. When he reached the door he kicked the manual release lever with his good foot. It was no use. He felt his heart racing and he caught himself hyperventilating. He had never been a believer in Satan or hell; now he suddenly found himself in the underworld with no escape.

He sat down with his back against the door and fell asleep. He dreamt a dark Kachina cloud came rolling over the desert. "Hekyapawu, are you going to rain?" he asked the ominous cloud. It became dark as midnight in the middle of the afternoon. He woke up with a start and remembered when the volcanic island of Krakatoa erupted, the entire world experienced night for almost a year. He could hear his rapid breathing echoing down the emergency tunnel.

Professor Sinclair, who was Jewish, had explained that *śatan* was an old Hebrew word that originally meant obstacle. "There has to be a way out of here. Come on, Mavin, you're a trouble-shooter," he challenged.

In this case, the obstacle was ironically the door he was leaning against. He formulated a plan.

"Gunnarson is gonna owe me big-time when this is over. All I need to do is override the emergency lock down code."

He climbed up to Level Five and went to work. "I may not be a programmer, but luckily I know someone who knows everything. Kep, how do I access the emergency code?" With Kep's help, it took him until midnight to isolate the lockdown code. He searched for errors, but the system was running at an optimal level. After three days of trying to alter the code, he realized it was tamper-proof. He wasn't qualified to reboot a supercomputer. If he did manage to initiate a shutdown, he doubted he would ever be able to restart Kep. Aside from the fact that Kep ran the entire facility, if he failed to restart the system he would be completely alone. It was not a risk he was willing to take.

He knew he had years of food and water, but if they didn't cut through the blast doors soon, he wondered how sane he would be when they found him. He was already talking to himself in the mirror.

"Mavin, you're looking a bit like a seed potato, too much time in the root cellar my friend." He missed the sun on his face. He knew the human body needed sunlight to produce the chemicals it needed to function.

When he was seven years old, his grandfather pulled up the ladder, leaving him in the bottom of a Kiva all night. He wasn't afraid. The old man was testing him. He searched in the dark for the Sipapu, the little hole where the ancestors first emerged. It wasn't until he was older that he got fed up with his grandfather's tricks. Once, when Two Feathers was too drunk to stand, he claimed he could travel through time. Maybe it was true. Grandfather had seen the future and had prepared him for life underground.

On day seven, he began an open log. The first week he watched what he said. After the second week, he no longer cared, "Captain's log, star date twenty-nine sixty-three point seven. Kep, why is your voice female?" He thought of Johannes Kepler.

"Unknown."

"And, what's with the British accent? Can you replace your voice patch with an Italian waitress?"

"Negative."

"No sweat my pet. But do me a big favor and never filter my spam again. I'm sorry that I ever asked."

"You have no new mail."

If the world ended, wouldn't he have felt an earthquake, or at least a tremor? Something. Anything. Kep would have received up to the minute information from every seismic monitoring station in the world. If there were a system malfunction, wouldn't he have found some errors in the code by now? Aside from the fact that there was no connection to the outside world, everything seemed to be in perfect working order. If there was a break in all the redundant fiber optics cables, none of the damage was apparent inside of the facility. All of the equipment was in pristine condition.

He thought about the first time he had seen a pig butchered. Grandpa Latigo shot their pig, Suzy in the head with his old revolver. He scalded the hair off Suzy's skin with a weed burner. The smell had turned his stomach. What could have seared all the antennae from the top of the mountain in a fraction of a second?

He was sealed in.

# Scarlet Poppies

Like the seeds dreaming beneath the snow
your heart dreams of spring.
—Kahlil Gibran

M avin wandered through the endless aisles of computer servers on Level Five.

"Nothing is, that thinking doesn't make it so," Mavin quoted the young prince of Denmark. It was his six-month anniversary of being trapped underground. His mother had told him that his father would spend six months beneath the ocean before seeing the sun again. Was that the limit of the boat, or did the navy notice that the sailors began to crack up during the seventh month? Why had nobody cut through the blast doors or tried to contact him?

The combination of loneliness and not knowing what caused him to be trapped underground slowly loosened his grip on reality. He was aware that he was slipping further and further into madness. He would take the stairs down to Level Five and not remember the reason he had come from Level Two. He'd climb back up to Level Two and try to remember why he had climbed up from Level Five.

"Never a borrower, nor a lender be," he repeated all the lines from the play he could remember. "Hamlet suffered from a kind of madness you know," he informed Kep. He stopped in front of a random terminal and ran a diagnostic. "There are several errors running in this bank of servers, my dear. Tighten down the thumbscrews, young lady. Get thee to a nunnery!"

All the other tables in the cafeteria were in serious need of dusting. He heated up a giant plateful of instant mashed potatoes and gravy. The first week underground, he had placed spoons in every serving tray and arranged the lids like dominos. "Mrs. Jenson is going to go ape when she sees her kitchen." He couldn't wait to see her go off.

He sat at his usual table and kept up his end of the conversation with Kep. "I'm sure you think knowledge is the cornerstone of civilization. I wouldn't expect anything less from you, my dear. I know you're not used to being wrong, but you're grossly mistaken. It's always been food. You're plenty smart, Kep. And you're the only woman in town. Sure, you may know everything in the world, but you can't make a blade of grass. You know everything about a potato—but you are not, nor will you ever be anything as wonderful as a potato." He stuck his fork in the remaining mound of instant spuds, like a flag on the moon and jumped to his feet. "The time has come, the Walrus said, to talk of many things... like dessert!"

He opened a gallon can of fruit cocktail and scooped a massive portion into a mixing bowl, digging for extra pale cherries. He thought about how many survivalists and seed savers would be jealous of his bunker. "I'm going to die like a pharaoh, surrounded by all the seeds in the world. I guess I'm as ready as I'm ever going to be for the afterlife. But I'll tell you what, my lovely. I can pass on being a mummy. Those dudes look rough when they dig 'em up. I mean, what's the point?"

Right after the emergency lockdown, Mavin had jimmied open Trish's locker and found her security lanyard with her key fob. He spent hours sitting in front of the airlock doors on Level Seven trying to guess her security code.

He sat in a plastic chair listening to Phil Chenevert read the *Wizard of Oz* audio book and punched in random series of numbers into the security pad. The first month he set up a system and kept a notebook. After six months of trying to break a twelve-digit alphanumeric code, he wasn't any closer. There were millions of possible combinations.

"They now came upon more and more of the big scarlet poppies, and fewer and fewer of the other flowers; and soon they found themselves in the midst of a great meadow of poppies. Now it is well known that when there are many of these flowers together their odor is so powerful that anyone who breathes it falls asleep, and if the sleeper is not carried away from the scent of the flowers, he sleeps on and on forever."

"Kep, I know that you know Trish's security code. Quit being such a bitch kitty and let me into the cryo vault. I promise I won't do anything crazy." He remembered his weekly chess games with Trish and had a sudden revelation. "Kep, what are the opening chess moves of the Dutch defense?"

"2.c4 Nf6 3.g3."

He punched in the sequence. The cryo chamber doors clicked open with a burst of gas.

# The Great Walrus

Birth, life and death—each took place
on the hidden side of a leaf.
—Toni Morrison

The five women made their way swiftly over the ice in the near dark. Their leader, Karin Ledin, was the only surviving member of the team with experience in the far north. Eleven months earlier, from the southern capital of Kashphera, twenty Peregrine Korps specialists set out on their quest.

Leto, the great seer had seen the treasure of seeds on the top of the world, buried under a frozen mountain. "In the heart of the mountain sleeps the past, present, and future," she had foretold. Every winter for the past eleven years, the celebrated Peregrines had sent expeditions into the north, but no one had returned. If crossing the ice was humanly possible, the cold of the first moon held the most promise. Their timing needed to be perfect if they were to avoid thin patches of ice, or worse, a freak storm that would push warm air up from the south causing the ice to break up and flow in unpredictable directions.

They were nearly to the top of the world. It was midwinter, and the sun remained below the horizon, even during the day, casting a morning-like glow for a couple of hours before it once again turned into dark night. The women covered great distances by starlight with very little food, water, or sleep. The company stopped and rested.

"I'd give my left tit for a piece of fresh fruit," Rani said chewing on a piece of dried squid.

"Melon for a melon." Sidta joked.

"In your case, raisin for a raisin." Charu kicked Sidta's shin and laughed.

"I'll take first watch," Karin said, "Then Charu, Rani, Simone, and Sidta. Sidta, wake us at dawn."

After her watch, Simone woke the jovial Sidta, helping her to brush off the thick layer of fresh snow that had fallen on her oilcloth.

Sidta stood up and shivered. "After I relieve myself, I'll relieve you."

Simone loved Sidta's impish sense of humor. "I know I'm not an officer like you, Sidta, but I think I can manage to pee on my own. Maybe instead, you could take a turn at watch while I grab forty winks."

At first milky light, the group set off breaking trail. Karin paused at regular intervals to thrust her harpoon through the fresh snow, testing the thickness of the ice.

When they entered a round basin, Simone tapped Karin's shoulder. The band immediately paused and listened.

Karin asked softly, "What is it, Simone?"

"An animal or something else, I'm not sure."

Karin made a circular motion with her hand and the band spread out in a defensive formation. They waited and listened to the wind. Just as Karin signaled for them to continue, a cloaked figure raised its head out of the snow.

"Strangers doing?" the small figure asked.

The band remained motionless, their finely tuned senses scanning the entire basin for the slightest sound or movement.

"More than three. Walrus people will cut you into bait." The diminutive figure pulled back her fur hood and stabbed her harpoon into the snow. "Strangers doing?" She shook her head and inched closer.

"Peace to you." Karin drove her harpoon into the snow and bowed. "We are the Peregrine people." Karin wondered, "more than three" what? More than three people?

"I am Malina, of the Snow Fox. We hunt over the floating ice. Strangers too many." Malina shook her head again.

"I am Karin. This is Sidta, Charu, Rani, and Simone."

Malina showed her perfect teeth. She was the size of a child, barely half the height of the strangers. As she came closer in the near darkness, Karin could see the stranger was a full-grown woman between twenty and thirty. She was not tall, but her thick bones and powerful frame made it hard to think of her as small. When she was at arm's length, she sat down and patted the snow.

Karin returned Malina's smile and sat across from her. The rest of the company formed a protective ring, watching in every direction as dry snowflakes swirled around them. Karin slipped the oilskin water bag from inside her parka and uncorked the stopper. She took a small sip, and then handed it to Malina. They drank together and laughed. Karin gestured for Malina to keep the water bag. "A gift."

Malina pointed to Simone and gestured for her to come and sit.

Karin nodded.

"I am Simone." She introduced herself and sat down bowing with her forehead on the snow.

"Simone smell Malina?" The small stranger pointed to herself and then acted out the earlier event with her hands.

"I didn't smell you." Simone pointed to her nose and shook her head. "I sensed you." She pointed to her heart.

This explanation pleased Malina greatly. "Walrus people not smell Malina. Simone true hunter." She unsheathed her walrus tusk knife, handing it to Simone to feel its keen edge.

Simone smiled when she saw the elegantly carved fox head on the end of the handle. She unsheathed her own blade and handed it to Malina.

Malina sprung to her feet as quick as a fox and sliced the air with the razor sharp knife.

In a blink, Karin and Simone jumped away in the same instant, though they had nothing to fear.

Malina dug into her oilskin bag and shared her assortment of ivory harpoon heads and an assortment of stone-scraping blades. She then produced a handful of small arrowheads, a flint, and a miniature whalebone oil lamp. As the tools and implements were passed around to each member of the company, they voiced their respect at the craftsmanship and quality. On the ivory awl was an intricate scrimshaw portraying two foxes chasing one another.

Malina acted out the various uses of each tool. Then, without explanation, she set off to demonstrate her skills. The group followed a respectful distance behind. Within an hour, Malina had found a fox's den and rigged a snare at the entrance.

With Malina's help the group covered greater distances and were able to hunt as they made the crossing. With each passing day, the ice became thicker. Karin realized the unpredictable harsh environment was simply the world to Malina. She was born on the floating ice. Before the next dark new moon, they were all wearing white fox fur pantaloons and *amauti*, the traditional hooded parkas.

Malina showed Simone how to sew a waterproof stitch. "The magic of the Snow Fox is powerful, but it cannot protect you from the Great Walrus," Malina explained. "She sees each of us in her dreams."

Karin overheard. "Don't worry, Malina. We also see the Great Walrus in our dreams." In a way it was the truth. The seer, Leto had seen the mountain on the top of the world.

Malina shook her head. "The Walrus people will cut you into bait. Only White Bear and Sedna battle the Walrus."

"Who is Sedna?" Karin asked.

"The great whale that hunts the other whale." Malina explained that nothing hunted Sedna. She was the goddess that devours all.

When they reached the shore of the island it was the first quarter of the Cold Moon, the longest night of the year, winter solstice. After more than a month on the ice, the frozen tundra felt soft under their feet.

Karin led them up a small ravine out of the wind. She held up her hand, signaling for them to rest. "Where are the Walrus people?" she asked Malina.

Malina explained how the Walrus people follow the herd of caribou as they roam the island searching for food. "Nibble, nibble." She picked a clump of lichen that was growing on an exposed patch of tundra and handed it to Karin.

Karin looked up the gentle slope. "Malina, what's on top of this mountain?"

"Grandmother sang of the Great Walrus on the mountain."

"Take us to her."

Malina looked over to Simone. "Simone smell Walrus?"

"Yes, Malina. Simone smell walrus." Simone put her hand on Malina's shoulder. "Don't worry."

Karin gestured for Simone to take point. They headed up the mountain and into a thick mist.

Six hours later they rested. Rani took first watch. Despite being in hostile territory, the travelers slept soundly with solid earth beneath them. At the first signs of dawn from the southeast, the party continued to climb into the heart of the island. The thick mist settled into a knee-high fog. Two hours later, the glow from the south began to fade into a star filled sky.

Simone abruptly halted. The band immediately formed a defensive circle. Against the starry horizon were two long tusks to either side of a massive head.

Malina dropped her hands to her sides and walked towards the Great Walrus. There was no escape from the one who sees all.

The rest of the company followed, their eyes trained on the tall shape against the sky. As they neared, the towering figure grew. Her shining eyes looked down on them. A ring of standing stones encircled the tower.

Karin and Simone passed into the ring of stones, approaching the goddess in silence. The rest of the company took defensive positions behind the ring of stones.

Simone touched the long ribbed neck and waited to see if the Great Walrus would awake. "She is made of stone."

"This is it." Karin let out a sigh and dropped her pack. "What do you think, Simone? Can you climb up and get a better look?"

Simone unslung her pack and began to scale the round tower.

Malina ran up to stop her. "Simone doing?"

"It's all right, Malina," Simone said softly. As she neared the top, she could see that the two fossilized mammoth tusks were lashed to the sides of the figure's head with thick cords of walrus hide, sealed with fat. The frayed ends of the cord looked like whiskers. Simone's toes found a small ledge that looked from below to be the upper lip of the goddess. The shining eyes were polished circles that had been etched into two smooth gray slabs. Simone gestured for Karin to climb up.

Malina jumped up and down. "Karin!" Were they trying to be eaten?

Karin joined Simone and steadied herself on the narrow ledge. She took out her knife and tapped the black slab. It rang like a forbidden bell. "Sweet Mother Crane! It's a door of metal."

"How does it open?" Simone felt for an invisible handle.

"Perhaps a prayer and an offering." Karin reached into her shoulder bag for her remaining dried fish and placed it on the narrow ledge below the door. The two chanted a prayer to the White Crane.

Sidta, Charu, and Rani knelt and bowed their heads and joined in prayer to the White Crane. The moon rose. A chilly east wind rattled the giant ivory tusks against the sides of the tower.

Simone had an idea. She reached around her neck for the small leather pouch. It was an amulet containing a pinch of earth from Avighna Island. She cut open the top of the tiny pouch and sprinkled a dash of earth on the threshold. A strong gust of wind blew the soil up into her face and hair.

Karin gave Simone a grim smile. She looked down at the others. Only five of them had survived the journey. The Walrus people would find them in the coming morning. There was little to be done but wait. An impenetrable iron door denied them. Their whole lives had been given for this moment. She wondered if the hundreds that had come before them had ever made it this far. Without realizing it, tears began to stream down her cheeks and freeze.

Simone looked down and pretended not to see. Karin's legs began to shake, her muscles slowly giving way. They had been clinging to the ledge through the long night. "We should climb down, Karin. We'll think of something once we've rested."

Karin nodded and brushed away her tears. The weight of the journey fell from her shoulders, and with it her purpose for living. She felt for a foothold below the narrow ledge, but she was exhausted; her toehold gave way and she would have fallen if Simone had not grabbed her arm. The tower began to vibrate. The earth shook.

Malina sat on the ground. They had poked the Great Walrus in the eye and awakened her. She would be hungry after her long sleep. She would eat them whole. Malina smiled, she decided she preferred this. She did not wish to be cut into bait.

The metal panel Simone was leaning against suddenly slid open. She fell backward pulling Karin inside the mouth.

The company watched from below, helpless, as the goddess consumed their leader.

Malina snapped the spell. She sprung to her feet and drove her harpoon hard against the thick stone neck of the Great Walrus. It glanced off, leaving a small nick.

Karin called to them, "I'm sending down a line, tie our packs and then climb up. Quickly!"

Once their packs were hauled up, Rani climbed up helping to pull Malina, while Charu pushed from below. When they were halfway up the tower an arrow struck Charu between her shoulder blades. She hit the frozen ground with a terrible crack.

A horde of dark figures raced up the slope.

Sidta, who was still on the ground, drew her blade and instinctively ran to meet the attackers. She waded into them, slicing tendon and bone.

When Rani reached the lit mouth, Simone and Karin grabbed her and then helped pull Malina inside. Arrows struck all around them in broken rhythm.

"Stay low! Keep away from the opening." Karin watched Sidta fall and be hacked to pieces. She pushed Simone's head down. "She's gone. There's nothing we can do."

When the arrows stopped, Karin knew their attackers were climbing the tower. "Get ready. They're coming."

The doors slid silently closed. They could feel themselves falling. A light flickered on. After months of near darkness, the light in the small room was blinding.

"It's said the goddesses are the bringers of light," Simone whispered. Is this what it's like to be swallowed by a goddess? She wondered. A moment later the doors slid open again. They expected arrows or worse. Miraculously, a frozen dark passageway replaced the night.

Simone crawled out on her hands and knees. The wind and the sky were gone. It was much colder. "There's no one here. I don't understand." She stood up, pressing herself against the frozen wall, allowing the light from the little room to travel as far down the ice cave as possible.

Karin helped Rani and Malina to their feet. They followed Simone a few paces. The doors of the small room slid closed. It was pitch black. They had been swallowed.

Karin voice was ordinary. "Rani, you're rear guard. Simone, you're point. Malina, let's see that little oil lamp of yours."

Malina struck her flint in rapid succession and after several tries the wick began to smoke. "If the walrus sneezes, we will be blown into the air," Malina warned.

"It's okay. Keep lighting the lamp, Malina," Karin said calmly. After a few more sputters and pops, the wick lit.

"Simone, go a few paces, then stop and listen," Karin advised. The shadows from the small flame danced along the narrow frozen tunnel. Simone took a few steps and listened, but all she could hear was the sound of their thick breathing. The group scraped through layers of hoarfrost until they entered a large chamber.

"We're in her belly." Malina's childlike voice echoed off the high ceiling.

The long room was filled with rows of shelves stacked high with black cases. Karin cracked open a black crate. It was filled with shiny packets. She sliced one open with her knife and poured a pile of tiny carrot seeds into her hand.

"Mother of us all! We've found them." Her voice broke. "They smell heavenly." She poured a pile of seeds into both Rani's and Simone's cupped palms.

The three took a moment to remember Sidta, and the other members of their team who had given their lives so that they could reach their destination.

Simone couldn't believe Sidta was dead. On the first day of their journey, Sidta had somehow managed to sneak a small bag of stones into her pack. Sidta walked beside her all day smiling and joking. That evening when Simone discovered the rocks, Sidta explained that she was doing her a favor. "You need the extra

training. Look how your butt is getting so big." The whole party
was in hysterics. Even Karin couldn't hold back a laugh.

"Leto's vision. It is all true." Karin interrupted Simone's
thoughts. "Now, the land can return to balance. The deserts will
return to green forests." They looked at the hundreds of black
cases stacked on row after row of shelving.

Simone opened another black case. It too was filled with shiny
packets. "How will we decide which seeds to carry back?" Then
added softly, "And how will we ever find our way out of here."

"Look for rice and wheat," Karin said enthusiastically. "First,
we need more light. Look for anything that will burn. We need
torches and a fire."

Rani looked at Simone and gave her half a smile.

Simone nodded, letting Rani know she understood the absurdity of their situation. After seeing their leader lose hope just
before the attack, Simone welcomed the return of Karin's unflap-
pable attitude. "She's right, Rani. We're going to make it."

Malina tasted the carrot seeds and spit them out. "Yuk! Caribou would not eat this." She didn't understand. She had cut open
many walruses and found whole fish in their stomachs. What
were these bags of dust doing in the belly of the Great Walrus?
She sat down and watched her new family opening crates and
sorting shiny bags into piles.

Karin saw the lost look on Malina's face. "Malina, come and
help me break this box into pieces. We'll make a fire to warm
ourselves and save your lamp oil." Karin opened more cases, di-
viding the silver seed packets into an ever-growing piles. "We'll
get an inventory of what's here, then decide what we should carry
home," Karin spoke as if it were going to happen. She had already
set aside packets of maple and sycamore seeds for her pack.

Simone held up her hand and everyone froze. A faint light
could be seen down at the end of the tunnel. The fire popped,
shooting a glowing ember onto the icy floor. It quickly turned
black.

Simone took up a defensive position just inside the chamber and waited. She could sense something coming.

"How many?" Karin whispered.

Simone shook her head. "I hear something. Whatever it is, it's moving very slowly."

"Rani," Karin whispered. "Use a crate and push the fire back into the chamber. Keep the coals alive, but dampen the flame. We'll fight in the dark; it's to our advantage. Malina come and stand to my right. We'll be a team. Rani, join Simone. Whoever gets past you, Malina and I will deal with them."

Simone listened as something slithered down the passage.

Malina cradled her harpoon and waited. The clawing sound from the passageway drew nearer.

Simone stood with her blade loose in her hand ready to strike. The fire unexpectedly flared.

A hideous shape raised itself on one knee and stood filling the doorway.

"Sweet Mother Crane!" Simone gasped. The naked figure's empty eyes were hideous. She had never seen a more grotesque sight. Glancing back to Karin, unsure of what to do, Simone gave ground and then once again squared herself to her assailant.

The thin figure was trembling and covered in a thick blue slime. He raised his arm and opened his mouth before falling forward, cracking his face on the icy floor.

"Check the passageway!" Karin called out.

Simone darted down the length of the tunnel. Her heart was pounding. She ran back again in an instant. "The passageway is clear."

"Rani, bring the coals closer," Karin ordered. "Make the fire hot and bright. Simone, check to see if he's playing possum. Be careful."

"It looks to be sick." Simone felt for a pulse. "Is it?"

"Yes. It's a man," Karin said.

"He's breathing, but cold as ice," Simone said. His upper lip was bleeding. A blue slimy gel covered his naked form. She rubbed the gel between her fingers. It had a syrupy sweet smell.

"Stack these empty crates together. Make a bed for him near the fire." Karin reached inside her shoulder bag for a soft piece of leather and handed it to Simone. "Use this to wash him." Karin pulled her baggy amauti parka up over her head. "We'll need to share some of our furs." Sitting near the fire, she carefully cut through the sinew seams.

None of them were anxious to be colder, but they welcomed the idea of the man being fully clothed.

Mavin woke up coughing. He rolled on his side and hacked up the thick lump in his throat. The light from the fire stabbed his eyes. He rubbed them with his numb hand. He couldn't tell if he was touching his face or not. He couldn't feel anything. His ears were plugged, but he could hear muffled voices. He tried to talk, but this only made him cough again.

"He's awake." Simone felt his forehead.

Karin sat nearby and spoke slowly. "Can you hear me?"

Mavin nodded his head and grunted, "Um hmm."

"Do you mean, yes?"

"Um hmm."

"Listen, you're going to be all right. You're safe. You need to sleep. Do you understand?"

"Um hmm."

Karin brushed the hair from Simone's face. "I need to concentrate on finding a way out of here. You need to take care of this man. He was sent to us for a reason."

"I understand," Simone said. She had never heard Karin sound so tender. "I'll take good care of him." She rubbed the man's cold feet and didn't look up until Karin had gone. They had come to the top of the world for a single purpose. They were in the belly of a monster. Now, instead of carrying bags of golden seeds on her shoulders, she was saddled with this beast. She cleared her thoughts and continued to massage his limbs. He did seem to have some power of reason, she reminded herself. He had answered, yes in his own fashion. Perhaps, Karin was right, maybe this blue man knew of a passageway out of the darkness. Who could say, maybe he would recover from his sickness and be able to walk? "It doesn't matter," she said to the sleeping man. "We'll never see the sky again."

Malina joined Simone. "He is Son of Sedna, made from one of the goddess's fingers the people chopped off. Blue, like a chopped-off finger. A Baby-man. Fully grown, the children of Sedna are born."

Simone reached down and tended the fire. She felt him move beside her. He was waking up again. She massaged his hands and forearms. His blue skin was drying and peeling. Underneath the papery blue layer his brown skin was soft as a newborn. She opened his eyelids one at a time. His pupils were cloudy and dilated. The whites of his eyes were red. "Can you hear me?" she asked.

He heard voices. "Is there sound in a dream?" he wondered. Light stabbed the back of his eyes.

"You're safe now." She repeated what Karin had said.

The red glow of the fire reflected in her eyes. He blinked. The snow fox was staring at him in his red brake lights. "You?" His vision cleared. It was the face of a beautiful woman framed in white fur. His breath caught and then raced.

Simone was startled at his clear speech. "You're safe. Don't be afraid."

Mavin looked around. Why was there a fire in the middle of the floor? He couldn't believe all the ice and hoarfrost on the walls and ceiling. The aluminum racks were corroded and cracked. When his nurse stood up to put more wood on the fire, he realized she was tall. Her cinnamon skin and Eurasian features were striking. Her wide shoulders and powerful build gave her the look of an Olympic athlete before the chemists became involved.

She felt his forehead. "You're much warmer. How are you feeling?"

"I'm hot."

# Raven

Deep roots are not reached by the frost.
–J.R.R. Tolkien

Karin returned from exploring the tunnels. "The mountain is hollow." She went over to the fire and warmed her hands. "How is the man? He looks much improved."

"He was awake for a brief moment and said he was hot," Simone reported.

"Is he too close to the fire?"

"His skin is cold to the touch, but his feet and hands are much warmer than a few hours ago."

"When he wakes up, I need to speak with him," Karin said.

Mavin opened his eyes to shouting and coughing. A dense black smoke was filling the chamber.

"Whale oil," Malina said to Karin. The smell was unmistakable.

"The Walrus people." Karin jumped to her feet. "They're trying to smoke us out."

"The man is waking up," Simone called out.

Karin bent down over him. "What is your name?"

"Mavin."

"Raven?"

"No, Mavin. Who are you?"

"I am Karin. I'll explain everything later. Do you know the way out of the mountain?"

He didn't understand why they were all wearing furs. "What year is this?"

"Year of the Monkey, 986."

"That can't be right."

"We're in trouble, Raven. We need a way out of here."

"There's an emergency tunnel on Level Six." He pointed down. "Why is it so smoky?"

"The Walrus people are attacking us."

"Who? What's going on? Kep. Are you there? Kep?"

The man was acting delirious. "Simone, can you and Rani carry him, along with your packs?" Karin asked.

"I'll manage," Despite Simone's promise to Karin, if it came down to it she knew what she must do.

"Raven." Karin knelt beside him and whispered, "What's the tallest tree?" Her pack was stuffed with every variety of tree seeds she could find.

"Sequoia sempervirens," he said without hesitation.

"It's time to go, Karin." Rani was getting nervous. The smoke was thickening against the ceiling, forcing them to stay low to the floor.

"Do you know where the seeds are for this tall tree?" she asked.

"Last row, fourth from the end, middle rack." He pointed to the far end of the vault.

Karin took a torch and disappeared into the maze of racks. They could hear her popping latches of the cases. She crawled back and threw Mavin a heavy packet. "Keep them safe. When we return home, we'll plant a tall tree for our gallant friends who have given their lives." Karin shouldered her pack. "Lead the way, Raven."

This struck Mavin as funny, considering he barely had the strength to crawl. He pointed down the hall to the stairwell door. "This way." He remembered all the times he had tried to break through the door at the end of the emergency evacuation tunnel. Kep must have opened the blast doors at the top of the lift. How else could these women have gotten into the facility? "I hope you have unlocked the emergency doors on six, Kep," he shouted.

Simone thought the man must be delirious, talking to shadows. She took the packet of seeds from him and tucked it into her already overstuffed pack. She crawled beneath the dense black smoke, pulling the thin man on his back by his arms. Malina was short enough to walk almost upright under the dense smoke. She towed Simone's pack by the straps.

As they neared the stairwell door, Mavin could see black smoke billowing through the cracks of the elevator doors. The fire was in the elevator shaft. "Through this door." He pointed.

Karin pulled on the door handle. The hinges were rusted shut. Malina drove her harpoon into the crack of the door and pried. The hinges creaked and then broke off. The heavy metal door crashed to the floor.

Simone threw Mavin over her shoulder and carried him through the doorway. The stairs were icy, but there was no smoke in the stairwell.

When they passed the door on Level Five, Mavin reached for the handle. "Kep! Are you there?" He realized he was thinking of her as alive. He thought of the angry mob of Christians that burned the Alexandrian Library. "Kep!"

Karin stopped. "Is there someone who needs our help?"

"No, not a person." He realized he couldn't explain. "A friend."

Karin didn't understand his cryptic response. They needed to keep moving. "Which way, Raven?"

"The exit tunnel is down one more level." He wanted to help Kep, but he needed to see the sky again. He had a faint memory of climbing into the cryo chamber. In that moment he realized Kep must have kept him alive, monitoring his vitals for years. Kep must have triggered an automated sequence to bring him out of stasis. He owed her his life, but at the moment he was in no shape to help Kep or anyone else.

Malina rambled about being smoked before being cut into bait.

Rani couldn't believe the sound coming out of Malina's mouth. "Listen to your voice, Malina. It's so high," Rani said and then giggled when she heard the childlike sound coming from her own mouth.

They all began to giggle in a high-pitch chorus and couldn't stop.

"What's happening?" Karin squeaked.

"It's helium," Mavin explained in a chipmunk's voice. "It's a type of gas."

Karin looked at him in disbelief.

"The fire in the elevator shaft must be at the bottom, on Level Seven," he explained. The fire was heating up the facility. The emergency fire suppression and ventilation systems weren't working. Judging by the derelict state of everything around him, it was reasonable to assume that all the emergency systems were offline. "This is not good!" he squeaked. "We need to hurry!" Luckily, helium was a non-reactive gas. It wouldn't explode if exposed to an open flame. However, if enough oxygen were displaced they would suffocate. "Through this door."

Once they left the safety of the stairway, the air was unbearable. They choked on the dense smoke billowing from the elevator shaft. They raced down the long emergency tunnel. Simone and Rani carried Mavin under his arms, dragging his feet.

By the looks of things, Mavin reasoned, a great deal of time must have elapsed while he was in stasis. Every system had been left unmaintained for perhaps hundreds of years. He thought about the frozen nitrogen tanks. The tanks were so cold, that left unchecked, oxygen would condense around them. Condensed liquid oxygen was highly explosive. The superheated nitrogen in the tanks could become exothermic. The whole mountain could explode.

When they reached the end of the tunnel, Mavin felt a mixture of relief and panic. "The outside world is behind this door." He heard his heart pounding in his ears. The smoke from the whale fat began to fill the long corridor. Did fresh air have a taste? He couldn't remember.

"This is it," Karin's voice rang down the round corridor. "If the Walrus people are waiting for us, they mustn't stop us. Do whatever it takes. Fight! Stay alive!" Karin put her shoulder to the door and pushed. It was stuck.

Malina drove her harpoon into the crack and pried. The door burst open. A wave of water washed them back down the tunnel mixing with the smoke.

Simone held onto Mavin's wrist with an iron grip and waded forward against the waist deep current. The tunnel quickly filled. When the water became too deep to stand, Simone held onto Mavin and treaded water. The pack floated, helping them to keep their heads above the rising water. When the tunnel was nearly filled to the ceiling the water pressure began to equalize. Mavin couldn't catch his breath.

"We're going to dive under and out the door!" Simone held his face and locked on to his eyes. "Take a deep breath, Raven. Kick and swim with everything you have!"

Mavin nodded his head and took a deep breath.

Simone dove under and pushed her feet off the corrugated ceiling of the tunnel, pulling him under and through the doorway. A swift current immediately grabbed them. The pack bobbed them to the surface. Simone caught her breath and soon realized they were in the middle of a fast moving river. She held onto the man from behind and kept his head above water. He was still breathing, but his body was limp. She tried to grip the icy bank with her free hand.

Malina swam out of the tunnel with the ease of a seal and used her harpoon to gain a purchase on the ice. She climbed up the frozen riverbank and drove her harpoon into a crack in the ice. She wrapped her knees around it and waited.

Simone saw the dark shape on the bank and reached.

Malina grabbed her hand, but the weight of Simone, the pack, and the man nearly pulled her back into the rushing torrent.

Simone rolled up on the bank, and together the two women pulled Mavin and the pack out of the water. "Malina, where are Karin and Rani?"

Malina shook her head.

Simone wanted to call out to Karin, but feared the Walrus people were near. They had to move.

Mavin was barely conscious and shivering uncontrollably. Their waterproof pantaloons and Amauti kept them from freezing to death.

Simone slung Mavin over her shoulder and dragged the pack behind her.

"Lucky, he is not fat like my brothers," Malina said and smiled.

Malina's joke helped lighten Simone's heart. With every step she held out hope that they would rejoin Karin and Rani. The air felt gentle and sweet compared with the smoke under the mountain. "It feels warm," Karin said.

"The weather has turned," Malina agreed. Any moment they would meet the Walrus people, and it would be over. "Simone, we need to cross the river." Malina pointed to the opposite bank and to safety.

Simone knew that Malina was right. If they followed the river any further, they would be seen from above. They needed to reach the opposite bank and head west.

"Leave him," Malina said with no malice.

"She's right," Mavin said. "Take the seeds. I'll be fine here."

Simone was shocked. It wasn't possible for a man to care about anything but himself. "We'll follow the river and search for Karin and Rani."

# Old Salt Woman

What is life? It is the flash of a firefly in the night.
It is the breathe of a buffalo in the wintertime.
It is the little shadow, which runs across the grass
and loses itself in the sunset.
—CROWFOOT

Mavin woke up to the sound of Simone's voice. "Take the man and keep moving. I will catch up." Mavin watched Simone run back up the mountain. Smoke bellowed from a tower with two massive tusks. He realized it was the elevator shaft. Thirty feet of sandstone had somehow worn away, leaving the concrete shaft exposed. It made no sense. Nor did a river appearing out of nowhere.

Malina grabbed his left foot. "Come on, Raven." She dragged him along on his back.

"It's Mavin," he protested, doing his best to hold his head up until he once again passed out.

When he awoke, Simone was staring down at him. "How are you?"

"To be honest, it's been tough sledding."

"Here, drink a little water, then we need to move."

He took two swallows before she threw him back over her shoulder. He drooled on her back. "I feel hot."

"Yes, I know." She could feel him shivering.

They reached the edge of the island at dawn. The river and the warmer air had broken up the ice. The dark open water stood out against the glowing white chunks of ice.

"Time to cross the river." Malina pointed up the slope.

They watched as a horde of dark shapes descended the mountain.

Mavin looked out over the broken ice field as it rippled from the mild ocean swell.

"Set me down," Mavin said.

"Hold still, Raven," Simone scolded.

"Set me down. Take the seeds and swim across the river."

"Quiet! Or we'll go back to dragging you." Simone followed Malina out across the broken ice field, jumping from one floating piece to the next.

In the growing light, Mavin studied the dark shapes of their pursuers as they spread out over the checkered landscape. "Checkmate in three moves."

They reached the edge of the ice and open water. Simone carefully set Mavin down and studied her surroundings. She called to Malina in a loud whisper, pointing to a seam in the ice.

The island of ice they were standing on had recently refrozen to a much larger floating mass.

Malina surveyed the crack and found a weak point. She drove in her harpoon, chipping and prying.

Mavin watched the figures swarming down the slope. They would be overrun soon. Casting themselves adrift was their only hope of escape.

There was a loud thunderclap in the distance. A deep hollow rumble rippled beneath the ice, followed by a high-pitched chorus of cracks.

To Mavin, it sounded like an explosion. His heart sank. As he feared, the fire must have ignited the liquid oxygen. A plume of smoke shot high into the air from the top of the mountain like an erupting volcano. He looked at the small pack. It was possible they had the only remaining seeds from the vault.

The ice under their feet began to rock and pitch. The earthquake had broken them free.

Malina wedged her harpoon in the widening crack. Simone grabbed hold and together they heaved. The seam opened. They moved to the other end of the long crack and pried. The large island they were standing on was free. The current from the mouth of the river slowly turned them like a heavy-laden ship warping out of port.

"Lay flat," Malina whispered.

A half an hour passed and they heard guttural voices. Simone held Mavin's head down when he tried to look. He guessed they had drifted less than a hundred feet from the next large chunk of ice. The power of the snow fox hid them.

Mavin thought of Kep. Was she still alive? What was the extent of the damage? If Level Seven blew up, would the seeds on Level One be safe? He squirmed. Simone pressed his face hard against the ice. An hour passed. He listened to the sound of the sea lapping the edge of the ice. The wind picked up. The voices grew louder. He fell asleep to the gentle rocking of the ice.

\* \* \* \*

When he awoke, he lifted his head slowly, not knowing what to expect. Malina was fishing off the edge. Simone was stitching a fur hood for him. Dark blue water surrounded them on all sides.

He drifted back into a hypnagogic dream. He was a boy sitting beside a red river. Old Salt Woman sat beside him. She pointed across the river where two men were under the shade of a poplar. Though they were far away, he could tell they were strangers. Old Salt Woman, without speaking, asked how he knew they were strangers and not Ashiwi.

When a doe beds down in the shade, she is a part of the tree and the grass. Ashiwi sitting under a tree are part of the tree and its shade. These strangers stick out like plastic coolers, he thought.

Old Salt Woman smiled, pleased with his answer.

Mavin woke up and watched the two women. The word primitive had always sounded bitter to his ears. It was impossible to imagine Malina and Simone separate from their surroundings. They were home. He was the plastic cooler. He crawled over to the pack. It had been tethered to the ice by an ingenious method. Malina had chipped a hole into the ice and tucked in the leather straps. She filled the hole with water, which quickly froze locking in the straps.

Mavin opened the pack and inventoried the seeds. The four-ply aluminum packets were in pristine condition. He was confident that no moisture had seeped through the layers. He thought of Captain Nemo's unsinkable casket washing up on Mysterious Island. Inside, were all of his books and papers sealed in waterproof zinc envelopes. Mavin had no idea how long he had been in stasis, but he doubted any of the seeds would germinate. It was a near certainty that the genetically modified seeds would not germinate. After only two years in storage they were no longer viable.

Simone watched as the man laid out the seed packets in order. She wasn't concerned. He had proven to her that he cared about them. She had never seen such a scrawny creature. She was surprised that he was still alive. She had sworn an oath to fulfill her mission and a second one to Karin, to keep the man safe. She wondered why she hadn't crossed the river when she had the chance.

# Ice Ship

Once more I am the silent one who came out
of the distance wrapped in cold rain and bells:
I owe the earth's pure death the will to sprout.
                                    –Pablo Neruda


slashing wave broke over the ice and ran underneath
Mavin who was curled up in a ball, sleeping.
"The sea is angry," Malina explained. "Sedna is not
happy. We should have left her ugly son on the island."

"You may be right." Simone watched as another large chunk
of ice broke off the edge. Their frozen raft had started out as a
small island, but was now quickly dissolving into the salty sea.
The soft edges gave way without warning. Simone was aware that
her attention was also dissolving, growing narrower by the hour.
She hadn't slept in three days. It was difficult to mark the passing
of time in the endless arctic night. The wind blew through her
thoughts like a broken spider's web.

The sun felt warm on her cheeks. She had traveled for months,
walking all spring and into summer to study with a great teacher.
Her mothers told her she was very lucky. She was to study the
art of ki with a true master. A dozen girls, around her same age,
sat in the middle of a green meadow pulling weeds. Thousands of
weeds grew between the grasses.

The girl beside her, named Edessa, complained, "My mothers
gave me away so I could learn to fight, not to pull weeds!" The other girls agreed. The girl closest to Simone stood up and dumped
the weeds out of her bucket and kicked it in the air. The other girls
screamed, tossing and kicking their buckets back and forth.

Simone dropped her head, afraid to watch. She continued to pull on the long root of a kuzu. Edessa chided her for not joining in their game, and then kicked over Simone's bucket. When Simone reached for it, the bigger girl stepped on her hand and kicked her in the ribs. The other girls laughed and took turns kicking her. Simone curled into a ball until they tired of their sport and ran off. She sat up and assessed the damage. Her ribs were bruised and her dress was covered in grass stains and mud.

That night, she went straight to bed without going to the dining tent. When she awoke the other girls were already gone. She went to the dining tent for breakfast. It was empty. Did she oversleep? On the long table was a single bowl of rice with a slice of yellow squash. She called out, but no one answered. She ate her meal and carried her bucket to the meadow.

When her bucket was almost full, the old woman who cooked their meals appeared on the edge of the meadow. "Young lady, come here. What is your name?"

"I am Simone."

"Simone, I am Maya. Let me see your bucket." It was filled with long rooted kuzu. "Come with me, I have more work for you."

"Where is everyone?"

"The other girls have gone home. Would you like to join them?"

"I can't go home. I've come here to learn ki."

"Oh," the old woman said without inflection. "Why are you covered in dirt?"

"I'm sorry, I tripped and fell down."

"Go down to the river and wash your clothes. You will find laundry there that needs washing. When you've finished, come and eat your evening meal."

Simone washed her dress and then started on the giant pile of sheets from the other girl's beds. It grew dark and still there were more sheets to wash. She hung the last of the sheets to dry after midnight in the silver moonlight. She walked through the sea of shimmering white fabric blowing in the breeze.

She opened her eyes; the moon on the water lit the glowing white chunk of ice. She said a prayer to the White Crane and another one for her teacher Maya.

Mavin woke up shivering. He rolled on his back and stared into the night sky. The quarter moon was setting in the west. "I should be petrified," he said to the moon. "I'm atop a slippery cube of ice floating in the middle of a black sea with no land in sight. And, that's exactly how I feel. This is a perfect moment." He closed his eyes and laughed. A large wave hit the jagged corner of their ice raft spinning them slowly in the opposite direction.

* * * *

At dawn, Malina watched the angry sea. Two frigate birds were circling above the waves. She watched them moving closer and closer. She saw a flash off the water. A black dorsal fin rose high above the mercury-colored waves. They should have left the man on the island. "Simone, Sedna has come for her son." Malina pointed.

Mavin woke up and got to his knees.

Simone scoured the surface of the water just as a massive wave hit. The section of ice that Simone was standing on crumbled under her feet. She was in the water before she could react.

"Simone!" Malina yelled.

Mavin turned just as Simone drop out of sight.

"Raven, Sedna is coming! Hurry, we need to make rope." She pulled off her fur Amauti and began cutting it into strips. She heard the whale's blow and turned to see the black fluke disappear beneath the wave. Sedna dove.

The large section entering the water had pushed Simone away from the main raft of ice. She was caught in the deep trough of a wave.

Malina frantically tied the ends of the fur strips together. "Raven, tie this around your ankle. Reach down and pull Simone up." Malina thrust her harpoon into the middle of the ice and tied her end of the fur chain to it. "Raven, when you look into the blue eye, you must eat the mushroom."

"What?"

"Promise!"

"All right, I promise." He had no idea what Malina was going on about. He watched her run to the opposite edge of the ice. "Malina, come and help me pull Simone out of the water before she freezes to death."

Malina guessed that the two frigate birds were hovering above Sedna. She ran and dove in the water.

"What the hell! Malina!" Mavin stood up and watched her swimming toward the frigate birds with the speed of a seal. He heard Simone calling for help. He gauged the length he needed and tied the chain of furs around his ankle. He leaned as far over the edge as he dared and stretched his fingers.

Simone gripped the icy ledge and managed to grab Mavin's hand. Her added weight stretched the chain of furs. Mavin's hips slid over the edge. He dangled by one leg.

Simone scampered up over him. Once on top of the ice, she pulled him up by his ankle. "Where's Malina?"

"She ran and jumped in over there."

"Malina!" Simone ran to the edge. She shielded her eyes from the dimly lit horizon and scanned the waves. "Malina!"

"She was talking crazy. She made me promise to eat a mushroom."

A frigate bird dove and came out of the water with something in its beak. The other bird gave chase.

"Malina! Where are you?" Simone was angry. "What happened?"

"I told you. She ran and jumped in."

"Why didn't you stop her? What's wrong with you!" She turned searching the empty waves. It didn't make any sense.

Mavin scanned the surface of the water and then fell to his knees and began to sob. "She swam towards those two birds."

A massive black form rose out of the water just in front of Simone.

"Sedna!" Simone instinctively leaped back. A fine spray from the orca's blow filled the air. The wake from the diving whale tilted the ice. Simone slipped fell and then sprang to her feet. She pried Malina's harpoon from the ice and ran as close to the edge as she dared. She stood still holding the harpoon above her head waiting to strike. A freezing rain began to fall. She glanced at the pack lashed securely to the ice and then to Mavin.

He stared back at her. "Please, don't be angry with me."

The drizzling rain made it impossible to tell, but she thought she could see tears streaming down his face. Malina had gone to meet her goddess Sedna. She had sacrificed herself to save her. A big wave lifted a corner of the ice. Another large piece of edge broke loose and slid quietly into the dark water.

Simone knelt down and tried to untie the knot around Mavin's ankle. The cold had robbed her fingers of the ability to follow her will. The knot had pulled tight and was cutting off the circulation to his foot. She used her teeth and loosened the lash. She pulled off his fur moccasin and rubbed his blue foot.

Mavin looked away, feeling ashamed.

She drove the harpoon back into the center of the ice raft and tied the remaining chain of furs to its base. She tied the other end around Mavin's waist.

He couldn't bring himself to look at her.

Simone dug around in Malina's bag taking out each of her prized possessions. She realized the source of her anger. She was the scout. It was her job to face the danger. Now Malina was dead. Everyone was dead. Her pain fed the deep prejudice she harbored against men. She wanted to hate him.

"Raven."

He looked up, but couldn't meet her eyes. All of Malina's tools were carefully arranged beside him.

"I'm sorry I was angry." She tried her best to smile.

Mavin wondered how many generations these same treasures had been passed from hand to hand. "Malina knew what she was doing," he said. "She wasn't the least bit afraid. Not even a little." He broke down again. He wondered why he was so completely devastated, he barely knew Malina. Trish was dead. For all he knew, everyone he'd ever known was dead. He hadn't cried for any of them. The warm tears froze on his cheeks.

\* \* \* \*

In the days that followed, Mavin was in and out of consciousness. He woke up and watched his guardian fishing. With what little details he managed to glean from her outward behavior, he wove into a loose tapestry. She wasn't, by any means, primitive, but she appeared to have no knowledge of the modern world. She was a sophisticated thinker. He recognized clear patterns, but her behavior was littered with inconsistencies. In his compromised state, he wondered if it was all some sort of hoax being perpetrated on him. He thought of his father and Malina deep beneath the waves. He would be joining them soon.

"Simone."

"Was is it?"

"Raven is hungry."

"I thought you were hot."

"We need to eat." He held up a foil packet. "To be honest, I don't think the corn seeds will germinate." He didn't finish his thought, besides we'll be dead and it won't matter anyway.

"You choose." She knew he cared about the seeds and had a deep understanding of them.

He read the packet to her, "Genuity® VT Double PRO® RIB Complete® a corn blend. Yum. A genetically modified medley of corn kernels," he said with mock enthusiasm. "We can soak the corn and mash it. Transgenic cornmeal mush, my favorite."

He was surprised how good it tasted. Hunger was the best sauce. "Slather a little famine-nnaise on wet dirt and it'll taste great," he tried to make light of the situation.

She gave him a quizzical look. "What's wrong, Raven?" She was used to his babbling speech, but the look on his face was different.

"We're going to die."

"Why would you say such a thing?" She smiled and then giggled.

It was the first sign of humor from his protector. The joyful sound of her high laughter brightened his spirit. "Like they say, nothing like a good hearty breakfast to start the day." He stared at the remaining dry corn kernels in the silver packet. "Hey, I wonder if fish like corn?"

"That's a very good idea." She soaked the few remaining corn seeds in salt water and tied them around Malina's ivory hook with strands of her hair. She cast the hand line out and within an hour, reeled in a young haddock. She cleaned the fish and saved the guts for bait.

After they finished their meal of raw fish Simone announced, "It's time for your after-lunch stroll." He was able to stand by himself. She gave him her arm. They walked around in a small circle. She smiled, remembering the first moment she saw him. "Do you remember when we met?"

"To be honest, not very well," he admitted.

"You stood up for a moment and then promptly tried to break the icy floor with your face." She didn't even try to hide her smile.

"Like Humpty Dumpty."

"Who?"

Mavin told her about the man who was really a giant egg and for some reason, just loved sitting on top of a high wall dangling his skinny little legs. Mavin explained about the fall and how all the king's horses and all the king's men couldn't put Humpty Dumpty together again.

For a moment, time stood still. Simone listened to the story and for the first time in memory, she let go. The pieces of the cracked world lay broken and there was nothing she could do about it.

Mavin ended the fairy tale, but his mind reeled through all the mythical falls of humankind. Adam and Eve's exile from the Garden of Eden and Tim Finnegan's mythical fall. Mavin loved Joyce's description of the mourners at the wake fighting and splashing whiskey on the corpse, bringing Finnegan back to life. Without skipping a beat. Tim Finnegan joined in on the fracas.

"Raven," Simone crashed in on his thoughts. "Why did Malina swim towards the whale?"

"I don't know."

# Tall Tree Tales

*A moment is to the universe as the seed is to the flower.*
—Khalid Masood

"Wake up, Raven."

He rubbed the frozen sleet from his eyes. It was barely light. Their craft of ice was listing at an angle. Simone had wedged the pack under his upper body to keep him more horizontal while he slept. When his swollen eyes adjusted to the dim light, he saw something dark and ominous filling the horizon. The adrenaline helped him to his feet.

A beam of orange sunlight pierced through a cloud illuminating the granite face of the fjord's western rim.

The two watched the dawn play against the solid rock. He listened to the waves lap against the sides of their tiny frozen craft. He was surprised at how little of it remained. It wasn't much bigger than a '64 Impala and with about as much buoyancy. By some miracle, it had transported them to the continent. He looked at all the pee stains. "Not a lot of resale value," he mumbled.

Simone double folded the top of the pack, sealing in as much air as possible. They had eaten all the seeds that Mavin said wouldn't grow. She slapped Mavin's legs and massaged his feet. The chain of furs was still tied around his waist. She tied the other end around her own waist and looked in his eyes. She could tell he was not able to focus. "Hang on to the pack. When you hit the water, hold your breath in tight. Even in your waterproof Amauti, the cold water will knock the air from your lungs. Kick your feet as hard as you can, it will keep you warm. We are going to make it." She couldn't tell if he was following what she was saying. "We're going to make it!" She lowered him into the freezing water and then dove in. She swam with all the strength she had left, pulling him along behind.

He hung on to the pack in a death grip. "Go, Sea Bass," he mumbled and kicked his feet.

When she reached the shallows, she pulled him to the rocky shore.

"Stand up, Mavin! Keep moving! Jump up and down!"

"I, I, I," his jaw shook out of control. "I like it when you call me by my name."

"Keep moving, don't stop." She cut green limbs and set to work making snowshoes. When she was finished, she lashed them to his fur moccasins and held his arm. "Start off slow, you'll get the hang of it soon."

In the years he spent living on Spitsbergen, he had become an expert at snowshoeing. He grabbed the short evergreen tree limbs and pulled himself up the steep slope. The spruce needles were much sharper than he remembered and punctured his fingertips like cactus spines. He did his best to keep up with her, crawling on all fours. "On the bright side," he said, out of breath. "It'll be nice to wipe my ass with something other than a chunk of ice." Near the top of the ridge he found a patch of thawed ground and dug his hands into the dark earth. It smelled alive. For the first time in weeks he believed they would live. Tears filled his eyes.

Simone noticed he had stopped. "Are you all right?"

"Yes."

"We need to keep moving." Her voice was harsher than she wanted it to be.

"Don't be cross. I need a moment."

"What's the matter?" Her impatience grew.

"I was frozen," he blurted out. "Frozen. Do you understand?"

Under the mountain she wondered how his skin could feel colder than ice.

"You saved my life." He couldn't control his emotions. "Thank you." He sobbed. "Thank you."

"You're welcome." She looked away. All twenty of her friends were dead. She felt ashamed. "Come on, Mavin, take my hand. We need to make it to the top of this ridge."

By mid-afternoon they had clawed their way up the razor ridge, out of the sunlight and into a frozen fog. A hard rime covered the stunted trees, bending the boughs low. He could still feel the rocking movement of the water. Believing that they were going to live gave Mavin's legs new strength.

Simone stopped and waited for him to catch up and then continued, urging him on. She couldn't believe how such a skinny frail creature could still be alive after their ordeal on the raft of ice.

The solid earth under his feet helped Mavin regain his senses. His mind began to sort things. The more he was able to add one thought to the next, the more the world turned red. He wanted to scream, "I've lost everything! Everyone! What's the point?" He kept his thoughts and feelings to himself. She'll think I'm crazy. "Perhaps I am insane?" he muttered.

The fog lifted and the sun burst through. His mind cleared. He looked out over the boreal forest of stunted firs. "It's a Krumholtz forest. The freezing wind causes this kind of deformation."

"Yes, they are trees." She gave him a strange look.

"The English call this elfin-wood."

Her eyebrows hung. How was it possible he had never seen a tree before?

"Simone, why are you looking at me like that? The trees get taller further south."

"Only in tall tree tales."

# The Shepherd

It is not down in any map; true places never are.
                                        –HERMAN MELVILLE

**M**avin caught up to her and tried to get a straight answer, "How much further is it to where we're going?"

"At the rate we're traveling? Two years."

"You're joking."

She wasn't smiling.

"Do you have a map?"

She didn't reply.

"How do you know where we're going?" He knew they were traveling southeast.

"During the day, the sun gives us the directions. During the night, the stars."

"You navigate by the stars?" He was surprised.

"It's not difficult once you learn the named stars."

Mavin wanted to impress her. He found the big Dipper and knew it pointed to the bright star Polaris at the end of the Little Dipper. "The North Star." He pointed.

Unable to hold back a high giggle, she shook her head and pointed to the constellation Cepheus. "The Shepherd, she points north." She knew being born a boy he would not have gone to school.

Mavin remembered the longest natural cycle visible to the naked eye, the procession of the equinox. The North Star slowly changed over time. When he was in Egypt, he learned from his mentor Dr. Sinclair that the pyramids were aligned to the star Thuban. It was the North Star 5,000 years ago. It made him shudder to think about how long he must have been under the mountain. Perhaps Simone was wrong about Polaris. One thing he was sure of, there were no satellites in the night sky.

He fell further behind. It was hard to walk and think. Were they in Norway or Denmark? Did Denmark have fjords? He would ask the prince. If Hamlet didn't know, the long-winded Polonius surely would. "Hamlet, I know who killed your father," he said, and realized the young Danish prince was perhaps the world's worst detective. "Who killed everyone? That is the question." He hoped it was a giant meteor, but his gut told him different. If there had been a nuclear holocaust, the radiation had not caused any abnormalities in his companion, quite the opposite; she was tall, athletic and stunningly beautiful. He thought of a way to test her scientific knowledge. "Simone?"

"Yes?"

"You're always telling me to pay attention to my feet. What is holding my feet to the ground?" He wondered if she knew about gravity.

"That is a good question." She thought about how to explain it simply, so that he might comprehend. "All that we see with our eyes is brought about by unseen causes and conditions. Our Mother Earth is so large, her mass so great, that we are like fleas on a mountain. It is nothing for her to hold us thus."

"Oh," he said, and wondered if could he have explained it any better.

# The Boundary

If you can look into the seeds of time, and say which
grain will grow and which will not, speak then unto me.
—William Shakespeare

Over the coming weeks, the snow hardened and thinned until they were walking on spongy permafrost. Simone had only one strict rule: they must cover as much ground every day as possible. She never bullied him, but she never let up. When he became too exhausted to continue, she would put her arm under his and give him the harpoon to use as a walking stick. Her encouragement never wavered.

"Where is everyone? Where are all the people?" Mavin had expected to encounter a village by now, even this far north.

"We're in the Boundary."

"What boundary?"

"It's a wide crease between the Eastern and Western Empires. It was agreed a millennium ago that no one was to live in the Boundary."

"A millennium?" It took all his concentration not to think about how much time he must have been in stasis. "Why don't we head for a city?"

"It's safer if we stay in the Boundary."

"That sounds like a load of BS."

"Be ess?"

"Less than true."

"Everything spoken is less than true." She motioned for them to stop.

"What now?"

"There," she whispered, directing him with her eyes.

Not knowing what to expect, Mavin grabbed hold of the harpoon with two hands. Sitting on a low limb a few feet away was a small owl. Gray feathers blended perfectly with the color of the inner branches of the dwarf fir. They stared into the owl's unblinking eyes until Simone tugged at Mavin's sleeve and he reluctantly left the owl's company.

"I can't believe how you see everything." He marveled at her powers of observation.

"More proof of the spoken word being less than true." She felt eyes on them this very minute. It bothered her greatly that she was unable to discover who was watching them.

"Well, I'm impressed," he said, just as he stepped on a small hole in the ground, the entrance of a hornet's nest. A black cloud erupted from the ground and swarmed around his head. He swatted a hornet, which turned in mid-flight stinging him in the nose beside his left eye.

"Cover your eyes, Mavin! They follow your eyes." She grabbed his arm and used her other hand to shield his eyes. They ran down a grassy hillside until Mavin lost his footing and tumbled down the slope.

She scampered down after him and slung off her pack. "Are you all right? Let me see." His left eye was already swelling shut. "Are you stung anywhere else?"

"Just my face. It feels like Malina's harpoon has been driven through my sinuses into my brain."

"Hornets don't like the son of Sedna."

He laughed and winced. "Luckily it only hurts when I'm laughing or not laughing."

"Children of Sedna have thick skulls. Why don't you listen? Am I not always telling you to watch your feet?"

"I listen." He touched his cheek and grimaced. "I just reserve the right to ignore what you say."

"If you want to survive you might consider paying attention to where you step."

"Why were all of the Peregrine people and Walrus people women?"

His question caught her off guard. "Why choose to be a man?"

"We don't get to choose what sex were are."

She looked at him and busted out laughing. "Men are not known for their wit. But you rival my friend, Sidta. She could always make me laugh, no matter the situation."

"You think I'm funny?"

"Let's just say, when we reach civilization, your lack of inhibition will hardly pass as wit in the modern world."

"The modern world?" He laughed and it hurt.

# Two Equal One

...The seed you plant in love, no matter how small,
will grow into a mighty tree of refuge.

—ALFENI SHAKUR

For weeks the rolling landscape seemed changeless, until slowly the ground began to harden under their feet. Small stands of miniature birch trees began to mix with the stunted Krumholtz evergreens. He had never encountered this tiny variety of birch; it had prickly thorns on its bare stems. Watching the buds on the colored stems burst into soft green leaves lightened Mavin's step. Spring was arriving to the north.

To his horror, it was just as Simone had said; all of the trees remained stunted, growing only shoulder high. He wondered what environmental conditions had caused such dwarfing, a lack of light? He remembered that plant hormones, called auxins, were a little like growth hormone in humans.

They rested in the limited shade of a short evergreen. It was a fir, but the needles were sharp like a spruce.

"Simone, do you know how to write?"

"Yes."

"Can you write something for me?"

"Of course." She had wondered if he could read or write, but didn't want to embarrass him by asking. She was grateful that he had brought it up. She picked up a stick and smoothed out a patch of bare earth and scratched a basic character with the ivory tip of the harpoon.

"This indicates a person," she explained. "The two lines represent two people leaning, supporting one another. Two equals one. Do you understand?" She knew the concept might be difficult for him. "A person cannot exist alone, it takes two to make one."

He didn't recognize the script. "Gotcha," he said automatically without really grasping what she meant.

"Can you guess what this character represents?" She scratched it out beside the first character.

She smiled, hoping he could guess by the shape. "I'll give you a hint." She pointed at the little fir tree beside them. It didn't help. "This character indicates a tree."

"Okay, I see how it looks a little like a tree." He thought he recognized the characters as Asian.

"Guess what they mean together." She combined the first character to the second.

休

It could hardly be simpler, she thought. "Take a guess, Mavin."

"I give up."

"It is a woman sitting under a tree." She knew he was frustrated and gave him a minute to think. "What are we doing right now?" She could tell he was no longer trying. "When you combine the two characters it means, to rest."

"Makes sense," he said. People have rested under trees for millions of years. Not that this stubby little fir was offering much shade. "Can you write it in English for me?"

She laughed. "Sorry. I can't teach you how to write in English."
"What is so funny?" She laughed at the oddest things.
"Nothing is written in English."

*   *   *   *

In the coming weeks, high formations of snow geese covered the sky. Their cacophonous roar unnerved Mavin. They circle overhead flying lower and lower. Their honks and squawking complaints turned to one vast unearthly agreement just as they landed, bombarding the soft tundra, blanketing the green rolling hills once again in white.

Mavin's ears ached from the constant verbal assault of thousands of geese. For hours they walked through the mass of white. At first they tried to walk softly trying to let the birds know they meant them no harm. By evening, Mavin had had enough of their squawking and took to running at them until the flock burst into flight and circled around them. Within a week, they were stepping around thousands of goose eggs.

In the evening, Simone gathered eggs while Mavin snapped off dead branches from the low-growing shrubs. Simone used her flint to light a handful of dry grass and thorny twigs. When the fire died down, she scratched a hole in the ash and added the eggs, covering them with the ash and hot coals. They ate three baked eggs apiece for dinner, and saved the other half dozen for breakfast and lunch for the following day. Simone showed him berries that could be eaten and those that were too bitter or poisonous. He was amazed how every plant seemed to have spines or thorns. Even collecting dry leaves for the fire was prickly business.

He knew it must be far in the future, but it felt as though he'd traveled back through time. He was Will Rogers in the old movie, *A Connecticut Yankee in King Arthur's Court*. Twain's dark satire had arguably been the first science fiction book ever written. Few doubted that Twain had influenced H. G. Wells when he published, *The Time Machine,* just six years later.

# The Field

The best time to plant a tree was twenty years ago.
The second best time is now.
−Chinese Proverb

Mavin measured his steps, stepping carefully between clutches of eggs covering the spongy grass. He paused and glanced over to his protector waving her harpoon to shoo away the ganders defending their nests. What would Darwin think of the evolution of the species? If Simone was to be believed, there were many more girls being born than boys. He had witnessed in his own time that the population of woman had grown to greater than sixty percent. Was it nature's way of protecting itself from Man the Toolmaker? Males were hardwired to protect their loved ones, no matter the cost. Mutually Assured Destruction, M.A.D. the military doctrine that guaranteed the complete annihilation of both attacker and defender, was the ultimate dark irony. It was impossible for Mavin to imagine mothers threatening the lives of children, even an enemy's child, as a means to provide safety and security to their own family.

He would spare Simone the knowledge that eventually the sun would explode and the great oceans would evaporate into space freezing into millions of comets seeking another dry earth. Would a single microbe of life survive frozen in the ice? He was living proof that stranger things were possible. "I've little doubt that irony will survive the vacuum of space," he confided to the glowing eggs spread over the endless green. Simone felt a tingling in the middle of her back. She looked over her shoulder and thought she caught a glimpse of something moving in the brush

behind Mavin. She couldn't shake the feeling that they were being watched. She waited for him to catch up. "Your practice is
improving."

"Why do you say that?"

"You're watching where you walk and you have more pepper
in your step today."

"I've little choice, but to look where I step." The grass was covered in thousands of eggs about to hatch. He wanted so badly to
leave her in the dust for once. He started the morning ahead of
her, but by mid-afternoon he was flagging, doing his best to keep
pace, despite her carrying the heavy pack.

By the next new moon, they had moved beyond the geese
mating grounds. Food once again became scarce. The open
rolling hills became a maze of narrow ravines, overgrown with
thorny brush. They were forced to backtrack when they ended
up at the bottom of a gulch that ended in a steep drop off. Mavin
was exhausted and frustrated at having to retrace their steps. He
watched Simone pick an egg and leave the second one in the nest.

When he reached for the remaining egg, she said in a quiet
voice, "Take what you need and leave the rest."

"Is that why you didn't kill that fat little owl that was right in
front of us when we were freezing and starving?"

"You don't look frozen or starving," she countered. "Besides,
could you kill and eat an owl?"

"No. Never," he admitted. "But I could eat this other egg."

She gave him the look. He decided to find his own nest and
make the rules.

Simone tied the harpoon under the pack straps and fell into
her natural pace. Once again Mavin felt the indignity of falling
behind. He heard a branch snap and turned up a game trail to
see what it was.

Simone stopped to wait for him to catch up. When she looked
back, Mavin was wandering up a ravine.

"No! Mavin!" She slipped off her pack and raced towards him.

He turned just as the bowstring snapped. An arrow arced down on him in slow motion.

In that instant, Simone pushed her palms forward projecting her ki.

A wave of energy knocked Mavin off his feet. The arrow struck the rocky path just in front of him.

"Run!" she yelled.

He stood up and ran past her in a full sprint.

She backed away, expecting a second arrow. When it didn't come, she grabbed the pack and raced after him. They ran for an hour without stopping.

"I need to rest for a moment," he said. "What happened back there?" His adrenaline had worn off, but he was still in shock.

"You wanted to know where all the people were," she said, out of breath.

"I mean, what happened? What did you do?"

She was about to give him grief, and then remembered he was still blind in his left eye from the hornet sting. Besides, it was her own fault. She should have told him they were not alone in the Boundary. The color of the arrow was familiar. She had seen it somewhere before. "You were lucky, Mavin."

"More than lucky. I saw the arrow coming right at me. How did you do that?"

"Do what?"

"Come on, Simone. How did you stop that arrow?"

"I don't know what you mean."

"Unbelievable." He got up and started back up the trail, if only to see another arrow magically fall to earth. The Zuni believed they were among the first people to hunt with a bow and arrow. By the time Mavin was ten, he could shoot a blackbird out of the sky with the little bow he had made. He lightly touched his tender left eyelid. Most of the swelling was gone, but the lid was closed and unresponsive. Without depth perception he couldn't fully trust what he'd seen.

"Come back, Mavin. I'll tell you."

He turned, still upset. "Back on Svalbard I watched you run back up the mountain. Malina told me you took on a horde of those walrus people by yourself."

"You were delirious."

"I've watched you in the hours before dawn doing some kind of Tai Chi."

"You know ki?"

"I've heard of it."

"Ki is energy. Everything is energy. Do you understand?"

"Yes, I mean, it's a proven fact that everything is energy." He didn't want to get into $E=mc^2$ with a woman wearing skins. "I know about martial arts, but I've never seen anything quite like that in real life."

"What do you mean?" she asked.

"I didn't know it was possible to stop an arrow in flight."

"I'm not sure that can be done. But it is possible to dampen some of the energy that the arrow has borrowed from the bow by using ki. Each of us has ki. Your ki is close to your body. When ki is away from the body, we call it the Field. I could teach you, if you really want to learn."

"Seriously?"

"For now, it's best if we keep moving. Whoever shot that arrow could be tracking us. Pay close attention to your feet. The Way of Balance begins with your feet touching the earth. As your focus grows and you're able to control your awareness, we'll move on with your training." She wanted to tell him that it really didn't matter what you were paying close attention to, so long as you were paying close attention. Since they were walking all day, she decided to make things as simple and practical as possible for him.

Mavin replayed the event over and over in his mind. He was compelled to consider the world from an entirely different perspective. Before that moment when the arrow was arcing down on him, the physical space between things contain only air, the perfect medium for an arrow to pass through. Now, like Ørsted discovering electromagnetism, he understood that ki was all around him. Simone didn't know about electrons circling the nucleus of an atom, but he was forced to consider that she had a real connection and understanding of the unseen forces that bind the world together.

# Rub a Little Dirt On It

It's not the deprivations of winter that gets you,
or the damp of spring, but the no man's land between.
—Kristin Kimball

There were no mountains on the horizon to gauge their progress. "Is there no end to this wasteland?" Mavin hated the desert.

"Concentrate on your feet," she said. Why did he constantly wish to be somewhere else? What choice was there, but to accept the world?

The only change to the flat barren landscape was the fast-growing grass that had erupted after the last heavy rain. In the span of two weeks, the short grass was already going to seed and turning brown. The late morning sun began to reflect off the cracked earth like a clay oven.

Simone stopped to dig a root with her harpoon. The stubby green top had only two small leaves, but the yellow root proved to be as long as her forearm. She drove the harpoon into the soft sand at a slight angle. "Let's make shade." It was far too hot to walk over the blistering flat during the middle of the day.

Mavin unrolled the mat he carried and tied one corner to the top of the harpoon and then scavenged a handful of rocks to weigh down the other three corners. They went through the motions with mindless skill, repeating movements from countless times before.

Simone had pulled handfuls of grass and twisted the fibers between her fingers as they walked, eventually creating a coil of twine. When they stopped to rest she wove the new length into the growing shade mat. She joined him under the small bit of shade and with her long knife quickly peeled and shaved the long root onto a small piece of woven cloth. She held up the cloth and squeezed drops of juice into Mavin's mouth like a bird feeding its young. The bitterness of the juice reminded Mavin of the worst walnut he had ever eaten. "This root juice is as bad as the medicine teas my grandmother used to make me drink," he complained. He was amazed how his throat felt drier than before drinking the astringent liquid. Nonetheless, he thanked her and returned the favor, squeezing a few drops into her mouth, careful not to miss.

They slept through the heat of the afternoon. A mild breeze woke Simone and she nudged Mavin. "It's time to walk." She helped him up and they quickly broke camp.

He followed behind her in a half-conscious daze.

The breeze picked up and the heat abated. She waited for him to catch up. "Why do you hate the desert so much?"

"Who said I did?" He walked by her without looking up. Everyone died sometime. His grandfather told him you couldn't enter the afterlife until you had finished walking your invisible path. Two Feathers made him crazy with his brujo bullshit. Grandfather was right about some things, there were too many ghosts in the desert.

"Ever since we started across the sand, you've barely spoken." She noticed how his mood was steadily growing worse.

"I grew up in the desert. When I was a fifteen, my grandfather called me an Air-conditioner Indian." He realized the words didn't make sense to her. "My grandfather was Joseph Two Feathers, but everyone called him TwoBeers." He chuckled to himself. He kept his legs going and looked around for something to focus his drifting attention. He noticed the rocks around his feet were getting larger. He remembered the low rope-swing on their front porch. Both his grandfathers would watch him during the day when his mom was at work. The two old men would drink warm beer and argue.

"Lat, only drunks start before noon." Two Feathers handed his oldest friend another beer.

"You people," Latigo said, disgusted. He tapped the can and popped the top deflecting the warm stream. The dripping foam disappeared into the thirsty grain of the porch. Latigo shook off his trigger finger and continued, "You're in high feather. One beer and you're on your ass. Never understood why they call you TwoBeers?"

"Bite me." Two Feathers swatted a fly on the back of his neck.

"And the horse you rode in on. It's no wonder you lost to the white man." Latigo's father had been Irish, and despite his mother being full-blooded Indian, he always thought of himself as a white cowboy.

"Dumber than the post you hitch your pony to." Two Feathers laughed. "A true warrior doesn't need to tie up his pony. Hell, Lat. You can't even whistle up your dog."

"That's a goddamn lie." Latigo stuck two fingers in his mouth and let out an ear-piercing whistle. His dog Pinto perked up from his nap under a nearby Pinion pine, then flopped back down.

Mavin appreciated Pinto's contribution to the proceedings. He loved the way papa TwoBeers's whole body shook when he was busting a gut. He could tell grandpa Latigo's feelings were hurt.

"Rub a little dirt on it and tough it out, aye, Pinto?" Two Feathers choked on his next swig. "Lat, you know the white man didn't win with heart. They were chicken shit. They brought diseases to kill the people."

"Oh, here we go again. You act like we brought the measles and mumps to America on purpose. Ever hear of the bubonic plague? Plenty of white people died of that. Think about it. If we wanted to get rid of you like you claim, we would have..." He stopped and kicked his friend in the shin to stop him from laughing. "Shit. TwoBeers, you don't even have a pony. You gotta walk everywhere you go. Now—that's goddam funny."

"I have a truck, dumbshit. They say ignorance is bliss. Lat, you lucky bastard, you must be having a perpetual orgasm." TwoBeers shook with laughter.

"That was your old lady, when she used to sneak into my bed after you passed out."

They had grown up together, enlisted together, and gone to Vietnam together.

Mavin's mom came home from work and found them drunk on the porch again. She grabbed her broom and took a direct path to Latigo. "Is this what you call babysitting?"

Latigo showed amazing agility for a big man, by jumping off the porch just beyond the arc of the broom. Pinto woke up and started barking.

"You three been on the porch all day?"

"No, Momma. We went down to the river and…"

"Raven, don't bother lying for these two good-for-nothings. As usual, they didn't even bother to hide their empties." She looked at the pile of cans, and gave her father the stink face.

Latigo didn't wait around. He gave a quick tug on the cinch strap and swung his girth into the saddle in one move. He rode down the hill in a mixed gallop, Pinto in tow.

# The Corners

Before the seed there comes the thought of bloom.
–E. B. WHITE

The sun mercifully dipped into the haze. As Mavin's head cooled he came out of his daydream. He quickened his pace to catch up to Simone before it became too dark. Soon they would have only starlight. It was the new moon, a full month since they entered the barren flats. The small rocks around his feet had grown into sizable stones. "Simone!" He ran to catch up.

"What is it?"

"I remember something." He grabbed his face with both hands and tried to think. "These larger rocks mean something." He could see Papa TwoBeers shaking his head. "Let me." He gestured for Malina's harpoon.

Simone handed it over, and Mavin poked the ground as he went. She was delighted to see him take the lead. His method of prodding the ground was preciously amusing. The lark's song faded with the last rays of the sun. She could barely see Mavin three paces ahead.

"Holy shit." He stopped abruptly.

As she stepped around him, he grabbed her arm.

"What is it? A snake. I don't see anything."

"Exactly." He tapped the ground in front of her feet and then there was nothing. A narrow canyon sliced through the desert floor. It was too dark to see the other side. Mavin carefully leaned over the ledge and dropped a rock. There was no sound. "It's deep." Mavin swallowed the lump in his throat.

"I should have known that it's too dark to travel without the moon," Simone said, disgusted. "We'll sleep until first light." It upset that her that her senses were dull. The heat and lack of food and water had compromised her more than she wanted to admit. It didn't help matters that he may have saved her life again. She had no right to call herself a scout. Malina, Karin and her dead compatriots flooded her thoughts.

A chill ran down Mavin's spine. He thought about many nights they'd walked through the night to escape the heat of the day.

"Mavin, I have something important to ask you."

"What is it?"

"If anything happens—"

"Nothing is going to happen, go back to sleep." As weary as they both were, neither could sleep.

"Promise me, Mavin, that you'll take the seeds to Kashphera."

"I'm not promising, because nothing is going to happen to you."

At first light, they wasted the cool hours of the morning following a long rock finger that ended with a long steep drop off. Despite Mavin's protests, Simone attempted to climb down the sheer rock face. When Malina's harpoon slipped out of its lanyard and silently fell to the unseen bottom, she climbed back to the top exhausted.

Mavin was lying in the dust barely conscious.

"Rest. I'll keep searching for a way down," she said quietly, careful not to wake him.

In the intense heat of the afternoon, she nudged him awake. "Get up, Mavin."

She put her arm under his shoulder and dragged the pack.

"Where's Malina's harpoon?" he asked.

"I lost it."

"But…" He didn't understand. "We need it."

"It's gone."

Just when the heat became unbearable, they dipped into the shade of a narrow ravine. Mavin let out a guttural shriek when his right foot found a smooth carved step. "Civilization!" The stone treads were worn in the center. His heart raced. "Where are the people?" Had they vanished overnight like the Anasazi, or the nine billion people of his own time? He followed Simone down the serpentine steps until he could touch both sides of the smooth canyon wall with his outstretched arms. Only a wavy sliver of blue sky remained high above.

Simone paused and cupped her hands over her ears. The un-mistakable sound of gurgling water echoed through the canyon. They raced down the steps. When they reached the bottom, their feet sank into a deep mound of fine sand that had blown down the ravine over the years. A thick wall of green shrubs blocked their way. Simone bent the prickly branches back until Mavin could grab them.

He wondered if the oasis was real, when a green limb lashed him in the cheek.

They picked their way through a patch of nettles growing in the shade of the high cliff. Simone stopped. Mavin bumped into her and nearly lost his footing on the ledge. Below, a shallow spring gurgled up through clean gravel. He couldn't believe his eyes. From the base of the hot dry cliff flowed an underground river.

Simone un-slung her pack, and crawled down the bank. She kissed the surface of the water, said a prayer to the White Crane, and took a long cool drink.

Mavin slid down the bank headfirst. He dipped his head un-der the cool water before taking a small swallow. He followed the wonderful cool feeling all the way down his throat into his chest. It seemed like months since he was able to breathe through his nose. He was convinced they were going to die in the desert. He rolled on his back and laughed. Against the blue sky, he watched the blood flowing through the capillaries in his eyes. Blue-sky sprites.

Simone pulled off her buckskin dress and jumped in. Her slender form glided beneath the clear pool to the far bank.

Mavin rubbed his eyes. She was a guardian nymph, the river's child. He pulled off his leather pants and dove in. His body vibrated like a brass bell. He surfaced and watched her from behind, slowly rising out of the water. Her breasts lifted as she tied her hair above her head. She felt his eyes and looked over her shoulder.

He looked down at the water, but not in time. He was taken aback by her lack of modesty or immodesty. It was as if she had no awareness of her beauty. She sat on the opposite bank, so close and so completely out of reach. He tried to hold her eyes, but turned away. Despite sleeping next to her for nearly a year, she remained outside his understanding.

"I'm a genuine throwback," he said to his reflection. "Frozen, sidelined from evolution." His physical stature didn't compare to hers. "Guess who's coming to dinner? A Neanderthal."

She watched in wonder at the water gurgling from under the dry rock cliff. He swam to the far bank and joined her. "Is this a spring?" he asked.

"It's the headwaters of the holy river Neda. Generations fought and died over this place. It's the reason the Boundary was created nearly a thousand years ago."

Water was life. He understood why this had been a holy place since the beginning of time. No matter which goddesses or god you prayed to, sweet water springing from barren rock was a miracle. "It doesn't make sense. Why fight over a miracle?" he asked.

"The world is under no obligation to make sense."

"Good point." He couldn't believe he had ever thought of her as primitive. "How do you know this place?"

"There are many stories of the holy waters of Neda. Water is the indivisible thing, the beginning and the ending. The giver of life."

"Have you been here before?"

"It's forbidden, punishable by death."

"But we came here by mistake."

"It won't change our fate if we're discovered. The modern calendar begins here on this very spot 987 years ago."

For months, Mavin clung to the hope that they would run into a regular person, and everything would return to normal. He played along with her, swapping old legends. It was only a matter of time before they came across a town, and the charade would be over. The months passed, and the world remained empty. He was clinging to a fantasy in order to remain sane. There were no jet trails, no satellites in the night sky. No glow of a nearby city. Nothing. It was the year 987.

Simone made a fire and picked nettles. She set them over a pile of hot rocks and drizzled water over them, steaming the long green stems.

He was surprised by the sweetness of the nettles after the bitter roots they had been eating. They filled their water bags and headed downriver. Stone foundations crisscrossed the bedrock along both banks. Mavin could see sections of fluted columns half-buried in the thick brush. "Was this a city?"

"These are ruins of old temples, one built upon the other. A new goddess devouring the old through the ages."

"Some things never change."

She sensed something and scanned the rim of the cliffs behind them.

"What is it?"

"I'm not sure, probably nothing." Her sense of unease grew.

They walked until dark and made camp on top of a large boulder. The next morning Mavin could tell something was wrong.

"We need to double back." Simone sounded out of sorts.

"Why?"

"I wish I knew. We need to make sure we're not being followed."

"By who?"

"Just keep your eyes open, Mavin."

By noon they reached the base of the dry cliff. Mavin watched the water bubbling up as they skirted the source of the river. They follow the narrow ledge winding their way through the thick green brush as before. Simone froze at the base of the steps where their feet had plunged into the mound of fine sand.

"What's going on, Simone?" He didn't understand why they had come back. "What is it?"

She held her finger to her lips and whispered, "Look down, Mavin. What do you see?"

"Nothing."

"Where are our tracks from yesterday?"

A gust of wind blew a cloud of sand down the stairway canyon. Mavin closed his eyes and mouth until the sand passed.

Simone caught a distinct scent.

"The wind erased our footprints," he said. There was no other explanation.

Simone tapped him gently on the shoulder and pointed back the way they had come through the brush. "We need to go," she whispered.

When they reached a place where the trail widened, Mavin caught up to her. "What's the deal?"

"Dog People."

"Dog People? I don't like the sound of that."

"The Dog People are known for their ability to track and to cover their tracks. If we hadn't just come through that soft sand?"

The way she left the question dangle made Mavin nervous. "It was the wind. It really gusts down that canyon." He couldn't believe anyone could have followed them across the desert.

"Trust me, Mavin. We're being followed." There was an unmistakable scent of men. "I've heard the Dog People can track an animal over solid rock." She smiled. "We'll test their skills." She set off at a blistering pace through the old ruins.

"What should we do?" he called after her.

"Do you want me to say?"

"No," he said sarcastically. He stared down at his feet in an exaggerated way and quickened his pace holding out his arms like a clown balancing on an imaginary tightrope.

# The Black Hair

By respecting the trees, you prove
that you are a person who deserves to be respected.
—Mehmet Murat ildan

After two days of crisscrossing the river and stepping on only hard stones to cover their tracks, they came to a wide valley. The meandering river poured into a shallow lake whose banks were choked with tule grass.

Simone waded into the shallow water. Mavin reluctantly followed before she was lost in the maze of tall grass. He held his hands above the pointy ends of the grass that stung if you brushed against them.

"Do you know this lake?" he asked.

"These are the holy waters of the Zūr."

He could see rings on the calm surface of the water. "Fish!" He was excited to eat something besides roots and bugs.

They waded through the maze of tall grass until late afternoon. Simone picked out a small island amidst an endless archipelago. She unslung her pack, and in short order, transformed the spiny dried grass into a soft welcoming nest. "Take a rest, Mavin. I'll try to catch us some fish."

"I'm beat, but I'd like to help fish."

"Fine." She pulled a large flat rock from the clay bank. "Help me find more stones this shape or bigger."

"If you say so." As usual he had no idea of what she was up to.

When they had a good-sized pile, she leaned four stones, one against the other, like an A-frame. She looked at him, expecting him to understand the plan. "Help me carry them." She stacked a handful in her arms and set off to a deep pool where the fish were jumping.

"You'll scare them," he whispered.

She handed off her stack of stones, save two, and dove straight to the bottom of the deep pool. She came up a moment later with no fish or rocks. "Let me see two more." He handed her two more flat rocks and she disappeared again under the water. When she was done, and the water cleared, Mavin could see a small village of rock A-frames on the blue sandy bottom.

"Great. Now all the fish are long gone, and I'm starving."

"Yes, the fish have all gone off to hide," she said and giggled.

For a moment, her carefree laughter made the air feel lighter and the sunshine more golden on the tall grass surrounding them.

"Come on, Raven. You're scaring the fish," she teased.

"Too late." Hungry and frustrated, he followed her back to their little grass nest. He lay down in the waning light and immediately somersaulted into a dream. He awoke to the sound of Simone cleaning a pile of small fish.

He leapt to his feet in excitement. "How did you catch those?"

She held up her hands and wiggled her fingers.

"Seriously, with your hands?" he asked.

"Our fish returned to their favorite pool. When I waded over, they hid in the nearest place at hand." She mimicked closing her hands around the ends of her little fish traps. She had dug a small pit in the clay bank of their island and began making a fire.

"Aren't you afraid the Dog People will smell the smoke?"

"The marshland will protect us. We'll rest a few days and dry some fish for our journey."

"You'll get no argument from me."

The following day was the first they had not walked since escaping the seed vault twelve months before. To Simone's surprise, it was not the Dog People, but her conscience that caught up to her while they rested. "How can I explain what awaits Mavin when we reach Kashphera?" It felt deceitful to keep the truth from him. She doubted his ability to understand the complexities of society. She wouldn't be able to protect him once they reached civilization. One thing was clear: he would have to learn manners if he hoped to survive.

After getting a painful puncture on his finger from a dorsal fin, Mavin decided he preferred fishing with a hook and line. Since Malina's ivory hook was much too big, he decided he would carve a smaller version from a rib bone he had found. Simone was happy to lend her blade. She watched him with noticeable pride, as he shaved the edges of the tiny hook.

It was the first day that Mavin wasn't mentally and physically exhausted since waking from his long sleep. He had been in a state of emotional shock for months. He couldn't accept what had occurred. Whenever he tried to think of his friends and family, a wall appeared. Now, the barrier in his mind was coming into clean focus. He reached for the courage needed to face whatever was behind the wall. The same questions ran over and over again in his mind. What had ended the world? How long had he been asleep? Where were all the people? Had there been a nuclear holocaust or did a giant meteor wipe out every trace of civilization?

He decided early on that he would play his cards close to his chest. He remembered the prime directive from Star Trek. Simone's worldview seemed to be shaped by mythical stories. Growing up in the Pueblo, he understood that stories explained the universe. Morality differed from culture to culture. If you're a Makah Indian, you hunt and kill whales. If your tribe is Greenpeace, you believe it's wrong to kill such a majestic creature. He finished carving the hook and tied it to the thick twine. He sat on the bank, baited the hook with fish guts, and threw in his line.

It floated before soaking up water and sinking, carrying the bait to the sandy bottom.

"There is nothing like fishing to ponder the big questions," he confessed to the fish, who were ignoring his bait. His thoughts found the same warn groove, what caused the end of the world? He imagined his fishing line as a mobius loop, with no end or beginning. Everything is a cycle, he thought. "But things do end." He thought about his father serving in the military. "America, the greatest country on earth!" he yelled, scaring the fish. What was America's contribution to the world, he wondered, the Bill of Rights? Or did ideas of freedom matter without a massive military to back it up? Mavin never had the chance to discuss Mutual Assured Destruction with his father. In this new world order that he found himself in, it wasn't that far-fetched to believe that the knowledge in his head was the most dangerous weapon in existence. All it took was mixing sulfur with charcoal to make gunpowder. It made him cringe to think how with one slip of the tongue he could start the whole cycle of destruction turning.

He regretted not being able to be completely honest with Simone, but it was impossible. Nonetheless, his omissions were making him increasingly uncomfortable. How could he tell her the truth? It didn't matter in what century you lived. His own mother wouldn't believe that he had been frozen. He didn't believe it.

"The other night. How did you know the cliff was there?" Simone interrupted his thoughts.

"Something I picked up from my grandfather Two Feathers."

"You're not Sedna's child?"

"No. Of course I'm not Sedna's child!" he erupted at the absurdity.

She cupped her hand over her mouth and throttled her laugh. "I'm sorry."

"Don't be." He realized she was pulling his leg. "Never be sorry for a joke. I enjoy being teased."

"You keep that well-hidden."

"You have some nerve talking to me about secrets," he countered.

She watched the fish feeding on the surface of the lake. "You knew your grandfather?" she asked, as if it were next to impossible.

"You would have gotten on well with Papa TwoBeers. You have the same philosophy when it comes to the great outdoors. If you're not on the edge of death from hunger, thirst, or exposure; then you're missing the full experience. TwoBeers about killed me a couple of times. Don't get me wrong. Nothing as hectic as camping with you."

She was continually surprised by his resilience. She didn't think he would live an hour when she saw him lying on the icy floor bleeding. "You said your people are from the desert?"

"Yes. I grew up in the Southwest, a very long way from here."

"So why do you hate the desert so much?"

"I couldn't wait to leave." Why not just tell her the truth? She deserves to know. Would she understand about the ghosts of his ancestors? "Where are your people from?" He hid behind his question.

She cut a thick shaft of tule grass and waded over to a high cut bank. He reeled in his line and watched in silence as she deftly scratched a map into the soft clay.

"We are here. The frozen island of the Walrus People is high on the top of the world. We're heading southeast to the Diamond Province." She took several steps to her right to keep her map in scale. "I was born here, in the Eastern province. I don't remember much about where I was born." She took several steps to Mavin's left and stabbed the clay. "I was raised here, just below the Black Hair layer."

"I've heard you talk about the days of the Black Hair. Was it a long time ago?"

She pointed to a thin black layer in the embankment. "It is here."

"What do you mean? This is it?" He felt the sharp line in the clay. "This is the black hair?" He dug some out with his fingernails. It felt brittle and flaky. "I think this is mica, a kind of natural glass." He rinsed the brittle flake off in the water and held it up to the sun. It wasn't translucent. He snapped the wafer-thin piece in half.

Is this from my time? he wondered. Or is this all that remains? He looked at the ten feet of sediments sitting on top of the thin layer of carbon-colored glass. Layers of clay and sand were not the same as tree rings you could count like years. Radiocarbon dating could tell how much time had passed. "Now, I just need an Accelerator Mass Spectrometer and I can measure how long I was asleep," he said to himself.

"In the old stories of men, their sky god exiled them from the garden." She watched his reaction.

"The garden of Eden?"

"You know the story?" She knew he was keeping things from her. "Do you worship the sky god?"

"My mother took me to Catholic mass, but it didn't take."

"Tell me more about your mother's people," she asked. How could he have no knowledge of the civilized world? How far away could his land be?

He noticed how she said, his mother's people. How could a man have his own people? He let it go. "The Spanish called us Zuni, but we call ourselves Ashiwi." He couldn't tell her about gunpowder or Einstein's theory of Relativity, but he could tell her about his childhood. "We trace our ancestors back through our mother. So, I guess you're right, they are my mother's people." He could see her face relax. "The Zuni believe the world has gone through many ages. Long ago we dwelt in a place of no light, deep under the earth called the Fourth World. Awonawilona, who created all things, took pity on the people and sent his two sons to guide the people to the light. To prepare for the journey, Awonawilona's sons planted four seeds. They became a pine, a spruce, a silver spruce, and an aspen."

"I enjoy your tall tree tales." She laughed. "But why are all the people in your stories men? Is your story meant to be humorous?"

"No, I don't think so," he said curtly. Maybe she had a point, but he didn't care for it.

She wanted to believe that he was different from other men. "My eldest mother told me of the Time of Water and the Age of Fire. Do you know these stories?"

"No, I would love to hear them."

She looked at the clouds passing overhead, collecting her thoughts. "I'm sorry, I'm unable to translate the verses exactly. They won't rhyme or have the pleasant agreements at the end of a stanza in English."

"That's fine, I won't know the difference."

"Before there were stories, women ruled in the Time of Water. Our ancestors observed nature closely and uncovered the secrets of ki, the energy that binds all things together. There was peace and equality. The Goddess Eirene gave birth to a male child. She named him Asura. On Asura's nineteenth birthday, he stole fire from the mountaintop and waged a bitter war against his mother and sisters. This was the beginning of the Age of Fire. Asura, Destroyer of Worlds, scorched the earth and burned women like logs on a fire. The sky became black with their smoke, neither the sun, the moon, nor the stars shined. In the never-ending night, the people, the animals and the plants withered. The trees stood silent witness as evil men destroyed the earth. The trees made a vow to each other that they would never again grow higher than man's shoulders to punish them for their wickedness. In the never-ending night the few remaining people hid under the earth. When I saw you the first time, I thought you were from the Age of Fire, before the Dark Hair." She looked at him, expecting him to deny it.

"Oh," was all he was able to say.

"Don't you remember? You said you were hot in the freezing cold?" She knew he was hiding something.

"Your old stories are very sad." he didn't want to talk about being under the mountain.

"The goddess you call, Awonawilona, who led the people out of darkness, we call White Crane. She is the Daughter of Avighna. Like your goddess, the White Crane led the people from the darkness deep under the earth into the light. It was the beginning of the Third Age."

He started to correct her and checked himself. Awonawilona was a god, not a goddess. Did it really matter? Did anyone really know? He wanted to ask her more about the Age of Fire. Maybe there were clues hidden in the story about the destruction of civilization. "Tell me more of Asura, the destroyer of worlds." The Age of Fire sounded eerily like the Medieval Inquisitions of Europe.

"It's time to sleep, Mavin. Tomorrow we travel before your calluses get soft."

# Crossroads

The flowing water makes the still mountain move;
the vivid trees make the obdurate stone alive.
—SHITOA

They climbed out onto a tongue of land that spilled out into the barren flats. The wind-swept dunes below looked like cuneiform script. Simone took a moment to watch for any movement behind them before studying the terrain that lay ahead. To the west a domed-shaped mountain rose out of the flat plateau.

"Look, Mavin. Do you see that yellow cloud near that round mountain?"

"I don't think it's a mountain."

She laughed. "So, a mountain is not a mountain?"

"I've seen this type of mound before. It's called a Tell. It's a man-made mound." He saw the sour expression on her face. "You know what I mean, human-made. That mound was a city a very long time ago."

"All right," she said. "Say I believe you. Do you see that smoke?"

"Yes."

"When is smoke not smoke?"

"When it's dust."

"You are clever, for a man." She hoped it was a dust devil, but the absence of wind made this an unlikely theory. "It may be a herd of goats and a shepherd."

"That doesn't look like a herd of goats." He had been around plenty of sheep and goats.

"Those far mountains to the west are where the Jara people live. They were never conquered. We don't want to meet the Jara. We need to be cautious crossing this flat."

"That's too bad. The area around that Tell would be very... interesting." It took all of his willpower not to make the pun.

"Why?" She was constantly surprised by his inquisitive nature.

"I'm not sure if any of the seeds in our pack will germinate. To be honest, the chances are slim to none. If you're looking to improve wheat, you need to cross breed your seeds with old cultivars. There's a good chance that whoever built that city thousands of years ago grew food. This is desert now, but way back when, this was probably a lush valley where they grew grains and tended orchards." For all he knew the mound could be from his own time.

"Leto would not have led us to the top of the world to bring back seeds that are not alive," she corrected him.

"If you say so." He knew how badly they both needed to believe the seeds would sprout, which made it all the more unlikely.

She started down the ridge and headed south across the erg. The mysterious dust cloud slowly made its way to the east of them. They wove through the high crescent-shaped dunes keeping to the hard parched clay. Crossing the high drifts of soft sand took more time and energy than going around them. In the late afternoon they cautiously approached a well-defined track in the hardpan. Simone studied the signs carefully before making a decision. "It's half a day old."

"Is it the Jara?" Mavin asked.

"Possibly. This track looks to have been made by a hundred or more disciplined troops. This is a serious violation. This great a number are not allowed in the Boundary. The Triumvirate must be made aware." She stepped into a boot print showing Mavin how to step completely inside of the next print. "It's important you concentrate, Mavin. Do you understand?"

"We're heading in the direction of the most feared people in the world? What's not to understand?"

"Pay attention to your feet."

"Don't worry, I never forget the Prime Directive." He was sorry the minute he said it. "No harm, no foul," he mumbled. She had no idea what he meant. "Are you worried the Dog People are still following us?"

"Do you want to turn around and ask them?"

"Not so much."

"At times, I feel we are still being watched." Her strategy was simple. If the Dog People were following them, would they want to take on an army of Jara? Why else, they will ask themselves, would we travel in the same direction unless they are our allies? She was very pleased with her plan. They would use one potential foe to rub off the other. Once they neared the hogback ridge that cut across the flat, they would follow it south.

# From Before

Give me the fruitful error anytime,
full of seeds, bursting with its own corrections.
–Vilfredo Pareto

Simone looked up from the track and studied the cloud of dust on the horizon. It took a moment for her to realize it was moving towards them. Her gamble was turning into a big error in judgment.

"Mavin. They're coming back."

"The Jara?"

"I don't think we should wait to ask. We need to run. That rock rise to the south is our best hope." The uplifted seam of sandstone cut a sinuous line through the flats. She set off in an aggressive pace despite the heavy pack.

Mavin fell into his own steady gait and was soon left behind. Two hours later, Mavin stopped to catch his breath and relieved himself. His urine pooled, refusing to seep into the powdery dry earth.

Simone reached the sandstone ridge first and began searching for a way to climb over it. There were thickening clouds all day. She prayed to the White Crane for a heavy rain to hide their tracks. The booming thunder in the distance grew steadily louder.

Mavin caught up to her and braced his hands on his knees trying to catch his breath. He unconsciously counted after every thunderclap, "One Thousand and one, one thousand and two, one thousand—"

Simone plunged her walking stick into the ground just as a bolt of lightning struck directly in front of them. The flash was blinding. The severity of the thunderclap knocked the wind out of Mavin.

"We need cover!" Simone scrambled around the rocks searching every crevice. She could feel the hair on the back of her neck tingling.

Small pellets of graupel struck the ground and melted into sludge underfoot. Round balls of hail bounced all around them. Then, as if heaved all at once from the heavens, chunks of ice came down covering everything in white.

Mavin held his hands on his head. Large hailstones stung the back of his hands. He remembered a story his mother told him. Awonawilona's son had a prayer stick of pine. When he struck the ground with it, the wooden staff became a bolt of lightning.

Simone found a narrow space under a rock ledge. "Mavin. Come quickly!" She slung off her pack and dug frantically with her stick. When the space was large enough, she helped him scramble under the rock. "Climb back as far as you can." She crawled on her belly and dragged the pack behind her. It wedged in the opening. She raked the loose gravel aside with her bare hands until the pack was free. "Mavin?" She choked on the dust and dirt. It was pitch black.

"I'm here." He was grateful to find shelter from the giant hail pummeling his head, but it was distressing being in a hole in the ground. He became nauseated.

Simone crawled back and joined him. She opened the pack and dug through Malina's bag. "Hold on to Malina's lamp." She struck her flint repeatedly, heating the wick until it sputtered and lit. The small flame flickered sending out pulsating shadows. She saw the look on his face. "What's wrong with you? Are you ill?"

He was about to retch. Having been trapped under the mountain for an eternity, he felt the weight of the earth on his chest. The lamplight reflected off the ceiling of the cave behind her. His eyes widened.

She turned and gasped. They were sitting on a high balcony of a massive underground theater. "Take care of the flame, " she said. "Don't let it go out. I'll be back in a couple of minutes."

She returned dragging a bundle of thorny grass. "It's wet, but it will burn." She wrapped a handful of grass into a tight bundle and lit one end with the lamp. The torch flame sputtered illuminating the massive chamber.

They stared, unable to find any words. The horns of a giant painted bull reached out to them in the darkness. The walls were alive with herds of wild animals.

"Are they real?" She had never seen such creatures.

"Yes. Those are saber-toothed cats." He pointed, "Those are wildebeests and giant mastodons." He looked in amazement at what he thought was a flying saucer, and then realized that it was a disc-shaped cloud with rain falling below it. The white dots of paint suddenly became giant hailstones. He laughed. "Look, the paintings are telling our story." He pointed to the very weather that had delivered them.

"Those round clouds, we call mercies." She could just make out a faded yellow bolt of lightning.

They picked their way through fallen rock and debris strewn over the cavern floor. Metal girders and aluminum struts were piled like massive Pick Up Sticks. It took Mavin a minute to realize they were standing in what had been a visitor's lobby. He recognized the remains of a ticket booth. Dilapidated sections of shelving were covered in three inches of fine dust. He followed his shadow from Simone's torch. "This area was a gift shop." The words fell out of his mouth. He stepped on a large flat panel that rocked under his weight. He brushed off a thick blanket of dust. It was a thick sheet of glass. The rubber seals holding it had long since disintegrated. The huge rectangles of glass had tumbled down like giant playing cards without breaking.

Mavin remembered reading about the Lascaux cave, how mold threatened the cave art. Glass had been installed and a special gas pumped into the cave to preserve the paintings.

Simone picked her way through the debris to the cave wall and held up her torch. "Are they goddesses?" She felt the colors with her fingertips, caressing a horse's mane.

Mavin thought about explaining how acid from her fingertips would damage the paintings, but checked his thought. Could irony be stacked any higher? This pre-historic art had survived, when every trace of modern civilization had vanished. He would never again doubt the tensile strength of irony. "They're not gods and goddesses." He stepped over a fallen stalactite and joined her. "My people call them animal spirits."

He began to feel ill again. He sat down before he collapsed.

She could feel the spirit of the wild animals surrounding them. "Do you know this place?" He didn't answer. "Mavin?" She shook him by the shoulder. "Mavin, are you okay?" His eyes were lazy and out of focus.

I'll tell her everything, he decided. These paintings are tens of thousands of years old. But when is now? The more he pressed for answers, the further he descended into the underworld. How long had he been frozen behind glass? His mind compiled the evidence, cataloged the facts, but couldn't perform the calculation. He looked up at Simone dressed in skins as she gazed at the extinct creatures depicted on the cavern wall. She melded into the paint and charcoal. He closed his eyes and saw green spots from the torchlight. He rolled on his side and fought off the urge to vomit.

He quit school when he was fifteen. A month later, he was caught siphoning gas from the church bus. He swallowed a mouthful of gas and was heaving when the priest showed up. Father Riley went to the tribal council and convinced them that the best penance was to have Mavin pick up trash along the highway until he decided to show up for school and church.

Mavin walked for miles along the empty highway with a black plastic bag slung over his shoulder. He reached down and shook out the sand from a Styrofoam clamshell container. He could just make out the golden arches.

Two Feathers drove up in his rusty Ford. "Get in, asshole."

Mavin tossed the trash bag in the bed of the pickup and jumped in the cab. They drove for two hours without saying a word.

Two Feathers glanced over and watched his grandson expertly roll a joint.

The broken spring in the old bench seat was poking Mavin in his left butt cheek. "Why don't you fix this seat?" Mavin grumbled.

"I don't sit over there." Two Feather's whole body shook when he laughed.

Mavin lit a stick match, burned the paper off the end of the fat spliff and took a big hit. He offered it to his grandfather without looking.

"Only losers smoke their breakfast." Two Feathers kept both eyes on the empty road.

Mavin coughed. "Oh yeah, forgot. You drink your breakfast." He took another long hit and held it. Mavin recognized Grandpa Latigo's lariat hanging behind the seat on the rifle rack. The braided honda knot was the finest he had ever seen. "Is it true that Grandpa Latigo died in a bar fight?"

"Dumber than a fence post, and tough as nails." TwoBeers smiled, remembering his best friend.

"Were you with Grandpa Latigo when he died?"

"Nope."

"Tad Parsons said that a logger down at the Forester's Bar called you a dirty Indian, so Latigo punched the logger in the nose, outnumbered ten to one."

"Tad Parsons wasn't there." The fracas happened in a bar on the Rue Catinat in Saigon with a table full of drunken Marines. It was one of many times Latigo saved his skin and lived to embellish the tale over and over again. The highway was straight, but Two Feathers had to fight the wheel to keep the old rig on the right side of the pavement. He slowed down and then abruptly turned off the shoulder into the thick brush.

Mavin coughed out smoke. "This ain't a road, TwoBeers!" He glanced at the gas gauge, and then remembered it was broken, along with the speedometer cable. He reached over and, despite the bumpy ride, managed to set the dash clock to 4:20. He smirked and waited. "Club 4:20?" He was disappointed when grandfather didn't get the joke.

Two Feathers was too busy swerving around giant cactus, zigzagging his way through the chaparral. The play in the worn steering box made for an exaggerated amount of steering.

Mavin got the giggles from the weed and grandfather's cartoon-like driving. Dust filled the cab, adding to the thick layer on the dash, and to Mavin's cottonmouth. "You got anything to drink?"

"In the back." Twobeers pointed with his thumb.

Mavin pulled the pair of vise-grips clamped on the broken door-latch and jumped out. They were crawling along at a snail's pace. He reached over the sideboard and grabbed the pack of Bud, and jumped back into the cab. He popped the top and handed grandfather the can of warm beer.

The old man grabbed the necker knob with his left hand and expertly maneuvered between the cactus while taking a long swig.

"You gonna tell me where the hell we're going?" Mavin was running out of patience with the senile old drunk.

"I've no fucking idea."

They were out of beer when the engine coughed and died.

"What's up, TwoBeers?"

"Out of gas."

"Why are we out of gas?"

"Beats me. Blame it on the Bossa Nova." The old man opened his door and laced up his boots.

"What do we do now?"

"Walk."

Mavin pretended not to be scared, but this was getting crazier by the minute, even for TwoBeers. After Latigo died, TwoBeers would disappear into the desert for months. Mavin got out his rolling papers and licked his fingers. When he looked up grandfather was gone. "What the..." Mavin climbed out of the cab and raced around the other side of the rig. He was too stoned, drunk and angry to think. He beat through the brush looking for the crazy old man. "TwoBeers!" He glimpsed a red headband through the blooming sage. He caught up, and pushed out his breath, expecting an explanation. They walked without talking until sunset.

Two Feathers gathered wood and made a fire.

Mavin pulled out his remaining stash and rolled a fatty. He stuck a twig in the fire, lit his last joint and unconsciously passed it.

"Only punks smoke their dinner," Two Feathers said before taking a prodigious hit. He coughed, allowing some of the thick smoke to escape. "What happened to you, grandson? I thought you made up your mind to become a man. Now look at you?"

"Screw you and the horse you rode in on." Mavin was proud to remember Papa Latigo's old saw.

"Grandson, words are not just sounds. Words are magic."

"Like the magic that erupts from the end of a bull?" Mavin giggled.

"Get some sleep. We've ground to cover tomorrow or we'll be dried bones."

The next morning Mavin opened his eyes to a coyote staring right at him. "What the hell!"

The coyote disappeared in a flash.

Two Feathers was sitting nearby. The old man's body shook in silent laughter. Mavin jumped up and dusted himself off. "Fuck, TwoBeers! Were you just gonna sit there and let him take a bit out of me?"

"He didn't want to eat you. He recognized you."

"From where?"

"From before."

"Very funny."

They walked through the heat of the day. Mavin chased his thoughts, but was unable to grasp the trouble they were in. He was light-headed from lack of food and water. A skunk staggered by in front of him looking blind drunk.

"Rabid skunk. That's a bad sign." Two Feathers said under his breath and looked upset.

"How do you know it's rabid?"

"Have you ever seen a skunk in the middle of the day?"

"It must be your animal spirit," Mavin said.

"If you weren't an Air-conditioner Indian, you'd know that it's dangerous to offend the spirits."

Mavin didn't like the look on the old man's face. He watched the skunk disappear into the bush. "I'll tell you what's dangerous—being out in the middle of bumfuck with no food or water! I don't remember agreeing to die out here."

TwoBeers smiled. "Oh? Grandson, what agreements do you remember entering into?" The desert was already healing the boy.

"I sure as fuck don't remember agreeing to this. When I jumped in your truck I thought you were going to give me a ride to town."

"Ha! People living in town are the lost ones. They're surrounded by familiar things and thousands of invisible agreements they don't remember making."

"If it's a choice between wandering around in the desert like a rabid skunk or eating pistachio gelato on a park bench? Gee, TwoBeers! You've really got me in a tight spot, I give up."

"Before today, Grandson, I thought you had given up." TwoBeers slapped the boy on the back. "We have to keep moving." The old man quickened his pace leaving the youth behind.

By late afternoon, Mavin's head was swimming in the heat. He followed TwoBeers up a meandering arroyo in a waking dream. The sandy banks of the dry riverbed narrowed into a red rock canyon. Mavin watched the old man scramble, like a spider, up a bank of scree and disappear under an outcropping of limestone.

Mavin clambered up the loose rocks, cursing under his breath. When he reached the top, the cool shade of the overhanging rock was a blessed relief. He laid flat on his back and caught his breath. He was about to bellyache some more when he noticed the rock painting above him. The tall black figures startled him. He closed his eyes and saw green spots. His stomach knotted. The images on the rock invaded his thoughts. The black shapes weren't threatening. Nonetheless, Mavin made every effort to block them. He clamped his eyes shut and covered his ears. When he finally got the courage to open his eyes, the dark shapes were floating around him.

He could hear their soft laughter. They were women carrying water from the river below, balancing water-vases on their heads. They seemed to delight in his pitiful attempts to keep them at bay.

Simone felt his forehead. He was panting like a dog, his skin was stone cold. She knew better than to try to wake him.

Mavin writhed on the ground—while in his mind—he ran naked through the desert. Balancing their full vessels, the women effortlessly kept pace without spilling a drop.

An hour later when Mavin opened his eyes, Simone was beside him tending the fire.

"How are you feeling?" she asked.

Her dark eyes glistened in the firelight like the first time he saw her wearing a white fur hood. Behind her, in the shadows, a herd of bison eluded a band of hunters. He got to his feet and pointed to a black horse. "Horses. That's what we need."

"They're real?"

"Of course they're real. I've ridden lots of horses."

"More tall tree stories?" She smiled.

He studied the paintings. "Look how the bison are running from those men?"

"Why would they be running from men?"

"Because they are hunting them."

"Men hunting?" She let out a high-pitched giggle that echoed off the cavern walls.

He had to smile. She was more of a mystery now, than when he awoke from his long sleep. He compared her physical stature to his own. She was slightly taller and by far stronger and more graceful. He looked closer at the painted figures. Maybe she was right; maybe not all of the hunters were men. He had to unseat his own bias, if he hoped to change her prejudices.

"Were you having a dream?" She was uncomfortable prying, but if he did have a vision it could be important to their survival. "You were tossing in your sleep."

"I dreamed I was with my grandfather in the middle of the desert without food or water. There were these figures painted on the rock. The dark ones." He couldn't think of any other way to describe them.

She noticed how his limbs were trembling. "Were they evil?"

"I don't think so. They were older than that." He realized that didn't make any sense. "I mean, they seemed old, really old, before good and bad. Sorry, I know that sounds crazy."

"It was more than a dream, Mavin. You had a vision."

"Why would you say that?" he barked. The rock painting of the women carrying water had not frightened him; what scared him to death was hearing their laughter and watching them floating all around him. He clenched his fists. Once you abandon reason—you've crossed over into insanity. He saw her downcast look. "I'm sorry, Simone, that I yelled at you."

"Tell me about the dark ones," she asked.

"They floated all around me, trying to get inside of me. I did everything I could to keep them away. I blacked out. When I woke up, I had a terrible fight with my grandfather. I screamed at him, 'We're lost, you old fool!' Grandfather said that I'd better find the way back to the road. I told him I didn't know the way. He said he didn't know either. I was so angry, I just marched back the way we came, or so I thought. We walked that second day in the heat with no water. My head was pounding. I was sure we were going to die."

"Now I understand why you don't like the desert," she said.

"At dusk, we came to a stack of red chimney rocks lit up by the last rays of the sun. Up against the painted cliffs was an old abandoned pueblo. No one had lived there for a long time. The roofs were fallen in, the wood timbers all rotted. Grandfather hugged me. 'I knew you were the one,' he said. 'Our ancestors, the Anasazi lived here. The ancient ones.' Underneath a fallen wall, I found a perfect clay jar sealed with beeswax. It was full of beautiful shiny beans with patterns on them like an Appaloosa horse. We slept in the old pueblo. The next morning grandfather tied his Barlow knife to a long stick and we gathered saguaro fruit to eat. I carried that heavy clay pot full of seeds all the way home."

He left out the part where TwoBeers led them straight back to his truck where he had a gas can stashed in back of the bench seat, along with an emergency six-pack of Bud. On the ride back to town TwoBeers gushed with pride. Not because Mavin had found the beans, but because his grandson had seen behind the smoke to the real world.

"Did the old beans grow?"

"They sprouted and the seeds spread quickly among the people. We plant beans, corn and squash together. We call them 'The Three Sisters.' When the corn is ankle high, we plant the beans and squash. You can hear the corn growing at night. The beans wrap around and climb the stalks of corn. The squash vines grow thick and keep the soil moist. I returned to high school that fall and wrote an article about finding the beans."

"Boys go to school?" She couldn't hide her surprised.

"Yes, all children go to school. Based on the strength of my paper I received a tribal scholarship to attend the University of New Mexico. When I graduated, my favorite professor, Dr. Sinclair asked me to go to Turkey with him to look for old cultivars." He saw her confused look. "Professor Sinclair and I searched for wild plants and collected their seeds. Sinclair was my dearest friend. I called him, Professor Aronnax, and he called me, Prince Dakkar." It made Mavin happy to remember his mentor. "After our final excursion, we took our collection of seeds to Svalbard, the mountain where you found me." He realized it was the first time he had told her the unfiltered truth. It was a great relief.

The fire sputtered and went out.

"I need out of here, Simone." Remembering being trapped under the mountain in Svalbard caused his heart to race.

When they emerged from the cave it was an hour after sunrise, the morning was still crisp. Mavin filled his lungs with sweet air. "The coast is clear." He stretched his back.

"The ocean is many leagues from here," she corrected him.

"It's an expression like... hope springs eternal." He tried again, "Bite off more than you can chew." He realized he had, when his examples fell on stony ground. "Never mind."

They headed south along the rocky seam. Mavin glanced back over his shoulder. The mound on the horizon behind them was calling. "If Professor Sinclair were here, Jara or no Jara, we would be headed back to that Tell."

# Garbanzos

*If you reveal your secrets to the wind you should not
blame the wind for revealing them to the trees.*
—KHALIL GIBRAN

The narrow arête ridge they were following rounded into a wide saddle as they dropped deeper into the canyon. They paused to take in the view of the river below. Stunted yellow pines covered the hot southern slope. Across the valley, on the shady north face, a forest of bonsai firs and spruce were artfully arranged on speckled granite cliffs.

They slid down a steep game trail to the cascading river. Mavin trained his eyes on the deepest pools looking for trout. He thought he saw a dark shape moving across the gravel bed. He looked up to see that he had once again fallen behind. He quickened his pace, while keeping a watchful eye out for fish. When he rounded a wide bend, Simone was in the middle of the trail holding up her hand.

At the confluence of two streams, a man was standing on a large rock. The stranger held a line in his hand and was oblivious to their presence.

Mavin was elated to see another human being.

Simone slid her pack silently from her shoulder. With both hands on her walking stick she approached the riverbank.

The stranger turned. After the surprise washed over his rugged features, his face softened into a smiled. Just as he called out a greeting, he felt a nibble and carefully reeled in the line. A fat-bellied trout leaped into the air right in front of him and disappeared. The empty hook danced on top of the current.

"Ahh!" The clean-shaven stranger let out a groan and gathered in the remaining line. He curled it neatly in his hands and jumped to a small rock. Just as he was about to leap on to the bank, Simone got there first. She pointed her staff directly at the big man, causing him to teeter on the small rock.

"Who are you?" she demanded.

The stranger reached down and regained his footing. "I'm Hester."

"What are you doing here?"

Hester laughed and held up his line. "Fishing."

The knife on his right hip made Simone anxious. "Are you alone?" The stranger had blue eyes with an orange ring around his left pupil.

"Until a moment ago."

*What was it about these men from the north?* She wondered, first Mavin, now this stranger is looking straight into my eyes. "Are you such a wild man that you have no manners?"

The man's mouth gaped open, but he continued to stare.

"What river is this?" She kept up her interrogation.

"I'm a traveler new to this valley."

"From which direction did you come?" She tapped her long staff hard on the rocks.

Mavin had never heard her speak so harshly. The stranger seemed harmless enough, despite his wide shoulders and powerful build. His short dark hair was wet from sweat. Mavin guessed he was in his late thirties, his face weathered from the sun. He was bare-chested and wore stained leather leggings.

"As I've just said, I'm a traveler. I'm not from anywhere." The stranger nearly lost his balance. "If I throw you my blade, will you let me off this rock before I fall in?"

"Where's your bow?"

"I'm but a humble fisherman."

"A humble liar, you mean," Simone countered.

Her tone unnerved Mavin. This stranger was the first person he had seen in months; he was anxious to make a new friend, not an enemy.

"I see the calluses on your fingers. I'll ask you for the last time. Where is your bow?" Simone looked ready to strike.

"It is hidden just there, under the cut bank." The stranger pointed upstream.

"Unfasten your belt and throw it to me. If you unsheathe your blade, I'll not hesitate."

Hester slowly unbuckled his belt and tossed his knife and fishing line unto the bank in front of Simone.

"Mavin, take the blade. Go look for the bow. Be careful; something isn't right."

"May I sit?" Hester was tired of balancing on the small rock and sat without waiting for a reply.

She knew the stranger could easily escape by jumping into the fast moving current. "Why have you been following us?"

Hester dangled his legs in the eddy of the rock. He laughed. "Why have you been following me?"

Mavin strapped on the knife and waded upstream. He reached behind where the water had undercut the bank and pulled out a long bundle. He climbed up the bank and unwrapped the oilskin to find a fine longbow and a quiver of arrows. Mavin anchored the tip of the bow with his left foot and bent it around his hip, expertly stringing the bow. He slid an arrow out of the quiver and notched it. He drew it back to his cheek and took momentary aim at the sitting figure. "Nice rig," he said to Hester and winked at Simone.

She didn't show any surprise at his ability. "Do you recognize the fletching?" she asked, keeping her attention on Hester.

"It looks very much like the arrow that was shot at me. But that was months ago, before we crossed the desert."

Simone thought about the cave paintings and Mavin's vision.

He was right. There are men who hunt. "Fisherman, why have you been following us for the last three moons?"

Hester didn't understand how she knew. "Please understand, it was only meant as a warning shot. When I saw my arrow bend in mid-flight, I couldn't believe my eyes. I thought you must be a witch. What will you do now, kill me?" Hester's voice didn't carry the necessary concern.

"I'm not a witch. And you're not a dog, you just smell like one. Tell your smelly dog friends to come out where we can see them. Then, maybe I won't kill you." Simone glanced up the hill behind her.

Hester smelled under his arm and laughed heartily. "Do I smell? Really?" When Simone turned to look at Mavin, Hester made a quick signal.

On the high ground above them, a thin man emerged from behind a rock. He had a bald patch on the side of his head that looked like a rat bite. To his left, a big black man emerged from a thicket with his bow drawn.

Hester shook his head.

The black man slid the arrow back in his quiver. Two more men appeared from nowhere.

"These are my companions; Melky, Bellows, Teak, and Jacoby." When Simone turned to face the greater number, Hester jumped on the bank and circled around her, keeping a safe distance. "Don't mind the ladies. They're not used to the company of men, or at least men who are not cattle."

His compatriots laughed, and eyed Simone's shapely figure.

"The tall one says I smell." Hester acted offended.

"You need a bath," she explained.

The men roared with delight.

She drove her staff into the ground. In one fluid motion she took a step in Hester's direction and pushed the air with open palms.

Hester flew backward into the river and was carried downstream.

The men stood watching, not believing what had just happened. The woman was nowhere near Hester and had no weapon.

Hester struggled in the strong current until he reached a rock bar. He waded through the shallows kicking the top of the water. "Don't do that again." He was smiling, but not pleased to be embarrassed in front of his men.

Mavin gauged the weight and thickness of the notched arrow between his fingers as the four big men slowly advanced down the hill. He wasn't confident he could hit a moving target at a distance. He planned his first and second shot.

Hester leaped up the bank and walked up to Simone. He made a mock bow before sitting down on the ground in front of her. "Truce?" He patted the ground for her to join him. "If we wanted to harm you, we could have easily done so by now."

"A hasty assumption," She kept her eyes on the greater number.

"For the love of cranes! What does it take for you and your hairless friend to extend a little courtesy?"

"The truth would have served you better from the start. Why have you been tracking us?" she asked.

"What's your name?" Hester decided to take control of the situation.

She closed her eyes.

Hester struggled to breathe. He pushed on his diaphragm to force the air from his chest.

Mavin watched Hester's face contort. A moment later the big stranger collapsed on his side gasping for breath.

The big black man, Melky drew his blade.

Mavin drew the bow. "Ah, ah!"

Melky and the other three men watched helplessly as their leader writhed and twisted. Fear permeated the ground.

Hester caught his breath and managed to get to his knees. "I was just saying to my friends, how we're not used to being in the company of a Lady."

"That much is clear." Simone looked at Mavin to let him know he could relax. "I am a Janjanbi. Do you understand?" she looked at Hester.

"Yes. I've heard of the Janjanbi. He had wondered if the Völur of Nabhi were real. We've no quarrel with you or your friend. I give you my word." Hester bowed and pressed his forehead to the ground.

The other men waited for her to say something. When she did not, they knelt and pressed their foreheads to the ground.

She waited counting to ten. "I accept your word, Hester." Her voice was once again soft. She took his hand and helped him to his feet.

The bearded men stood up, noticeably relieved and kept their gazes lowered.

"You've been following us for months, so you know that we're heading southeast. We're bound for Kashphera."

"I've heard of this place, it lies in a high valley beside a vast lake." Hester had always wanted to see how it compared to his own high valley. From the moment he saw her, he knew she was no ordinary woman. In the months trailing them, he had had many occasions to observe her. He was amazed by her stamina and survival skills. He had grown impatient and hoped to catch her off guard. He had no idea how far out of his depth he was until the trap had already been sprung.

She followed his eyes to her pack. "Do you think we carry treasure?" She untied the top of the pack. She could feel their anticipation. "Is this what you're after?" She poured the foil packets on the ground. "Go ahead, Hester. Pick one. Mavin, give the man back his blade."

Mavin wasn't happy about any more packets being opened, but he understood why it was necessary. When Simone told the strangers she was a Janjanbi, he saw the fear in their eyes. He handed Hester back his knife.

Keep the knife as a gift. It's sharp enough to shave with, not that you have to worry about that, my tawno friend." Hester cracked Mavin on the shoulder.

The wild men laughed heartily. They had never seen a full grown man incapable of growing a beard. Hester drew a blade from his boot and cut open a packet of garbanzo beans. He poured them in his hand. A full-bellied laugh escaped his lips. "What is this?"

"Bean seeds," Mavin said, defensively. "What's so funny?"

The bearded men roared. They were hunters. They ate meat. They had watched these two carrying their heavy load of bird food for hundreds of miles. The joke was too much for them. They were inconsolable. They slapped each other in fits of hilarity like bearded children.

Hester squeezed the other seed packets to make sure he wasn't being gulled.

She knew he was a cheater, so naturally he assumed he was being cheated.

"Beans don't grow in the snow." Once again Hester looked straight into her eyes.

Simone was surprised by how quickly Hester recovered from his disappointment and moved to the next logical question. Why would there be seeds in the far north? Mavin was the first man she'd met with higher powers of reason. She realized it couldn't have been easy for Hester to predict where they would enter the river valley. This ill-mannered man was too clever by half. It troubled her to think of Hester watching her for months. He must have reasoned that she would be uneasy meeting a group of strange men and contrived to meet her alone. *How arrogant, she* thought. Did this fool really believe he could charm his way into my confidence? "We're sorry to have disappointed you," she said. "As you see, we carry nothing of value. Now, you can be on your way." She helped Mavin repacked the seed packets.

"Perhaps, we also travel to Kashphera?" Hester posed his question while pouring the round wrinkled beans back into the foil bag. He sliced a thin strip of deerskin from his leggings and used it to tie the top of the packet. When Simone turned away, he tossed the packet wide of her.

She snatched it from the air without looking and then faced him. "It might come as a surprise, but the Triumvirate doesn't tolerate marauding bands of feral men. Trust me, return to where you came from, while you still can." She shouldered the pack and gave Mavin a look to let him know it was time to leave. She turned her back and headed downriver.

Hester shook his head and laughed. "Hey, what's your name?"

Mavin hastily nodded his goodbyes and thanked Hester again for the knife. He was reluctant to leave. He had so many questions. A part of him wished to remain in the company of men. It felt good, even if they couldn't be trusted. When he turned around, Simone had already disappeared. He panicked and ran after her. "Simone, wait!"

The bearded men roared in amusement at the hen-pecked youth.

Mavin ran up beside her. "Why did you leave so suddenly? They seemed like men of honor."

"Ha ha!" Her high-pitched laugh cut through the sound of the river. "At times you rival Sidta with your wit." She looked upriver and laughed. "Men with honor?"

# The Two Captains

If what I say to you resonates with you, it is merely
because we are both branches on the same tree.
–W.B. YEATS

Simone tended the fire, raking the un-burned ends into the center of the glowing embers. She had picked a camp well away from the sound of the river, so she could hear if Hester and his men approached. The altercation had drained her energy. She needed sleep.

Mavin looked up at the Milky Way and then stole a look at her while she watched the fire die down. "Who or what is the Triumvirate?" He had heard her mention it a couple of times.

"You've never heard of the Thrice-blessed?"

"Sorry, doesn't ring a bell."

"The Triumvirate is the three blessings: the Sisters of Nabhi, the High Council, and the Merc." She thought the Triumvirate was known throughout the ten directions. "Together, they are the Three Pillars that hold the world in balance."

"Oh." He knew it was high time he learned more about the world he was living in. The more immediate mystery was the woman he had been sleeping beside for almost a year. He had seen the arrow bend in mid-flight with one eye. Time and doubt had eroded his conviction that something beyond the ordinary had saved his life. Watching Hester flying backward had removed any and all doubt. "Where did you learn the Way of Balance?"

"I learned from my teacher Maya."

"She taught you how to fight?"

"Maya taught me how to recognize the connection between all things. The Way of Balance is the opposite of fighting. It is learning to be grateful, and giving thanks."

"I watched Hester sail backward into the river. I saw him rolling on his side unable to breathe. Is this what you call giving thanks?"

"Do you know what a magnet is?" she asked.

"Yes, I know about magnetic energy."

"Magnets both attract and repel. In a similar manner, it's possible to redirect the energy of your opponent."

"You told me once that you would teach me about ki."

"I remember. It may be possible for you to master your own ki. But first, Raven, you have to learn to stay out of trouble."

"My father called me Raven."

"Your father?"

"Yes, some of us have fathers. I know, hard to believe." He rolled on his back and became lost looking at the bright stars of the Milky Way. He remembered Veteran's Day as a kid. The fire popped. He looked over. She was fast asleep.

"Hurry, Mavin," his mother said. "At this rate we'll miss the fly-over." Every year she went on and on about missing the fly-over, but he'd never seen one yet. She pinned the Dolphin insignia on his best shirt and combed his hair again. He didn't remember much about his father. When he asked Grandpa Latigo about his dad, the old man had read him *Twenty Thousand Leagues Under the Sea* before bedtime. "Your father worked on a submarine like the *Nautilus*," Latigo explained.

Mavin grew up worshiping Captain Nemo. Most of the games he played as a kid were twenty thousand leagues under the salty ocean, which was bizarre for several reasons. The primary one being he had never seen an ocean. Later, he was disappointed to learn that twenty thousand leagues was twice the circumference of the earth—so quite a bit deeper than any ocean. When he began college, he learned that a single Boomer, a ballistic missile submarine, could single-handedly end the world. That was when he truly understood the madness of Nemo.

Captain Nemo, like Odysseus, called himself, "Nobody." Nemo's nineteenth century nuclear-powered submarine could sink any ship on the ocean. With technology, Nemo had become a modern Poseidon. Captain Ahab had an outdated approach to gods and monsters. "Don't waste your life obsessed with destroying the white whale," Mavin advised the stars. "Better to become the white whale and swallow the whole world."

# The Time of Water

The pine tree seems to listen, the fir tree to wait...
—FRIEDRICH NIETZSCHE

"Sex with a man?" Simone burst out laughing. "You are so funny." She held her side in pain.

"Hey, sex with a man is great."

She gave Mavin a look and burst out laughing again.

"That's not what I meant. It's a natural thing." It still didn't come out quite the way he'd hoped. "A woman and a man having sex together is natural."

"Because it's what cave people did?"

"It's how we all got here."

She couldn't tell if he was being serious. She fought off the giggles.

Mavin knew he had been sidelined from evolution for centuries, but how was it possible for two women to have a child together? It would require a high degree of medical knowledge. He wanted to ask her more about it, but decided to take advantage of her light mood in another way. "Can I ask you something?"

"You may." She could tell he was gathering up his courage for something.

"What happened back in the day of the Black Hair?"

"You're such a terrible liar, Mavin."

*She knows*, he thought. A deep shame filled him. He should have told her the truth from the beginning. He was no good at keeping secrets. Why did he think she wouldn't figure it out? He obviously wasn't from this time. "So, I suppose you blame me for the end of the world?" he blurted out.

"Only a man could make the end of the world about himself." She had never known anyone so convinced that they were the center of the world.

"And only a woman could…" he caught himself and held his tongue.

They walked in silence: both feeling the tension. A low rainbow appeared in the west and followed them. The mustard green hills shown through the wide bands of color in a way Mavin had never seen.

"Men forgot their mother," Simone said while scanning the area around them for movement. "When you forget your mother for long enough, she forgets even her own children."

"Do you mean our biological mother, or Mother Earth?"

"It's so easy for you to cut your own mother into pieces."

"I see your point, but Mother Earth is everything and my mother is… my mother."

"Your sky god peers down on all things and sees them separate and apart. The Unities are a joke to you. Your eyes tell you we are separate, so it must be so."

"Who is this sky god?" He pleaded ignorance. Did she mean, God the Father of the Catholic Church?

"The wild tribes of men call him the one true god." She looked into Mavin's eyes hoping he would finally tell her the truth. "Do you worship the sky father in the clouds and his son who came to earth."

"I don't know this sky god or his son." He returned her gaze, doing his best to believe the lie he had just told.

"In the Age of Fire when Asura ruled, he separated all things from each other. They set fire to the sky, saying that it was prophecy."

"Do you mean the end of the world?" He looked away. Men did destroy the world.

She noticed he was trembling. Why was he so upset?

Mavin felt the weight of the world pressing down, crushing his organs.

"Mavin, when someone tells you they know what happened before the Black Hair, even a child knows it's a tall tree tale."

That night Simone cooked the small eggs she had collected. They ate their meal in silence.

For nearly a year, he had studied her every gesture and expression. Yet, he was no closer to solving the mystery. It was clear that her entire understanding of the world came from stories. It wasn't much different than the traditional Zuni view of the universe. Her mythology placed her in time and space, not Newton's gravity or Einstein's theory of relativity. He decided the best way to understand her and the new world he was living in was to start at the beginning. "Tell me about the Time of Water."

"It was long ago, before men stole fire." Since the previous evening she sensed a change. He was distressed about something. She had no idea men were so complicated. "Before there were stories, there was Ice."

"Are you making this up?" He was afraid she was about to tell his story, the man from the ice.

She tried to ignore his interruption, "Before there were stories, there was Ice. For a million ions, Ice drifted through the void in a wispy dream until she met Sun. As Ice neared Sun, she melted and became Primordial Sea. She circled Sun until one day as Primordial Sea; she awoke and realized who she was. She let out a sigh that became the clouds and sky. Primordial Sea circled Sun until one day she felt swollen. From below her deep currents emerged Earth. In the beginning she covered Earth with her curling waves. Earth grew and grew until one day only her high clouds could shroud his wide shoulders. She felt joy at not being alone, but deeply saddened to be half, when once she had been whole. Her tears, the first rain that fell, gathered into a great river that sliced through Earth's fresh skin."

"Earth is a man?" Mavin chuckled. When he saw the look on her face, he was sorry he had interrupted. Her story was not unlike Zuni creation stories he had heard as a kid.

"Primordial Sea's tears fell for an age, mixing Earth slowly back into her. Sun grew jealous of Earth and hurled a massive yellow bolt towards him. Seeing the flying bolt, Primordial Sea turned to shield her companion. Thus, setting the world into motion, creating Day and Night. Sun's dagger struck her with such fury that it wiped away all recollection. Primordial Sea lay in an empty, dreamless sleep.

For a thousand eons Sun shone, but for Primordial Sea, only darkness existed. The energy from Sun's golden bolt created the tiniest bubble. After a hundred thousand eons the tiny bubble grew into another and then another, until Sea was froth. She became the tiniest floating plant, and much later the tiniest animal. Age upon age passed and Primordial Sea became all things. When at last she awoke, she was a White Crane. She took flight and remembered everything. She was whole again."

# Swan's Ford

*I like trees because they seem more resigned
to the way they have to live than other things do.*
—WILLA CATHER

Simone woke to the smell of smoke from a village several leagues to the east. She dug through the ashes from the evening's fire and found a glowing ember. She blew on it and added dry grass. "Mavin, wake up. We are about to leave the Boundary. You need to pack your knife away. From now on you must carry the seeds until we reach Kashphera." She saw the smirk on his face. "This isn't a joke. I'm serious. When we meet a traveler—"

"I know. Look at my feet," he said sarcastically. "You've been telling me the same things for over a year."

She shook her head and gave him a withering look. He seemed incapable of comprehending the importance of manners and time had run out. What was the sense of bringing him to Kashphera? What other choice was there? If he survived his initial encounter with the council, in time he could learn to conduct himself properly. No one would take responsibility for him with his current argumentative behavior. In any case, once she delivered her charge, he would no longer be her concern. She swore to Karin that she would take care of him, and she had fulfilled her side of the bargain.

The fall equinox was already upon them, more than a month too late to travel safely by the northern route. The first travelers they met confirmed Simone's suspicions that the high pass to the north was snowed in.

There was no choice but to cross the river at Swan's Ford and travel the longer route to the west. The distance was greater, but the southern pass into Kashphera was gentle by comparison. What difference would a few more weeks make after more than two years?

"We're approaching the ferry crossing, you must look at the ground in front of whoever we meet. Do not look directly at them. Don't speak, unless you're asked a question," she reminded him sternly.

Her repeated instructions stuck in his craw. "Yes, I know!" He pictured himself as a eunuch holding a wooden box containing his two shrunken jewels. As they neared the bank of the river, he peered up in a conspicuous stoop, which made him appear like a hapless idiot.

A group of old aunties sat on cushions under a sun-bleached awning, gossiping. When they caught sight of Simone, the aunties jumped to their feet and ran to hug her.

The cacophony of high voices pierced Mavin's ears. They babbled all at once. It was difficult to understand their thick accents. He waited for an introduction that never came. Simone completely ignored him, as did all the women.

Three old men sat on the hot ground next to their loads. Mavin walked over to them and said hello. They didn't look up or offer any greeting. He slung the pack to the ground and sat down, directing his sullen look at Simone.

Auntie Sharine, who had recognized Simone, poured tea and seated the young woman in the place of honor. "The ferry will not arrive till the afternoon," Sharine explained. The regal older woman introduced Simone to her friends. "Simone is a keeper of the histories." The aunties begged her to sing them a ballad while they waited.

"What would you like to hear?" Simone blushed.

"Sing of the great river." Sharine folded her hands in anticipation.

By the end of Simone's first long clear note, Mavin witnessed a transformation. His fierce guardian was now a little girl sitting in the shade without a care in the world. Though he didn't understand the words, Simone's expressions brought the story to life. Sweet recognition washed over the faces of the women. Mavin noticed repeated phrases and wondered if they were mnemonic clues.

Two hours later, her song finished, Mavin looked around. Not a dry eye. "Where did you learn to sing like that?" he asked.

His lack of manners startled the women. They hissed as if shooing a cat off the table.

Simone said something to calm the elderly women. She went over to speak with him, barking something he didn't understand for show. "Have I not warned you over and over not to speak to me directly?" she yelled in a whisper.

"Yes, all right." He wasn't going to apologize.

"The river is too high to cross at the ford and we've no money. When the ferry arrives, you must join in pulling it to the other side in exchange for our passage."

He nodded and kept his eyes lowered, knowing the aunties were watching him like a hawk. "You have a beautiful voice, Simone. Where did you learn to sing like that?"

"The main duty of a Janjanbi is to keep the histories. Maya taught me the stories of the people. She would say, 'The old stories repeat themselves over and over again and that someday I would understand.'"

He couldn't believe how many verses she had memorized. The delicate semi-tones of the melody still haunted him.

"Remember, Mavin everything is vibration. Ki. The tiniest thing in the universe is singing, the rocks, and the planets, everything in existence. Creation is a chorus. Everything is connected to everything."

"Ten out of ten physicists would agree." He was impressed by her simple, yet elegant explanation.

"Will you visit Saudhra, the valley where you were raised?" Sharine interrupted. She was concerned that Simone was spending far too much time with her manservant.

Simone rejoined the aunties under the shade. "I'm traveling to Kashphera on an urgent matter."

Mavin was chapped that she left out any mention of him.

"It is a pity." Sharine poured more tea. "You will be passing so near to Saudhra."

Simone dreaded taking the southern route for this very reason. She had her mission to complete. There was no middle ground. She watched the ferry slowly making its way towards them. Not a single day passed without her thinking of Maya.

During the ballad, the aunties had dug around in their bags for a bit of this and that, trading small scraps of fine material. They set to work sewing while they listened to the history of the people and the Great War.

Mavin watched the ferry in the middle of the river. A green-knotted rope lifted out of the water as it approached. Now, he understood why the boat didn't drift downstream. When the ferry docked, Mavin took his cue from the other men and helped to load the crates and sacks on the dock into the flat-bottomed boat. When they were ready to disembark, a gray-haired manservant showed Mavin how to grab the slimy thick-knotted rope at the bow and pull while walking to the stern the boat, then how to let go of the rope and walk to the bow and pull again.

The women gossiped and sewed while Mavin helped pull the ferry across the wide river. The wet rope was slick with green moss. Soon the deck was slippery as well. He listened closely to the women as he passed, gleaning a word here and there.

"Simone, we've finished," Sharine said enthusiastically. The aunties held up two sarongs as a screen while she slipped out of her stained leather wraps and into a newly made Phiran-style dress. Sharine combed Simone's hair and braided it. She coiled her long braid and held it in place with a black wooden comb.

When Simone emerged from behind the sarong screen, Mavin was stunned. He let go of the rope and stared.

Sharine saw the way the beardless manservant was looking at the girl. She reached over and swatted him with the hard rib of her fan. "Mind your manners, Pudding Head!"

Mavin grabbed the rope and pulled, never taking his eyes off Simone. Nothing remained of the young woman dressed in animal skins; even less it seemed of the kinship they had forged during their long journey together. The dress left her right shoulder bare like the traditional mantas that Zuni women wore when dancing at harvest time.

Simone was embarrassed by the way Mavin was looking at her.

Mavin pulled on the rope, feeling like a slave on an Egyptian barge.

When the aunties had finally stopped fussing over her, Simone brought Mavin a cup of water. "Stop staring," she said, making a face.

"I'm not." He turned and looked to the far side of the river.

"It's Paramitta." She wanted to change the subject.

"What's that?"

"Paramitta is the fall equinox, halfway between summer and winter. Right now, the day and the night are equal. The Way of Balance holds this day as one of the most important of the year. We're crossing to the further shore on the most auspicious of days."

"I'm sorry. I don't understand your holidays."

"The English word, arrive can be divided in two," she explained. "The first part, a, means to reach. Rive means, river. To cross the river is to arrive. Paramitta is the day we contemplate the further shore, crossing over to a higher understanding, one that we are as of yet unable to comprehend."

"Where am I crossing over to, Simone?"

"Hopefully, adulthood." She knew it sounded harsh, but she meant it. She left the rest of her thoughts unsaid. *You foolishly believe you can act however you please. In the world of adults there is duty and responsibility. Sacrifice.*

# The Jāti

The season of failure is the best time
for sowing the seeds of success.
—PARAMAHANSA YOGANANDA

When the ferry landed on the western bank, and the goods were all unloaded, Sharine waved Simone's manservant over to where the circle of women were resting in the shade. Sharine said something to Simone that Mavin didn't understand. Simone's face turned crimson.

"So... young man." Sharine began her interrogation. "I understand you and Simone have been scraping the root."

"Yes. How did you know?" Mavin remembered the many roots that Simone had dug up in the desert. He grimaced remembering the bitter taste.

The aunties were giggling, cupping their hand over their mouth to be polite. When Mavin contorted his face, they howled with delight.

Simone covered her face with both hands.

He couldn't tell if she was laughing or crying. She abruptly got up and ran down the road.

"Simone. Wait!" He made a quick bow to the aunties who were doubled over with laughter. He grabbed the pack and hurried after her.

When he caught up to her, she had tears streaming down her cheeks. "Why did you say such things?"

"What things?" He was confused.

"Why did you tell them, we were...?"

"I can't believe that you're angry with me after the way you treated me back there?"

"Scraping the root means to have sex with a man!"

"Hey, sex with a man is great." Once again, it didn't sound quite the way he wanted. "Look, I'm sorry if I said something wrong. I honestly didn't know what they meant. But you treated me like a leper."

"If you would listen, you would understand that we're entering the civilized world. You must behave." Her voice was trembling.

"I'm beginning to understand why you told Hester and his men not to come any further south."

"Hester? Even if he wasn't a feral outlaw, he was born man."

"And that's a sin?"

"It is a fact, Mavin. You're a man. You're unable to own property; and so you are the responsibility of another. Soon, I won't be able to help you. If there's no one willing to take up the burden, then you are without place."

"What are you saying, that I'm a lower class or a lower caste?"

"You are Jāti. Even if you find someone who will take up the burden, you're outside of society. We've been over and over this, but you don't listen."

"Fine, explain to me again. How can I enter society?"

"It is highly unlikely that you will ever enter society, but you may survive, if you learn basic manners. You must learn to act passive and demure. Then, by some miracle, you may find a matron."

"If by demure, you mean completely vacant like those men back at the ferry, then forget it. There must be another way."

"Be reborn a woman."

"Very funny." He doubted the operation was available. "Simone, why are you taking me to a place where I have no place?" He watched the color in her cheeks go pale.

"I've been doing my best to prepare you, but you're stubborn. It's not your fault. I'm sorry. I should have realized you're not capable of comprehending."

"I'm not an idiot. I know things that you can't even imagine!" He took off the pack and slammed it to the ground. In his anger, he was tempted to tell her everything. That would shut her up. "When you told Hester you were a Janjanbi, I saw the look on his face. All of those men were afraid of you. You must have some clout."

"I'm Janjanbi, foreign born."

"So you can't own land?"

"This is what I mean." She was reaching the end of her patience. What was the point of trying to explain? "Yes, I'm unable to own land or property." She wanted to say, And that's why very soon I will no longer be able to protect you.

"Do you at least get to vote?" he asked.

"I don't understand."

"Do you cast a ballot to decide who will represent you in the government?"

"Only a goddess may question the world." His absurd comments aggravated her. "Why would a goddess question the world? The world is as it should be."

"Sure. You were born a woman."

"You chose to be a man and now you complain."

"Wait a minute! Who said I chose to be a man? And who said I was complaining?" Mavin remembered why he was reluctant to ask her questions. "What's going to happen when we get to Kashphera? Are they going to give me a lobotomy?" The dull eyes of the men on the ferry unnerved him.

"I have no idea what will happen when we get to Kashphera. I've only been to the capital once."

"Are you're saying that I survived everything just so I can have my nuts handed to me in a box. Fine. Fuck it!" He threw his hands in the air. "But what about the seeds? What happens to them?" He pointed to the beat up pack they had been carrying for over a year.

"I delivered them to my superiors, after that, I have no idea. I imagine they will be planted to help to feed the people."

"You sure seem to have gone to a lot of trouble for things you don't know much about." He was tired of trying to make sense of her. The further south they travel, the less either of them mattered. "Auntie Sharine said you grew up near here?"

"Less than a week's journey." She pointed due west. "It was a small village on the coast."

He turned and walked into the direction of the setting sun.

"Mavin! Come back!" She shouted after him, but he didn't listen.

# Saudhra

Do not spread compost of the weeds.
—WILLIAM SHAKESPEARE

Simone approached the rim of the valley with trepidation. She had been unable to dissuade Mavin that this was the last place on earth she wanted to be. There had been a steady rain for a week. She expected the river below to be running high. She peered over the edge and held her breath. The surf rumbled in the distance, but the low clouds obscured the coastline.

Mavin looked down into the valley and wondered why they'd stopped. "What is this place?"

"This is Saudhra, where I grew up."

"There's nothing here."

She started down a set of stone steps. Mavin followed close behind. When they reached the valley floor, it was flat as a tabletop. The brush was so thick it made it difficult to tell where the riverbank ended and began. Mavin noticed a few inches of water running over river rock no matter where he stepped.

Simone set the pack down and stared at a thicket of blackberries. "A survivor told me that a great wall of water rolled to the back of the valley. When the wave returned to the sea, everyone, everything was gone, even the soil."

He wanted to comfort her. She was staring into a patch of brambles. "Was there something here?" he asked.

"Maya's house."

He had been angry with her from the very beginning. She couldn't understand how he had lost everything in a single moment with no explanation. A wave of shame washed over him. He sat down in the wet gravel and buried his face in his hands.

She stared at him. "You don't listen." She seethed. "You never listen! I told you that I didn't want to come here."

A chukar burst out from the brush and glided down the valley towards the sea. Mavin jumped.

Simone turned in slow motion, numb to the world. She walked towards the muffled surf.

He shouldered the pack and kept his distance. It worried him to see her so unsteady on her feet. They beat through the thorny brambles until the leached river rock turned to sand. Ice plant and clumps of pointy grass grew in patches over the dunes. The wide beach was swept clean except for a white rock being lapped by the surf. Mavin walked beside her on the firm wet sand just out of reach of the waves. He could see tears streaming down her face.

As they neared the white rock, Mavin could see that it was hollow. It wasn't a rock at all. He sat and stared at the massive whale vertebra half-buried in the sand. He tried to guess which way the tide was running. Four pelicans flew low in tight formation following the curl of a wave. The tidal flats to the north mirrored the clouds. He never knew what happened to his father. It was a military secret. He was only told that he died in the performance of his duty. He imagined his father's last moment inside the belly of a black behemoth, manning his post.

Simone sat next to him and took his hand, caressing his fingers. She had argued with Maya that day so many years ago. She didn't even remember why she had been angry. In the end, she had done what she was told and went into the mountains to pick winter cherries. Maya told her many times, "When you are a grown woman, you cannot return home." Now she understood. Maya believed that life began in the sea and returned to the sea. Simone remembered Malina swimming to meet her goddess, giving Mavin the time needed to rescue her. She looked at the massive bone being lashed by the milky surf.

Mavin felt her icy-cold fingers laced between his. He wanted desperately to comfort her. He put his arm around her and felt her trembling.

She leaned her head against his and whispered, "Sedna."

# A Rising Mist

Twisting inland,
the sea fog takes awhile
in the apple trees.
−Michael McClintock

Mavin woke up and felt a chill. A thick fog blocked the rays of the afternoon sun. Drops of dew hung in Simone's dark hair. She opened her eyes. The sun-bleached whalebone a stone's throw away was barely visible. He could hear the surf pounding, but couldn't see the water. It must be low tide, he thought. "What do you call this ocean?"

"The Near Sea."

"Is it often foggy like this?" Mavin wondered.

"Yes, this time of year the fog reaches many miles inland."

"Does the ground freeze in the winter?" he asked.

"No. Never."

Mavin sprung to his feet.

"What is it?" She didn't sense any danger.

"We must find the right place." He shouldered the pack and climbed the headland.

She hurried after him. "What is it, Mavin?"

"Remember what Karin said, 'When you get home, plant a tall tree and remember those who gave their lives.'"

"She meant Kashphera. It's not for us to…"

"Karin gave the Sequoia seeds to me, remember?"

Simone remembered every moment under the mountain. She could taste the black smoke in the back of her throat.

"Redwoods only grow in just the right environment," he

explained. "They need coastal fog. We need to find a sheltered spot away from the salty breeze."

She was out of breath trying to keep up.

They followed a ravine inland and crossed over a series of rolling hills. A leafy vale opened up to a wide grassy meadow. Mavin guessed the meadow had once been a lake. Around the edge of the meadow, scrubby big leaf maples mixed with laurels and miniature madrone. The fog hung heavy in the ferns and grass. Mavin kicked at the soft earth and grabbed a handful. "Smell that." He held the moist soil under her nose. "What do you think? Does this place feel right?"

She recognized the meadow. She had pulled many a deep-rooted kuzu from this glade as a girl. "Yes, Mavin. This place feels right." The ghosts of Karin and Sidta had been following her every step. It was time for them to find peace. It had been Karin's idea to plant a tree. "I want to help. Show me what to do. I've never planted anything before."

To Mavin, she had always seemed too serious for such a young woman. He was the sole survivor of his time. He understood too well, the guilt she carried for surviving the wave. He knew she felt responsible for the death of Malina and Karin. He dug through the pack and found the fat packet of seeds. "These little broadleaf maples will act as nursing trees, helping to protect the young seedlings."

"Nursing trees?"

"The truth is, there's a very low germination rate for Sequoia Sempervirens. The good news is there are 120 thousand seeds in this one pound bag."

"We can't plant all of them," she protested.

"Why not?"

"It's for the Merc and the other members of the Triumvirate to decide such things."

"I was the caretaker of these seeds before Karin entrusted them to me, besides, is Kashphera on the coast?"

"No. It's in a high mountain valley."

"Redwoods won't grow there. Trust me, this is the perfect place. Even if we planted just one seed and it grew, a single tree wouldn't survive on its own. It's like the symbol you showed me of a person. You can't have just one person; it takes at least two to make one. Redwoods need other redwoods to grow."

"I understand."

"Do you want to say a prayer or something?" he asked.

She closed her eyes.

He watched and waited in the long silence that followed.

"Mavin?"

"Yes?"

"Are they very tall trees?"

He wondered why it was so hard for her to believe. "They're the tallest trees in the world. When they're full-grown, you can't see the top."

This made her smile.

He cut open the foil packet and poured the fragrant seeds into her cupped palms.

She held the seeds and closed her eyes again. "Thank you, Karin, and Sidta. Thank you, Malina, and Rani." She named her companions who had perished on the journey north. "Thank you all for seeing us safely home. Now your long journey has ended. Rest here under the gentle wings of the White Crane."

Mavin poured a small pile of seeds in his left hand. Each seed felt like a tiny vibrant city. He thought of Kep and thanked her for saving him. He thought of Lars and Trish and his mother. He thought of his grandfathers and his people. He thought of the whole wide world once full of ten billion souls. The soft damp earth smelled alive and sweet. He opened his eyes. The silky mist around them began to rise.

As the seeds sifted through his fingertips, Mavin let go of his old view of the world. Facts and figures were cardboard. Existence was a burning, roiling, continuous funeral and birth—immeasurable. He walked in a spiraling circle feathering the living grains thru his fingers.

She waited for him to speak, wondering which goddess or god he would call upon. When his hands were empty, he shouldered the pack and walked into the fog.

# The Philosopher Queen

A seed hidden in the heart of an apple is an orchard invisible.
—WELSH PROVERB

Simone knew the land around her childhood home well. She picked young, tender roots of Taadi and leafs of Dusseru to make a curry. As the sun began to dip behind the foothills, they gathered firewood and made camp.

After they had eaten, he wanted to ask her how old she was when the wave destroyed her village, but decided against it. He knew she was suffering and it made his own heart heavy. He had spent more than his fair share of time feeling sorry for himself for surviving. Instead, he decided to distract her. "What is a Janjanbi?"

She was lost in the firelight, listening to the cicadas. "Why do you wish to know?"

"Is it a secret?"

"Yes."

"I can keep a secret."

"The Janjanbi have a dark history. Long before the Triumvirate, the Empress Raela ruled the southern empire. She sent raiding parties across the eastern border to kidnap young girls. These girls were trained in the fighting arts. The young girls grew up unaware that the people they eventually fought and killed were their own blood relatives. The Janjanbi became the most feared warriors in the three provinces. This early Janjanbi sect was very influential. They developed a high form of poetry and became skilled in the healing arts. They studied ki and developed the Way of Balance. They set into motion the seven levels of merit. In traditional Janjanbi society, officials did not inherit their status, but advanced through merit. The story of the Philosopher Queen comes from this time."

"Why didn't you tell me any of this before?"

"It's forbidden to speak of such things. You must never breathe a word of what I've told you."

"I promise I will never speak of this to anyone. Now please tell me about the Philosopher Queen."

"My teacher Maya did not believe the Philosopher Queen to be an historic figure, but regarded her as an ideal. During a dark time of violence between the three provinces, the Philosopher Queen became an adviser to the Empress. She took the opportunity to spread the Way of Balance. As with any spiritual practice, there are those who interpret inner knowledge as a means to gain power over others. The Way of Balance is both spiritual and temporal."

Mavin was amazed at how all the major world faiths were about love, and yet they were at the center of most every major conflict in history. "What do you mean by temporal?"

"When you learn to control your ki, it is an inner experience. But it also affects the outer world."

The sight of Hester flying backward into the river was proof enough for Mavin. "And the Triumvirate?"

"The Triumvirate was formed centuries later by the Founding Mothers."

"I thought you told me that the Janjanbi couldn't be in the military?"

"In the Second Age, the Janjanbi rebelled and assassinated the Empress. For centuries they were hunted down and killed. A few Janjanbi masters survived in the wilderness. When the White Crane brought the people out of darkness and began the Third Age, she founded the Sisters of Nabhi and reinstated the Janjanbi schools. Although the Janjanbi are tolerated today, we are also feared. Janjanbi are not permitted to be in the Peregrine

Korps. When my village was swept away, there were many in Kashphera who said the Janjanbi School had brought on the wrath of the goddess."

Mavin was not surprised that blame had survived the end of the world.

# Milk Name

The creation of a thousand forests is in one acorn.
—RALPH WALDO EMERSON

Mavin wished he could take Simone home and show her McKinley County where he grew up. He wondered if it was still there. If the pavement had long since crumbled, it wouldn't be much of a change. He chose to believe his people had survived.

Simone walked ahead. More than ever he wanted to tell her the truth. They had more in common than he ever imagined. "You told me that Maya named you."

She shot a glance back at him. "So often you break a perfectly good silence with one of your strange questions."

"Why didn't your mother? I mean, why didn't your mothers name you?"

"You told me your mentor named you, Prince Dakkar. So why is it strange that my mentor should give me my name?"

"I didn't mean to say it was strange. My mentor and I were only playing, having fun. He was the only person who ever called me Prince Dakkar."

"In the East, parents often wait to name their children until the end of the third moon after their birth. They give babies a milk name."

Mavin wondered if there was a high infant mortality rate. He waited hoping she would finish her story. "And?" he prodded.

"My mothers never gave me a proper name. Maybe they knew they had to give me up."

"So what did they call you?"

"They called me by my milk name."

"So, what's your milk name?"

"You must promise not to laugh, or tell another soul."

"I promise."

"Little Fatty."

Mavin's eyes grew bigger, but no sound came out of his mouth. She could tell he was holding his breath. His face turned bright red.

"Little Fatty!" He sputtered and fell over holding his stomach.

She wanted to jump on him with her knees. "Mavin! You promised."

He rolled over on his back and looked up at her. He could see she was hurt. "I'm sorry, Simone. I mean, Little…"

"Don't you dare!" She was about to jump on him.

"I'm sorry." He covered his mouth and did his best to stop laughing. "I can't help it."

"If you breathe a word."

"I would never." Little Fatty, he whispered to himself.

\*     \*     \*     \*

Simone scattered the ring of stones from the previous night's fire. "Our detour to Saudhra has left us little choice but to travel through the Mirror Valley."

Mavin shouldered the pack. "Is that bad?"

"Maya warned me to go around this place."

"Is it dangerous?" Mavin did not like the look on her face.

"Only for those who stay."

By early evening they came upon a small village. Mavin had longed to see people. Despite Simone's warnings, he wasn't prepared for the hollow eyes of the villagers and the round bellies of the children. He wondered how they could still be alive. A woman, hardly more than a bare skeleton wrapped in a sari, smiled and escorted them into the center of the village. It took all of Mavin's self-control to return the welcoming smiles of the villagers. He became terrified that the villagers would discover the seeds and boil them for food. He was ashamed when he realized their hosts were preparing what little food they had to share.

Simone disappeared. Mavin played with the children and then helped them to gather twigs and straw for the cooking fire. Simone returned with a bundle of wild plants. She separated them out and explained to the elders where she had found each of the leaves, roots and bark. Together the women pounded Simone's gatherings and made tea and a clear soup. After their meal, Simone made poultices for the open sores of the sick.

They awoke early the next morning and said their goodbyes. Mavin did his best to follow Simone's example to not show emotion. When the children began to cry, he turned and walked away hiding his face. The next village they encountered was much the same. Mavin helped Simone pick the medicinal plants and prepare the tea and poultices. The next morning they awoke early and slipped out of the village without saying goodbye.

"As much as they need our help, we need to travel at night, away from the river," Simone voice shook.

"They have water nearby, why don't they plow their fields?"

"The grain turns black and rots before it sets fruit."

"Can't we give them some of our wheat seeds to plant?" he pleaded. "I doubt they'll sprout, but we have to do something."

"You know very well, they're not our seeds to give."

Her archaic sense of duty infuriated him. "Are you telling me there's someone in the world that needs our seeds more than these people?"

"Do you think this is easy for me?" She tried her best, but tears streamed down her face. "It's for the Triumvirate to decide such matters."

He wanted to scream. Out of frustration, he picked up a rock and threw it as far as he could.

# The Thousand Steps

Words that have not changed much in twelve thousand years
are those of tree names: birch- bher, willow-wyt, alder- alsysos,
elm- ulmo, ash- os, apple- abul, beech-bhago.
—Paul Friedrich, Gary Snyder

They left the river and climbed up endless series of switchbacks for the next three days. Behind them, the tract became crowded. Mavin stepped aside, but the smiling travelers refused to pass. The temperature gradually became cooler. The steep trail finally gave way to a gentle alpine valley carpeted with orchids and anemones. Lime butterflies floated from blossom to blossom. Lace-leafed red maples and yew trees mixed with rhododendrons and azaleas.

"This place is called the Valley of the Flowers. It's half a day's trek to the thousand steps and then another hour to the summit," Simone explained.

"I need a breather." He looked back. The track was packed for as far as they could see. "Are we really that slow?" It hurt Mavin's pride to know he was holding up the line. He stepped off the path again, but the travelers behind only bowed and smiled refusing to pass. "I thought I was in decent shape." He had his hands on his knees and was huffing and puffing. "Is the pass always so busy?"

Simone could see the elevation was already affecting him. "Perhaps there are so many travelers because the northern pass is closed," she offered. Though that didn't explain why everyone was headed in the same direction.

Once they had crossed the ferry at Swan's Ford, news of Simone's return raced like wildfire. It didn't hurt that she had crossed the river during Paramitta, the most auspicious day of the year. Rumors abounded that a young Janjanbi had traveled to the top of the world and was now on her way to the capitol with a golden offering to the White Crane. The Way of Balance would be restored.

Simone explained to Mavin that Kashphera was the high jewel of the Diamond Province. "The thousand steps have protected the upper lake country from invaders for centuries. The floating gardens of Lake Avighna are famous throughout the three provinces."

It didn't sound to Mavin like the Triumvirate was in dire need of food.

Their fellow travelers offered to carry their pack, but Simone politely declined. Mavin was proud that she had so much confidence in his stamina. As the air grew thinner, his pace slowed to a crawl. He tucked his thumbs under the pack straps to give his shoulders a break. He wondered if she was trying to increase his worth? "Look at this rugged beast. He's quite handy at toting heavy things," he said to an old woman who came up to him. She smiled and offered him a paper cone filled with wild strawberries she had just picked. Smaller than the end of a baby's little finger, Mavin was amazed by the sweetness of the tiny berries.

He dropped the pack and sat down. The travelers behind them also set down their loads and rested. The wild strawberry woman made a small fire to make tea. Soon small cooking fires were burning. Bowls of hot tea and spicy curry were passed up and down the trail.

A small girl wandered about picking wildflowers. When she had as many as she could hold she gave them to Mavin.

"Is everyone so nice in Kashphera?" he asked. "You made it sound like we were going into the gates of hell."

Simone lowered her voice. "The generosity of the Jāti, poorest of the poor, never fails to surprise me. Their pockets are empty, but their hearts are full."

Mavin felt refreshed by the hot food and was able to quicken his pace, despite the thin air. Two hours later, they reached the base of a cliff. Mavin's heart sank. "I thought you said the southern pass was easier?"

"We're almost to the summit. Look, the Thousand Steps." She pointed to a narrow crease where steps were carved into the dark granite. "Don't worry, there are not really a thousand." The altitude was affecting him more than she had anticipated.

Mavin dug his thumbs under the pack straps and started climbing. Halfway up, his legs started shaking. When they reached the top step, Mavin turned around. "Eight hundred and eighty-eight."

She smiled. "You're ready to begin your next lesson in ki."

"Move on from my feet? Shocking! Now what? Start paying attention to my ankles?" he joked.

"I don't care what people say, you're smarter than you look."

When they reached the summit, they rested and took in the view of the snow-covered peaks to the east. "Your face is puffy, Mavin. We have to keep moving. We'll rest on the other side." She helped him to his feet.

An auntie who was sitting nearby offered Mavin a handful of ginkgo leaves to chew. He bowed and thanked her.

"Ginkgo will help you adjust to the altitude," Simone explained. It was difficult for her not to carry the pack. "It's mostly downhill from here."

He smiled through the pain, unsure if she had just made a joke.

His vulnerable state brought up emotions she couldn't allow herself. She prayed to the White Crane that the High Council and the Merc would take pity on him. Very soon he would no longer be her responsibility.

When they dropped down below the snowline, spectators began to line both sides of the track. By the time they reached the valley floor, it became obvious that the entire population of the valley had turned out to welcome them.

The council received word that a Janjanbi scout from the Peregrine team, which left Kashphera two years hence, had returned from the far north. A special session of the High Council was called. There had never been an incident on record where a mob had prevented anyone from entering the city. The councilwomen waited patiently for the Janjanbi.

When the sun began to set, Councilwoman Khalsa remarked, "Who is this scout who can find her way back from the top of the world and then get lost on her way to the capital?"

"Her name is Simone Kita. She was in this chamber two years ago, before your time." The elder councilwoman Asra took the opportunity to take her freshman colleague down a notch.

The council member's voices were drowned out by the thunderous crowd pouring into the upper galley and main hall. Everyone looked around, searching for the returning heroine.

The sea of humanity parted and a tall woman emerged followed by a thin man with an overstuffed rucksack. An enthusiastic cheer broke out.

Mavin unslung the pack and handed the straps to Simone.

The Janjanbi shocked the crowd by turning and bowing to the man.

"Take the pack, Simone," he said, but it was too loud for her to hear. "Take it!" He was embarrassed to see her bowing. He was unsure of what to do, so he returned her bow. When she remained bent at the waist he got nervous and unlaced the pack and poured the contents on to the marble floor. Simone remained looking at her feet. He backed into the crowd, leaving her alone in the center of the Rotunda with the pile of silver packets. The crowd became restless and then suddenly became silent when the Merc entered the chamber.

"Welcome home, Specialist Kita," The Merc said before pulling back the hood of her crimson robe. "Tell us, daughter, what have you brought us from the north?" The Merc's smooth voice echoed against the high-domed ceiling.

"We bring bountiful seeds, my Maharani."

"Come here, child. Don't be shy." The Merc's gentle voice put everyone at ease.

Simone chose a large silver packet and climbed the steps to the podium. She tore open the foil packet, gesturing for the Maharani to hold out her hand. She poured a pyramid of wheat into the beautiful woman's cupped palms.

The imposing figure in red held the golden grains high for everyone to see. "After too many years of famine, now the world will be made anew."

A wild cheer broke out.

Even from the far end of the rotunda, the tall figure in red was striking. Simone did her best to become invisible. Mavin was struck by her humility. He was impressed at the excitement the seeds were generating. It would take a miracle for them to spout. He had to believe there was a reason he had survived. What other purpose could there be but to deliver these seeds? He looked around at the smiling faces filling the massive hall. The size and height of the dome were impressive. The crowd was nearly all women and young girls, though there were a few demure looking men mixed about. He hoped Simone had exaggerated his situation. He was being completely ignored at the moment, but that was understandable. The whole journey home she acted as though she would hand the seeds over to a clerk. By the look on the councilwomen's faces, no one had expected anything like this. Mavin could see Simone searching for him.

The crowd outside continued to push their way in, pressing the onlookers closer and closer together.

The Merc poured her seeds into Simone's palms and then raised them, giving the crowd a chance to cheer the returning hero. The applause was deafening.

Soon Mavin was pressed against the back wall and unable to see a thing. An hour later when the crowd thinned, he couldn't find Simone. He called out, but she was gone.

A large woman in a saffron sarong greeted him. "I am Farzana, follow me." She turned without further explanation and headed out a side exit.

"Where's Simone?" He ran to keep up. "I need to find the Janjanbi."

Farzana barreled down a narrow winding street. Mavin followed, quickly losing how many turns to the right and left they had taken. She opened a faded green gate and crossed an inner courtyard. Mavin followed her down a hallway into a small room with a bed and a wooden chair.

"There is a shared bathroom down the hall," Farzana said. "I will bring you something to eat and drink."

Mavin kept his gaze lowered, never looking the large woman in the eyes, just as Simone had instructed. "Thank you, Farzana." He bowed. Tomorrow he would find Simone, with or without Farzana's help.

When she returned with his meal, he was lying on the bed asleep.

# Without Question

Trees are the poems that the earth writes upon the sky.
–Khalil Gibran

Simone's finely tuned senses were slow to adjust to the noise of the city. She remained vigilant all night, unable to sleep. Early the next morning, a barracks full of young officer cadets gathered around, peppering her with questions.

She folded her hands and repeated, "I'm unable to discuss details of the mission at this time." She was scheduled to report to her commanding officer for a debriefing. She wanted to ask after Mavin, but knew how that would be perceived. He was beyond her help now. She had expected a great weight to be lifted. She sat on her bunk and listened to the cadet's questions. "They are almost as big a pain as Mavin," she said to herself. "No, not by half. He's a pain even when he's gone."

After a shower, she sat on the bench in front of her locker brushing her hair. She massaged her scalp with the stiff brush. It felt divine.

A newly pressed dress uniform hung in the locker, along with underwear, stockings, a pair of polished black shoes, and a cap. It was unheard of for anyone but an officer to wear a dress uniform. "They must want me to look the part," she told herself. When she crossed the courtyard to report to the Special Forces commander, everyone she passed stood at attention. "What's going on?" she wondered.

The High Council and top brass were caught off guard by the events of the previous day. Colonel Bina and Commander Shazia of Unified Command had been in a joint meeting with

Councilwoman Asra and Councilwoman Khalsa late into the morning. If Specialist Kita's story was to be believed, she had crossed over the northern ice field and returned, a feat never before accomplished. There seemed little choice but to offer the returning hero a commission. The rank of second lieutenant was decided upon.

"What's the rush?" Col. Bina objected. "Allowing a foreign-born, civilian scout into the officer Korps is one thing. Offering her a commission is quite another. This flies in the face of history and sets a dangerous precedent." Bina was repulsed. *How can they even think of letting a Janjanbi into the service*, she thought.

"This foreign civilian, as you call her, has shown conspicuous gallantry and skill." Commander Shazia reminded Bina.

"May I urge the Council to allow us to follow procedure? There's no compelling reason to run ahead of ourselves," Col. Bina suggested firmly. "My priority is to debrief Specialist Kita and find out what happened to my people out there. This should be the priority. Politics shouldn't affect the natural order of things."

"Those of us who witnessed what happened yesterday," the elder councilwoman Asra interrupted, "are trying to maintain the natural orders of things. I don't care where Specialist Kita was born. A once in a lifetime event is not something to ignore. The people believe the Janjanbi to be a hero. There are rumblings."

"This is the capital. There are always rumblings." Bina hated compromise.

"Like it or not, the woman is a hero." Asra easily dominated the room. "She must be treated with honor or it will reflect poorly on all of us."

"When I've finished my debriefing, I'll submit my recommendations in writing and not before." Col. Bina was not going to be run roughshod.

"If memory serves, Colonel, you opposed having a Janjanbi join the expedition." Asra was about to remind the colonel that the military served the Triumvirate, not the other way around. "Under the circumstances, you're hardly the person to debrief Specialist Kita."

Simone arrived fifteen minutes early, but was led directly into the hall by an aide.

"Welcome." Councilwoman Asra met SPC Kita at the door. "Please, take a seat."

Simone sat at a low table. Her superiors were seated behind a raised podium with an embossed crane emblem.

"Specialist Kita, you are the sole survivor of your team?" Commander Shazia's first question went to the heart of the matter.

"Yes, so far as I'm aware."

"As a scout, was it not your responsibility to carry out reconnaissance and alert the team of any possible threats?" Cmdr. Shazia continued.

"Yes."

"Then how do you explain the fact that you're alive, and everyone else is missing in action?" Col. Bina squeezed the file she was holding with both hands.

"I take full responsibility." Simone let out a sigh of relief. She welcomed a quick and sturdy verdict.

Councilwoman Asra seized the opening. "Will you accept the decision of this joint committee without question?"

"Yes." Simone felt the weight lift from her heart. If she were found to be negligent in the performance of her duty, it would put her heart and mind at rest.

For three days, the Joint Committee questioned Specialist Kita. Colonel Bina recommended that the Janjanbi be awarded a civilian commendation for acts of heroism and meritorious achievement. She was over-ruled by the other members.

On the morning of the fifth day of their return, Simone found Mavin in a shabby house on Vico Road lying sick in bed. "As usual, you ignored me. I told you what rich food would do to your system." She wasn't going to waste her sympathy. It was his own fault he had been a glutton. "Drink tea for the few days with a little fruit. You've been eating wild things for over a year. You have to give your body time to adjust." She could tell he wasn't listening. "Have you been learning anything since our arrival?"

"Yes—the meaning of demeaning." He had been suffering from diarrhea for days. "My two feet have missed you," he jibbed.

She tried to keep a straight face. "I see you've found a place to sleep."

"I'm getting by. Tell me where have you been? What have you been up to?" He was shocked to see her in a uniform. "What's been happening?"

"They've made me second lieutenant." She pointed to her shoulder insignia.

"Congratulations, Simone." He was happy for her. "You're an officer, what you've always wanted."

"Why would you say such a thing?" She felt herself getting upset.

"You told me Janjanbi couldn't become officers. You should be proud." He didn't understand the look on her face.

"I never wanted this," she said. They were going to pin a medal on her chest and say, job well done. You're a hero. If that were true, then why was her entire team dead? It compounded her shame to wear their uniform.

"Look, I'm sorry, I didn't mean…"

She rushed out of the room before he could finish.

"Wait! Simone. Come back." He rolled out of bed, pulled on a pair of pants and ran across the courtyard. By the time he made it out into the busy street she was gone.

# Ceremony

There is a tale… it tells of the days when a blight
hung over our land. Nothing prospered. Nothing flourished.
—Cameron Dokey

Farzana knocked and entered Mavin's small room.

"Come in," Mavin said, after the fact. His sarcasm went unnoticed.

Farzana had a black dhoti suit and pants folded over her arm. "We need to get you dressed, Sri Mavin. You're to attend a formal ceremony."

"What kind of ceremony?" Her usual silence followed his every question. "Can you at least wait outside, Farzana?"

"Have you worn a dhoti before, Sri Mavin?" She doubted his ability to do the simplest thing.

"I've worn pajamas before. I think I can manage." He chased her out. Whenever he'd ventured out alone, he was told again and again by those he met how lucky he was to have Farzana taking care of him. Luck, he decided, had many faces.

He followed close behind the big woman weaving through the maze of narrow streets. He compared the view with tailgating a delivery van down an alley. They entered the capitol rotunda by the side entrance. Mavin waited on a stone bench until his backside was numb.

The voices of the crowd in the main hall echoed off the high-domed ceiling. He had no idea what the event would entail. His heart raced at the thought of seeing Simone. A guard escorted him through a side door onto a raised platform. The crowd came to life when they caught sight of him. He was left alone beside the podium. He was shocked to be on the stage. It was unclear if he was supposed to do something. He went to default setting and looked down at his feet.

Simone appeared from the wings in a formal dress uniform of the Peregrine Korps. The crowd burst into spontaneous cheers. She walked calmly across the platform amidst the deafening roar and stood to Mavin's left.

"Hello, Simone," he shouted over the crowd.

She ignored him.

She looked older, though it had only been two days since she stormed out of his room. The dark bags under her eyes concerned him.

Lady Miranda stood in the wings and watched the Janjanbi bathing in the adoration of the people. A few short years ago she received that kind of love from the citizenry. Not every decision that needed to be made was a popular one. To explain would be to show weakness. To properly fulfill the office of the Merc, it was necessary to make the hard decisions. She waited for the crowd to calm down. Over the years she learned how to deal with rivals. *I'll pin a medal on this Janjanbi and send her to a border posting where she'll end her days in obscurity.* The deafening cheers of the crowd unraveled her nerves. She returned to her antechamber. Her faithful advisor, Edessa knocked and entered.

"The Daughter of Avighna's barge is just now docking." Edessa reported. "The priestess should arrive shortly."

"Thank you, Edessa. Have Col. Bina and Cmdr. Shazia take their places. Then seat the council members."

Lady Miranda had carefully choreographed the event, but the new young priestess had ignored the timetable. In public theater, it was vital for the most important personage to appear last. She would soon train this new upstart, or she would be replaced.

An uncomfortable hour passed while everyone but the Merc stood waiting on the platform. As soon as White Crane arrived, she was led to the Merc's antechamber. "Welcome, your Grace." Lady Miranda rose and kissed the young priestesses's ring. "This way, please." She gestured for the young woman to go first.

"After you." The young priestess bowed at the neck.

When Mavin saw the Lady Miranda bound onto the platform in her crimson robes, he thought of Aphrodite revealing herself to mere mortals. He knew he shouldn't be staring, but he couldn't take his eyes off the lady in red. The crowd applauded as the Merc greeted Second Lieutenant Kita and stood by her side.

When White Crane entered, a hush fell over the hall. Her white robes draped the marble. She seemed to float. For many it was the first time they'd caught sight of the Daughter of Avighna. She was the earthly representative of White Crane who had delivered the people out of darkness nine centuries ago. It was said her eyes were as clear as the bottomless waters of Avighna.

To Mavin, it seemed impossible for any woman to compare to Miranda, whose form appeared divine. How wrong he had been. The silence deepened as White Crane's enchantment held the great hall.

Cmdr. Shazia footsteps could be heard as she approached the priestess. The decorated soldier held a small black silk pillow with both hands.

The Daughter of Avighna's delicate fingers plucked the shimmering star from the pillow and held it high for the crowd to see. The young woman's smile made whatever object she was holding insignificant.

Simone stood and waited, using all her energy to conceal the emptiness inside. Ever since she returned and handed over the seeds, she felt hollow. She had no appetite and couldn't sleep. Whatever meaning her life once held, it was lost. It was as though she were in the next room listening to the event.

The Daughter of Avighna took her time pinning the small star onto the chest of Second Lieutenant Kita. The priestess turned and faced the crowd standing directly in front of Lady Miranda. The Merc was forced to move to her left in order to be seen.

Murmurs and whispers mixed with the cheers and applause.

The council members filed out and then Mavin was escorted off the platform. He called out to Simone, but she didn't acknowledge him. Farzana led him back through the maze of streets. "What was that all about?" Mavin asked.

The big woman broke her own rule and answered his question. "The foreigner was given a medal. Did you not see? You were standing right beside her?" She shook her head in disgust.

"Yes, Farzana, I caught that much. But what does it all mean?"

"Nothing to bother your pretty little head about." Her own standing had diminished beyond repair. "Taking care of a man?" she mumbled. She never dreamed her fortunes would fall so low. "You stood right beside the Daughter of Avighna, ignorant son of a man!" It riled her that he should enjoy such fortune and yet be born too ignorant to know what it meant.

"Farzana, I beg you. Please explain what just happened." He tried to squeeze around and walk beside her.

"The Lady in red just got upstaged by the young high priestess. It will be a miracle if there isn't blood in the streets. Did you see the look on Lady Miranda's face? Sweet Crane! Mark my words, there's a storm coming over the lake." Farzana was barreling down the narrow street forcing people to dodge out of her way.

\*     \*     \*     \*

Lady Miranda stepped out of her heavy crimson robes and looked out over the city from her high balcony. "Edessa! The maiden has gone too far this time!" She lifted her long hair off her shoulders and felt the cool breeze against her bare skin. Her servant draped a thin silk robe over her shoulders and scurried away.

Edessa poured wine. "You've every reason to be upset."

"This little priestess thinks she can hide behind her white robes and innocent smile?" Miranda closed her eyes and imagined a skewered white bird roasting over a bed of coals. "It's not just the Nabhi slut. The Janjanbi and the beardless man complicate matters."

"A fitting arrangement will present itself," Edessa said calmly. "You'll think of something. You always do. The priestess is young and foolish. It will be months before the solstice. The people will have forgotten her by then." Edessa rubbed Miranda's shoulders. "You can see how loyal the Janjanbi is to you. She will jump off a cliff if you ask her. As for the thin man, you saw him. A half-wit, like the rest."

"They mustn't be allowed to communicate with one another." The applause in the rotunda had unnerved Miranda. "This Janjanbi must be sent to a border post as soon as possible. Let it be known there's trouble brewing along the western frontier."

"I desire what you desire." Edessa loosened her robe and leaned back on the cushions pulling Miranda close. "It is a shame all three can't be on the border when the fighting breaks out." Edessa kissed her mistress on the neck and nibbled her earlobe.

"You excite me." Envisioning the death of her rivals whetted Miranda's appetite. She reached under her lover's robe and raked her long nails across Edessa's breasts.

Edessa writhed and pretended to try to escape.

# House of Merlas

So in the dark we hide the heart that bleeds,
and wait, and tend our agonizing seeds.
—COUNTEE CULLEN

The icy peaks in the distance sent a prickling numbness into Mavin's toes. He turned and watched Simone in the bow of their little fishing boat. She was cold and aloof, distant as the snow covered Mercies rising out of the mist. She had aged five years in five months. He wondered what had happened to her over the winter to cause the change.

"You should reach Mizurria by nightfall." Their river guide broke the silence.

Simone didn't respond. She had spoken very little during the nine days of their journey. The merchant city of Mizurria was in the heart of Diamond Province. It was said to be a grand city built on the banks of the River Sky.

Traveling night and day, they slept on fishing nets, often changing boats in the early hours before dawn. Mavin was humbled by the kindness shown to them by the poor fisherman and villagers. The misery of the poor opened his eyes to the importance of the seeds they'd brought back from Svalbard. The children of the Mirror Valley never left his thoughts. When he learned that his expertise was needed to help germinate the seeds, he was thrilled. He thought Simone would be too. Instead, she was irritable. She spent all her time staring at the riverbank.

Simone had been recalled from her border post without explanation. She should have known it was to babysit. She didn't question orders. Still, she had hoped this chapter of her life was behind her. For months she'd been unable to sleep. Karin and Sidta haunted her dreams. Being near Mavin again made her heart even heavier.

Mavin had not anticipated how awkward it would be traveling together. He had missed her every moment she had been away. He wanted to tell her, but her attitude was impossible. She left without saying goodbye. For five months he heard no news of her. She had made it sound like he would be an indentured servant when they reached Kashphera. Now he was summoned to the great city of Mizurria by a noble house. If the way she was behaving towards him was any indication, it must have irked her to no end to see how well he was treated. He almost said something clever about how much better this little fishing boat handled than their ice raft, but the sour expression on her face curbed his tongue. He wanted to yell, "What's your problem?" He couldn't stop ruminating. He was tempted to push her over the side with his foot.

Their river guide beached the fishing dory beside a gondola-like shikara that was waiting for them on the edge of the city. A mermaid figurehead was carved into its high prow. The ornately painted craft had a wide cushioned seat covered with a domed shade awning. The shikara driver smiled and offered Mavin her hand. He stepped aboard and comfortably settled into the high-backed seat. Then the driver barked something to Simone that Mavin didn't understand.

Simone loaded their bags from the fishing boat and sat aft on a wooden crate in the hot sun.

Remembering their ferry crossing, Mavin ignored Simone and chatted with the comely river guide. Iron gates dotted the shoreline framing dozens of large stone mansions in the distance. As they glided with the current, large ornate residences became more frequent and nearer the shore. Soon palaces fronted both riverbanks. People in brightly colored garments filled wide steps that led down to the water.

Arched entrances, like sea caves, beckoned the mermaid on their prow to enter. As they came around a wide bend, the scale of the city astounded Mavin. Multi-storied palaces lined the banks for miles. After two hours he asked the driver how much further.

"We're still on the outskirts of the city. With the high flow of the river today, we should reach the central canal by sunset. Relax and enjoy yourself, Sri Mavin. The sacred waters of the River Sky flow from the heavenly peaks of the Mercies to Mizurria, the greatest city in the world."

The guide wrapped a cord around the tiller and unfolded a small table beside him. She covered a wooden tray with white linen and poured a glass of red wine into a hand-blown glass. She gave him a warm wet towel to freshen up before producing a plate of small cheeses and grapes from a wooden ice chest.

Simone watched Mavin being served. It appeared that despite his lack of manners, he had found a place in society. By the looks of it, a wealthy house had taken a keen interest. She had never been this far downriver. She had been brought up to serve and imagined the world was made up of people like herself. The tremendous wealth of the merchant class was an open secret. A sense of shame permeated her thoughts. A chorus of voices accused her of having no imagination. "Why wouldn't the world be full of such splendors?" she told herself. "The world is as it should be."

He thought of sharing his tray with her and then reminded himself that they were living in the civilized world now. How often she had scolded him. What was she sulking about? At least she didn't have to look down at his feet or pull the boat along by a slimy rope, while half a dozen aunties hurled insults. He left a piece of cheese on the platter.

As the sun went down over the widening river, torches were lit adding golden reflections to those of the reddening clouds. The water was alive with painted shikaras carrying thickly robbed passengers in every direction. Mavin picked out Venus in the crepuscule light. He remembered one night asking Simone if she knew that the morning and evening star were the same planet.

Their ironic reversal of fortunes was yet another contradiction. His star had risen, whereas she had been sent to a remote border post in the western desert, miles from the nearest village. She sat arm's length from him in the same little boat, as unreachable as ever. He was getting fed up with her negative attitude.

Their pilot turned into the central canal and explained that the island to their left was the hub of the city.

"I thought you'd be excited at the prospect of the seeds coming to life," he said to Simone's back.

She turned around, indignant. "Excuse me!" *How dare he say she didn't care?* Out of reflex, she stood up as their shikara glided under a stone archway.

Mavin caught a glimpse of the grand palace before they slipped into the boathouse beneath. He felt as though they had entered the sacred grotto of Neptune. The dock was lined with lavishly dressed attendants. The lines of the shikara were quickly secured. Torchlight reflected off the water illuminating a half-submerged fresco. A tall woman dressed in lavender held out her hand to Mavin.

He noticed steps descending beneath the emerald water. Their river guide had mentioned that the river was running high this time of year. He realized he was standing like a statue. He took the lady in lavender's soft hand and stepped onto the tiled landing. She held his hand leading him up the steps. He paused. Simone had not yet stepped out of the boat.

"Sri Mavin, we must hurry. You've arrived much later than expected." His guide pulled him up the remaining steps and down a long hallway. They crossed an inner courtyard lined with aediculae-like shrines that led to a massive foyer. He followed her up a grand curved staircase that led to a lavish penthouse suite.

Candelabra ringed the large chamber. His feet sunk into the thick magenta carpet. Silk pillows surrounded a black lacquered table. The lady in lavender gestured for him to make himself comfortable before she disappeared.

Mavin wandered out onto the generous balcony and breathed in the vibrant feel of the city. Lanterns from dozens of shikaras reflected off the busy canal below.

A gentle voice interrupted his musing. "Welcome to my home, Sri Mavin. I am Lady Merlas. Please call me Erica." She made a deep courtesy, and held it.

The generous neckline of her gown left Mavin with an immediate quandary.

She looked up and followed his eyes. "Oh, you've noticed my necklace." It was made of a fine golden mesh of interlocking chains. She fingered it. "It's a map of our city. Each of these tiny links represents a family palace on the river."

"Yes, breathtaking. I mean it's quite lovely," he stammered. The thin fabric of her dress clung to her generous curves.

"Would you care for some refreshment?"

He had been drinking wine all day while they floated through the city. He realized he was light-headed, still feeling the movement of the water. "Yes, thank you."

*It's so easy to seduce a man*, she confided to her portrait on the wall. "Red wine?"

"Yes. Perfect." *That's the last thing I need right now*, he thought.

She knelt on a cushion beside the low table and poured. Women are infinitely more complex. She thought to herself. We require the hundred unseen things to be in harmony. With men, we need only appear mildly interested in them. She handed him the glass, making sure to touch his hand. "What do you think of my humble abode?"

"I've never been in a more beautiful room." He hadn't noticed his surroundings since she appeared.

*This youth is easy to like,* she confessed to herself. She took a small sip and looked in his eyes.

He watched her white teeth slowly harvest a stray drop of wine from her bottom lip. He unconsciously bit his own. He became lost in the tiny curve at the corner of her mouth. A small dimple appeared and disappeared when she smiled. He struggled to guess her age. She looked in her mid-thirties, but something in her bearing told him she was older. "Lady Merlas."

"Call me Erica."

The flutter of her camel-like lashes interrupted his thought. There were shards of orange crystal in her brown eyes. When she closed her eyes he took the precious second to study her bare shoulders. Now, she didn't blink, holding his gaze while her chest heaved. Her scent enveloped him.

Poor thing. She wondered if he would ever take a sip of his wine, or finish his sentence. If it were simply a matter of physically seducing him, she had nearly succeeded. It was vital that he never learn how much she needed him. The bidding had started outrageously high and then soared for every allotment. The seeds had garnered the attention of every major house. She had taken a big gamble. If the seeds lived up to their billing, she would control the commodities market. He was the key. That meant setting the hook deep. "Is this is your first visit to Mizurria?"

"Yes. It's an unbelievable city. All day we floated by so many elegant palaces."

"You traveled from the north?"

"Yes, from Kashphera."

"Tomorrow we must show you the rest of the city. We are here in the center." She brushed her long nails slowly across the golden links of her necklace. He was caught in the black ringlets of her hair. The thin weave of her gown had him guessing what was fabric or flesh.

"The city reaches yet another hundred miles deeper down river."

He followed her fingertips raking across her breasts moving slowly downriver to the small ruby in her belly button. Unlike Simone, Erica was more than aware of her beauty. "Simone."

"Excuse me?" Lady Merlas looked up.

"I was wondering about my companion, the Janjanbi. Do you know where she is?"

"I've no idea."

Mavin watched the softness leave his host.

So, it's true, she confided to herself. He is different. She tried to put aside her personal feelings. This was business. *Have I lost my bloom?* She set down her glass. She had grown accustomed to getting whatever she desired. "You seem tired from your journey." She rang a small bell.

A servant entered.

"Sri Mavin is anxious to be shown his accommodations." Lady Merlas rose and disappeared behind a painted silk screen.

He was worried about Simone, though part of him was sorry he'd blurted out her name. The spell was broken. "You certainly blow hot and cold," he said to the portrait of the grand lady. He followed the servant down a set of stairs to his apartment. "Where is my Janjanbi?" He tried to sound like an important personage.

"I do not know, Sri Mavin. I will inquire." The servant bowed and closed the door behind her.

*Why didn't you get out of the boat? What's the matter with you?* "You're not my problem anymore!" he said to the empty room. Why did he even bother asking her to come along? "You're more trouble than you're worth." He sat on the bed and buried his head in his hands.

Mavin woke up with a dry mouth and a headache. He pulled open the soft thick curtains. A set of leaded glass doors opened onto a small balcony. Across the water he could see the central island. On its highest point, the first rays of the morning sun filtered through jade-green columns. He wondered if it was a temple of the White Crane.

The young servant knocked and brought in a breakfast of sweet breads and sliced mango. "Good morning, Sri Mavin. The Janjanbi that accompanied you to the palace has returned up-river."

She was gone. He steadied himself against the railing. He should have insisted that she remain with him. Now it was too late.

\* \* \* \*

Simone watched the six rowers move as one. Their perfect rhythm was hypnotic. After the humiliating ride in the shikara, it comforted her to know she merited a fast vessel on her return journey. She gleaned that only important personages traveled upriver in this fashion. A craft propelled by six rowers widened the eyes of those they overtook, as well as everyone traveling downriver.

She thought back to the previous evening. She let herself be distracted by her feelings. She failed to anticipate events. "I couldn't very well fight my way through a half dozen unarmed attendants for no reason. You're on your own now, Raven.

# Mercury Rising

Put your faith in the two inches of humus that will build
under the trees every thousand years.
—Wendell Berry

It was a hot humid morning when Mavin set off downriver
to the Jamurra district. The smoke from the evening torches
still hung over the water. His river guide was a heavyset
woman in her late fifties. He didn't know if she spoke English.
From the moment he stepped in her boat she refused to acknowledge his presence. He was no more than a sack of grain
she was hauling to the mill.

He was eager to be reunited with the seeds. They were a connection back to Svalbard, and to his lost friends and family. If
the seeds were still alive, then he wasn't the lone survivor of his
time. *Where had Simone gone,* he wondered. *Didn't she want to
stay? Did I do something wrong?* He didn't understand why she
had treated him so coldly.

Just as Erica Merlas had promised, the wonders of Mizurria
extended many miles south. Lavish palaces with ornate spires
lined both banks of the wide river. Just as they floated past a
high wall, it was as if a gray curtain had been drawn over the
dome of the sky. They had suddenly entered another country.
The few people Mavin saw on the riverbanks were like moving
scarecrows. Though they were but a stone's throw from the riverbank, no one onshore seemed to notice their boat. The thin
faces and sunken eyes of the people unnerved him.

The Jamurra district was in the heart of the south, the cul-
tural center of Diamond Province. In the late morning of the
second day, his guide maneuvered along a wooden jetty and

jumped out to fasten a line. She pointed across the green field to an ornate wooden gate.

He thanked his silent guide and walked across the green to where the director of the gardens was waiting.

*     *     *     *

Dr. Mirza, the director of the gardens, was anxious to show off the conservatory. She held the glass door open for him. The Merlas Botanical Gardens held one of the largest plant collections in the world. Doubtless, the tallest tree on record would impress the foreigner.

Mavin breathed in the leafy moist air. It smelled alive. The elegant oval conservatory had a thick sandstone foundation topped with high-arched panels of leaded glass. He wondered at the immense height of the cathedral-like glass structure. Wishful thinking, he assumed. There certainly wasn't anything high as an elephant's eye growing. They walked through exotic ferns and plants, many of which Mavin didn't recognize.

Dr. Mirza paused beside the long wooden table and smiled broadly. She had carefully arranged the finely crafted wooden boxes containing the famous seeds.

"What are these?" Mavin read the labels on the boxes and panicked. He opened the wooden lid and smelled the stale wheat. "Why were the sealed packets opened? These boxes are not moisture-proof!"

"Calm yourself, Sri Mavin." Dr. Mirza was not at all surprised by the foreign man's lack of manners. "This is how we received the seed allotments," she said calmly. Lady Merlas had sent a letter asking that she wait for the foreigner to arrive before attempting to germinate the seeds. What a surprise, she thought. The first thing out of the foreigner's mouth is to complain. Everyone knew that seeds packed in a finely crafted box were of greater value than seeds in a plain sack.

"These seeds are extremely old," he explained. "There's very little moisture, if any, remaining in the inner embryo. It was a huge error to open the packages prematurely!" He realized it probably wasn't the director's fault, but her pompous attitude wasn't helping to cool his temper. What could be done about it now? He noticed that the ten boxes were wheat and rice seeds only. "Where are the rest of the seeds from Svalbard?"

"These are all of the seeds that arrived," she said stiffly. Dr. Mirza had never experienced a man speaking down to her. She was grateful they were alone or she would never recover from the shame. If the Lady Merlas had not personally written instructing her to assist the man in every way, she would have him beaten and thrown into the river.

Mavin tried to settle down. What could be done about it now? It is what it is. He surrendered to the reality of the situation. He had a few preliminary thoughts on how to best approach the challenge of bringing the seeds to life. "We'll divide each variety into ten small batches and re-seal them," he informed the director. "That will provide us with ten trials. We'll take detailed notes of the temperature and moisture levels of each trial. We may need to use some abrasion techniques on the seeds's outer shells, as I'm sure they're very thick and hard at this point. We'll need thermometers."

"What is it you wish?" Did not the uncouth man understand that she was the director?

He wanted to ask her if she even knew what mercury was, but checked his thought. His decision not to interfere with the natural scientific development of the culture was proving to be much harder than he imagined. *What if the first test batch doesn't germinate? Will I break my own rules?* He realized he was grinding his teeth and glaring at the director.

She needed to wash her hands of this soon, or she would have this son of a man beaten regardless of the repercussions. "You'll have a full-time assistant during your stay." She wanted to say, "During your *brief* stay." Who did he think he was? "Now if you will excuse me, I have matters that require my attention." She didn't want to burden her staff with this barbarian. Instead, she would lend him a boy.

"Forgive me, Dr. Mirza." Mavin could see he had gone too far and offended the director. "I carried these seeds on my back for over a year. They mean a great deal to me. I'm sorry if I was rude."

The director turned her back to Mavin without acknowledging his apology. On her way by, she spoke to the country boy who was watering a bed of seedlings. "What is your name?"

"I am Jai Rey, Madam Director." The young man said while looking down at his feet.

"Jai Rey. This foreigner is here to germinate the seeds that arrived from Mizurria. He is your responsibility as of now. Do you understand?"

"Yes, Director." The young man looked at the ground until the director was well out of sight before presenting himself to the foreigner. "Welcome to Merlas Gardens. I am Jai Rey, at your service."

"Thank you, Jai. I am Mavin Cedarstrom. I'm very pleased to meet you. I hope you will forgive my rudeness. I meant no disrespect to Dr. Mirza. I've had a long journey and I'm very concerned about these seeds."

"Please do not apologize, Sri Mavin. I was watering and did not hear."

Mavin laughed. The boy was well within earshot. "I'm sure you heard every word."

"Sri Marvin, I understand the importance of these special seeds. Children in my village are going without enough to eat as we speak." He wanted to say that, "Children are starving to death, while I water rare flowers."

Mavin couldn't get the shrunken faces of the children in the Mirror Valley out of his head.

"Would you like to see how we germinate seeds here at the Merlas Gardens?" Jai asked.

"Yes, very much." Mavin had a degree in biology, but he reminded himself that he had very little experience actually growing anything.

"Sri Mavin, I can't express how grateful we are that you have come."

*   *   *   *

Jai quickly proved to be a young man of many talents. Mavin was amazed by his sheer competence. Jai had never attended school and yet had a broad understanding of agricultural practices. Jai showed Mavin a recent experiment he had developed using lower water levels to control rice neck rot. The approach had yielded some positive results, but after a heavy rain, black fungus once again spread like wildfire.

"I very much hope that you are successful in germinating the special seeds, Sri Mavin."

"I hope we are successful, my young friend. But I have to be honest, Jai. It's a million to one chance." In his heart, Mavin believed the seeds would grow, even though he knew it would take a miracle.

After work, Jai took Mavin home to meet his family. His mother, Zia put the kettle on for tea. In all the excitement of her guest's stories, the teapot was completely forgotten. "Sweet Crane! I've let the water boil away." Zia admonished herself.

"You need a whistling teapot," Mavin suggested.

"A teapot that can whistle?" Zia laughed. "I've never heard of such a thing."

Mavin admired her brass teakettle. He had an idea. He needed a way to measure the spout. He compared it to his thumbnail. "Give me a couple of days Zia, and I'll show you how a pot can whistle." He turned to Jai, "Is there someone in your village who repairs pots?"

After work the following day, Jai introduced Mavin to the tinsmith Vinita.

"I'm pleased to meet you, Vinita," Mavin suddenly became shy.

"Jai tells me you wish to make use of my hammer and tongs." The jolly tinsmith was more than curious to see what the beardless man had in mind. "You are most welcome to anything in my humble workshop."

"Thank you, Vinita. Do you have a teakettle that I could measure?" he asked.

"A tinsmith without a teapot? Ho!" Vinita laughed. "Nearly every teapot in the valley was made by my grandmother, my mother or myself."

"Oh, I see. Yes, the spout on your pot looks to be almost identical to Zia's."

"You may find this iron shoe helpful." Vinita showed Mavin her workbench. "I use this tapered shoe to make the teapot spouts."

"Yes, this is just what I need." Mavin set to work at once, hammering a flat piece of copper around the iron shoe and then added a second layer. He center-punched the cap before drilling a hole in the center with a brace and bit. He held the brass cap to his lips and blew, but no sound came out. "It's ready to try."

Vinita stirred the coals in her cook stove, added some dry kindling and set the kettle on.

"May I?" Mavin fitted the bright copper cap tightly on to the kettle's spout. "We'll soon know how I did."

"What is it we're waiting for?" Vinita looked at Mavin and then to Jai.

"You'll see." Mavin crossed his fingers. "Knock on wood."

Jai played along not giving anything away.

"Knock on wood?" Vinita laughed. "May I ask, Sri Mavin, where you learned to work with copper?" She admired his unorthodox technique.

Mavin explained that he had gone to school, but had a difficult time deciding on what to study. "I majored in biology, but I tried a little bit of everything: woodshop, metal shop, auto shop, electronics, and computers." Mavin could see Vinita's eyes getting bigger and bigger. He had gotten carried away.

An uncomfortable silence followed.

"What brings you to Jamurra, Sri Mavin?" Vinita rescued her guest from the awkward moment.

"I came to help Jai, of course," Mavin announced proudly.

Vinita was impressed by the stranger's humility. "And what are you helping Jai to do?"

"We are attempting to germinate some seeds that are centuries old. If we succeed, it will change the world," Mavin explained.

"Oh, is that all?" Vinita liked this fellow well. "And what will happen if the seeds do not sprout?"

"I don't know," Mavin hadn't allowed any thought of failure to enter his mind. "Then I suppose it will all be for nothing."

"Dr. Mirza will have us beaten to death and thrown in the river," Jai said, in a flat tone.

"You're joking?" Mavin tried to read his new friend's face.

Jai was grateful when a high piercing whistle came from the boiling kettle.

"Delightful, Sri Mavin! Very good!" Vinita jumped to her feet laughing.

"This first cap is a gift for Jai's mother. If you're interested, Vinita, you're more than welcome to the design." Mavin felt it was the least he could offer.

Vinita used a tea towel to remove the cap and examined the small hole closely, making note of the double layer. "I will try my hand at making your whistling caps, Sri Mavin. If I'm successful, I will split the profits equally with you."

"Thank you, Vinita. Let's just say, we will not have you beaten and thrown in the river." His attempt at humor was not well received. He tried to recover, "I appreciate your generosity in sharing your workshop with me. Let's call it a trade."

\*    \*    \*    \*

Three days later the first test batch of wheat sprouted. Mavin was beside himself with excitement. "It's a miracle!" He hugged Jai. "What's wrong my friend? You look like you've seen a ghost."

Realizing they had escaped the wrath of Director Mirza, Jai's face turned a pale white. Had the seeds not sprouted, they would surely have been beaten to death. "No, Sri Mavin, I'm very happy."

"You have a green thumb, my friend."

Jai looked at his hands. "No, Sri Mavin, my thumbs are fine."

"More than fine, you have a gift. You understand plants and they understand you."

"You are too kind, Sri Mavin."

The first test batch of rice also germinated, but three weeks later the new rice shoots exhibited the same brown diamond spots as all the other existing varieties being grown. Mavin recognized it as a common disease called 'rice blast'. A week later, he also identified both stem rust and powdery mildew in the wheat test beds.

If not for Jai's infectious positive attitude, Mavin would have lost hope in the project. What was the reason he had survived? What was the point of the seeds surviving just to immediately succumb to the same diseases in a single generation? It didn't make sense. As dire as the situation seemed, he promised himself that he would wait until the end of the growing season before drawing any conclusions.

On the eve of the summer solstice, Vinita, the tinsmith came to visit Jai and Mavin. She walked into the conservatory, exaggerating the weight of the small pouch she carried. She pretended to have a hard time lifting the pouch. She plunked it down on the wooden table with a loud thump.

"Sweet Crane! What do you have in there, Vin?" Jai asked.

"I told, Sri Mavin that I would split the profits. I'm here to make good."

"What have you got there, Vinita?" Mavin had instantly taken a liking to the jovial tinsmith the moment they'd met.

"Silver."

"You're joking." Mavin picked up the pouch. It was amazingly heavy for its size.

"Open it," Vinita insisted.

Mavin dug in the leather pouch and pulled out a handful of silver coins with a crane on one side and a tree on the other. "Where did you get all this money?"

"It turns out, Sri Mavin that everyone in Jamurra wishes to own a teapot that whistles. I can't make the brass caps fast enough. I've taken on an apprentice to help. This is your half of the profit, as agreed."

"You agreed," Mavin pointed out. "How much money is this?"

"Enough to treat all of your friends to a grand feast," Vinita said in earnest.

"What do you think, Jai?" Mavin was in shock.

Jai was likewise stunned. He shuffled his feet and thought for a moment. "The tea cap is your invention, Sri Mavin. This money is yours, as agreed."

"I don't remember agreeing. Besides, I thought I was Jāti? He remembered Simone saying he could never own anything.

"You are, Sri Mavin." Jai shook his head.

"Are you teasing me? I can't tell when you're being serious."

Jai looked at Vinita hoping she would help explain. "Sri Mavin, I think perhaps you do not have a complete understanding of Jāti. It can indicate one's birth, but it can also indicate one's trade, the guild in which you are born into, or trade that is passed on to you. In any case, none of this applies to you. You are Sri Mavin. You are of the House of Merlas," Jai held open his palms, as if to say it was all so obvious.

"Yes, I met with Lady Merlas," Mavin admitted. "And she sent me down here to help germinate the seeds, but I'm just an employee, like you." He looked at his two friends unable to read their faces. "What?"

Jai took a moment and then decided to speak plainly. "Sri Mavin, no one has ever met the Lady Merlas, not even the director, Dr. Mirza. I don't know who told you that you were Jāti, but with all due respect, they don't know what they're talking about."

"Okay. I'll tell you what, Jai." Mavin slapped his young friend on the back. "I'm putting you in charge of my half of the operation. Take the money and do something good with it." The look on Jai's face was precious. "Don't forget to save something for a rainy day." Mavin loaded a shovel and rake into a crude wheelbarrow he had cobbled together and headed to the test fields.

Vinita turned to Jai. "Do you think Sri Mavin will mind if I try my hand at making one of his wheeled carts?"

Jai's eyes lit up. "As Sri Mavin's assistant, and your new partner, I find myself in desperate need of such a cart."

As the crops grew, none of the test bed seeds showed any resistance to disease. What's more, the leaf shapes and colors were identical in every way to the current crops of wheat and rice. By the end of the growing season it was obvious something was wrong.

"Occam's razor," Mavin pronounced.

"I'm sorry, Sri Mavin. I do not understand."

"The simplest explanation is often the best. These test seeds are the same seeds being grown everywhere. They're not the seeds I helped to carry from Svalbard." Thinking back on it, he suspected as much the first day when he saw the seeds in the wooden boxes.

"I agree, Sri Mavin. The rice and wheat look like any other being grown in Jamurra."

Many times in the course of their work, Mavin wanted to explain to Jai how these two grains had evolved under human selection for ten thousand years. He knew there was no way to explain to Jai how he knew such things without opening up Pandora's box. By domesticating wheat and rice, humans played a big role in why they are now vulnerable to disease. Wild plants are seldom threatened by disease. No matter what the history, they had reached the end of the road. There was nothing left to try.

"Jai, please inform Dr. Mirza that I'm returning to Mizurria. I must speak with Lady Merlas. I need to know if she is a party to this deception."

"Sri Mavin, Mizurria is a dangerous place. Many have gone upriver and never been heard from again. Please do not speak to the Lady Merlas as you have to Dr. Mirza."

"Not to worry, Jai. Take care of things while I'm away."

# Invitation

It is good to know the truth,
but it is better to speak of palm trees.
—ARAB PROVERB

Lady Merlas was in the mood for good news. She had been following the progress, or rather lack of progress on her investment. The seer Leto had a vision of the seeds sleeping under the mountain on the top of the world. Against all odds, the seeds had been found and brought back. Lady Merlas had allowed herself to be caught up in the fervor. She couldn't resist the temptation to own a piece of destiny. If one seed sprouted, it would be the stuff of legends.

Mavin climbed the winding staircase to the lavish penthouse, remembering the Lady's unpredictable temperament. He kept his eyes lowered, but stole a glance. He was relieved to see she wore a simple black dress and very little makeup. "Lady Merlas." He bowed and waited.

"Have you brought me good news?"

"I've come to tell you that I've successfully germinated the seeds in the boxes that were waiting for me at the botanical gardens. However, the rice varieties were not resistant to disease, nor were the varieties of wheat. The reason for this, in my opinion, is that all of the seeds are common varieties." He watched her reaction.

"What is it you're saying, Sri Mavin?"

"The seeds that you bought at the auction are not the seeds that I helped carry back from the north. You have been cheated."

Lady Merlas took a long slow breath and exhaled slowly. "You are certain?"

"The seeds were not in the original sealed bags, which was suspicious. The wheat and rice that sprouted are identical in every way to that being commonly grown."

The word "common" enraged Lady Merlas. *There is was nothing about me that is common.*

Gauging by the level of self-control that Lady Merlas was exerting, Mavin doubted she was a part of the conspiracy. She had nothing to gain by keeping the Svalbard seeds hidden.

*Who would dare to cheat me in such an obvious way? she wondered. It had to be the Merc or the High Council. It would be suicide to openly accuse either. If word got out that I paid a fortune for ordinary seeds, my reputation would suffer irreparable harm.* "What do you propose, Sri Mavin?"

"I have no idea." He couldn't believe that Lady Merlas thought he knew what to do. "Perhaps, you could tell whomever you bought the seeds from that you know you've been cheated?"

"The Triumvirate put the seeds up for auction. You must know the Triumvirate is beyond questioning."

"Then say there's been a mistake."

"The Triumvirate is divine. It does not make mistakes. I suggest you think of something useful, Sri Mavin."

Her meaning was clear. If he was of no use to her, then he was back on the street, or worse.

"There may be another way to end the famine." Mavin thought of his mentor professor Sinclair. "We may be going about this all wrong. We don't need new seeds, we need old ones."

"I thought the seeds from under the mountain were old."

"Yes, that's true, but relatively speaking they're recent. For example, original strains of wheat are millions of years old. They're basically weeds and as such, immune to disease. If we were to find this type of old plant it could be cross-pollinated with the current varieties of wheat. I believe this could be one solution to ending the famine."

"You have my attention." Lady Merlas was interested in recovering her investment, not in feeding the poor.

"When Si..." He almost blurted out Simone's name before remembering what happened the last time. "When the Janjanbi and I were returning from the far north, we came across a mound in the desert. It was once an ancient city. I need to return to that mound and search for old cultivars."

"What do you need to fund your expedition?"

"Not what—who. I need my Janjanbi."

"I will see what can be arranged." She rang the little bell on the table and Mavin was shown to the same apartment where he had stayed on his previous visit.

Lady Merlas sent a communiqué upriver by messenger. A week later she received word and sent for her guest.

"I'm sorry, Sri Mavin," she perused the letter. "It appears your Janjanbi is otherwise engaged. She has accompanied the White Crane priestess to the Gathering at Nabhi. It's a very special honor to guard such an important personage." Lady Merlas regretted that she had not taken the opportunity to keep this Janjanbi for herself. "Why is it you require this Janjanbi, Simone Kita? I have several in my employ."

Mavin tried to hide his disappointment. "It's unlikely that your Janjanbi can lead me to the mound in the northern desert." He thought of a possible solution. "Can one of your people take me to this gathering?"

"The Gathering is for the sisterhood only. No one is allowed to visit Nabhi."

"I've been invited." Mavin produced a letter and explained, "I received this the day before I left Jamurra. It is from someone named Leto. Is this gathering near Jara country?"

"Nabhi is many leagues from Jara territory." Lady Merlas took her time reading the invitation. She smiled, realizing that a key opportunity had just presented itself. "With the possible exception of Sabina the Elder, Leto is the most respected of the living seers."

Mavin cringed at the thought of a group of prophets and seers. Growing up with TwoBeers and his brujo antics had put him off believing in magical powers.

"Althea, my most trusted Janjanbi, was trained at Nabhi. She will personally deliver you." *What better way to place a trusted spy at the Gathering?* A plan began to take shape in her mind. *Althea can gain intimate knowledge of the coming year. I'll soon recover my losses,* she thought. When they reach Nabhi, Althea will feign a sprained ankle and need to stay until she is healed.

# The Gathering

Acts of creation are ordinarily reserved for gods and poets.
To plant a pine, one need only own a shovel.
—ALDO LEOPOLD

"How many more days to the volcano?" Mavin asked his guide.

"We entered the caldron yesterday. Now we follow the stream," Althea explained.

The terrain was flat. There was no mountain in the distance. "I thought Nabhi was a volcanic mountain."

"Yes, Nabhi is a volcano, a very old one. When is a mountain not a mountain?" she asked.

"I don't know." He hated riddles. When she didn't answer he became frustrated. "I give up, Althea. When is a mountain not a mountain?"

"Nabhi is not a place that can be explained."

He could feel steam pouring out his ears. Althea was maddening. To the north, clouds of white steam billowed on the horizon. It made him smile to think of the gray matter in his skull as molten lava.

By midday, nearly every trace of plant life had disappeared. The dark soil gradually turned into swirls of otherworldly black lava. Mavin noticed a few small ferns growing deep in the cracks he was stepping over. When they made camp, there was no wood or sticks for a fire. The lava field was completely barren of life. The usual chorus of insects and frogs was replaced by an eerie silence.

"We're fortunate there is no wind." Althea wrapped her cloak around her and rested. "We'll arrive at the Gathering tomorrow."

The lava was hard and unyielding on Mavin's spine. His bones vibrated. Unable to sleep, he traced the stars of Sagittarius, the mighty centaur drawing his bow. It made him nervous how the nearby stream was void of anything living. Althea assured him the water was safe to drink. He couldn't wait to see Simone. The thought of her soothed his restless thoughts.

Mavin opened his eyes to deep crimson clouds in the east. The vivid colors momentarily diverted his attention. It was too quiet. "Where are all the birds?"

Did this man never tire of questions? Althea gave him a cur-dled smile and ignored him.

"Wake up on the wrong side of the bed, again? I've noticed you're not a morning person." *Or afternoon or evening person,* he said to himself. Her sour expression had intimidated him at first. "One part vinegar, two parts bitch," he said under his breath.

"You'll see what being clever brings." She made an involun-tary sound that Mavin didn't immediately register as laughing.

They walked into the late afternoon without speaking. After traversing a series of small depressions, they reached a narrow bridge that led into a spherical opening in the rock.

"It looks like a lava tube." Mavin's excitement ended when he realized it meant going underground. He stopped in his tracks.

Althea disappeared into the tunnel without looking back.

*What choice was there?* He concentrated on his feet and en-tered the dark passageway. When his eyes adjusted, there was a faint glow from an iridescent moss covering the black basalt. Water seeped through fissures into an ankle-deep pool. He tried to keep his breath steady as the light from the tunnel entrance faded. The sound of rushing water ahead made his heart quicken. He remembered vividly the emergency tunnel filling with ice-cold water. It was the first time Simone had saved his life. There was a faint smell of sulfur. He cautiously approached the end of the tunnel. A wall of water blocked his progress. He reached his arm into the heavy curtain of falling water and then quickly stepped through. He wiped the water from his eyes. A dark basalt rim framed the sky like a round mirror. Three cascading falls poured over the smooth edge of the rock into a dark blue pool. He stood entranced.

Althea stood beside a young woman in a brown robe. "Welcome to Nabhi," the young woman greeted Mavin.

Mavin returned her bow and with considerable effort continued to look down at his feet. Remaining silent was appropriate and convenient since he was unable to form a verbal response. Althea was right: Nabhi wasn't a place that could be explained.

"I'm Juni. I will be your attendant during your stay." Juni was surprised by his good manners. Althea had just been telling her about the feral man.

A ray of light shone through the mist rising from the base of the three falls.

"Come, Sri Mavin. Stand just here." Juni invited him to come closer to the pool. "Look." She pointed into the mist.

A ball of iridescent light shone in the circling mist. "What is it?" he asked.

"A round rainbow. It's quite rare." *Not as rare as having a man in the sanctuary*, she thought.

Althea skulked away, mumbling under her breath.

"Is Simone Kita here?" Mavin's heart raced.

"Yes. She is an attendant of White Crane."

"I need to see her," he said impatiently.

Juni searched for a polite way to inform him that his needs were of little importance. "First, Sri Mavin, you are to have an audience with the Elders. There is very little time for you to prepare."

"I understand." He looked across the water at the dozens of caverns that lined the blue hole. Hexagonal pillars of basalt created the natural honeycomb chambers. The moss-covered geometric shapes reminded Mavin of huge quartz crystals. Steam rose from smaller pools and mixed with the mist from the falls. "Are those hot springs?" he asked Juni.

"They are healing pools, each has its own unique energy. We haven't much time, Sri Mavin. Please listen closely. When you meet the Elders, it is important to keep your gaze lowered. Looking into the eyes of those with the second sight can cause madness. Bow from the waist, not the neck. Never speak directly to an Elder. Respond only when answering a direct question. End your reply with the formal address, 'Divine Council.' Do you have any questions, Sri Mavin?"

Simone had drilled him with this same tiresome etiquette for months. Mavin made a formal bow. "Thank you, Divine Council."

Juni was horrified. "Sri Mavin, your mocking attitude is showing all over your face. You must be sincere. You will be able to hide very little from the Elders."

"Which is it, Juni? Am I to be sincere, or am I to behave?" If he looked at the seers would he turn to stone? "I need to see Simone Kita. It's very important."

"Sri Mavin. You must understand that you've been invited here for a specific reason. I can assure you that it has nothing to do with your needs. Understand that every thought, feeling, and desire is magnified here, your words—even more so. Words have great power. Choose them carefully. Althea should have been preparing you on your journey here. Nabhi is no place to be if your intentions are not completely focused." She needed more time to prepare him for an audience. "One word from the lips of the Divine Council and the past, present, and future are altered." Juni's voice was shaking. "Sri Mavin, I urge you to remember the most humble feeling you've ever experienced. Concentrate on that feeling and linger there as long as possible."

Mavin looked into Juni's eyes and pursed his lips.

*Althea was right*, Juni thought. He does lack basic respect. She feared for his life.

"It's time, Sri Mavin." Juni had done her best to prepare him, now it was out of her hands.

Mavin followed her into the large chamber and kept his gaze lowered.

Sabina the Elder looked over the scruffy foreigner. "What day were you born, young man?"

Mavin bowed. "February the Second, Divine Council."

"Which month?" she asked again in a scolding tone.

"The second day of the second moon. My people call it the Hunger Moon."

"The Snow Moon." Sabina softened her tone, but continued to regard the man with conspicuous disdain. "Rani of Mazarin was born on this day."

"Well, that's good." Mavin didn't believe in astrology.

"No. This is not good. It is however, significant. You must not enter the waters of the tritiya pool."

"The third pool." Mavin remembered Simone explaining that water was tritiya: ice, water and steam. He turned his head to look for Simone in the crowd. Juni stood beside him and tugged on his sleeve to remind him to behave.

Sabina regarded the unwashed man. "What do you know of the Winter Solstice?" This would flummox the uncouth beast and put an end to this unfortunate meeting. She would find out soon enough who was responsible for the man's presence at the Gathering.

"On the ninth day after the shortest day of the year my people perform an ancient ritual called the Shalako. It's taken very seriously." Mavin had never taken it seriously. He was however grateful that his childhood was providing an easy way to bullshit the cranky old witch. "The Shalako are messengers between the spirit world and this world. They come to the human realm and gather the people's prayers and carry them back to the Kachinas."

"Are these Kachinas goddesses?" Sabina set a trap.

"I've been told that the Kachinas are the clouds, makers of the rains, the stars, many things. I do not know what the Kachinas are, or what they are not. I am only a man, Divine Council."

A gentle hum echoed in the chamber. The women were astounded by the youth's words. They looked at the Janjanbi, expecting Althea to explain. "The stranger must be an ugly woman dressed as a man," they whispered. There was no other explanation. She had no hair on her face. How long did she expect to keep up this charade?

Just before it was Leto's turn to question Mavin, Juni whispered last-minute instructions, "Remember to look at your feet, and do not speak unless answering a question. Sabina and the other seers pierce the veil into the shadow world of humans and animals. Leto is not like the others. Her visions are often impossible to interpret because she senses the world through plants, not animals. It was Leto who became aware of the seeds sleeping beneath the mountain."

Mavin stole a glance at the old woman seated in a natural alcove in the basalt cavern. She appeared nearsighted as a bear, relying on her other senses. He wanted to stay downwind.

"Raven." Leto pointed. "Come closer." Her voice had grown thinner with each passing winter. She wore a silver ampyx band inset with purple garnets.

Mavin tentatively approached. If what Juni said was true, this old woman had set everything into motion, the expedition to the north, meeting Simone, carrying the seeds back from Svalbard.

"The way is clear through the long darkness." Leto's thin voice could hardly be heard over the rushing waters. "Invisible as the sky, yet we drink her life giving breath." She whispered so only Mavin could hear, "Have the seeds sprouted?"

"Yes, Divine Council." Mavin kept his gaze lowered. "But, the grain succumbs to the same black blight as any other grain."

Leto shook her finger at him and her voice came alive, "Seeds are sacred gifts, they are blessings, not coins to be hoarded or weapons to be wielded!"

The old woman's insight struck Mavin like a bolt. He thought of the greedy corporations of his own time who raced to patent seeds they purported to invent. How much different the world would have been had seeds been revered as sacred gifts to be shared. "Truer words were never spoken, Divine Council."

"If you believe this in your heart, Raven, why is it you serve the House of Merlas?"

"I'm a man, Divine Council. It is not for me to decide who I serve."

Another warm hum filled the chamber. Men were known for two things—their ignorance and their arrogance. This man had unexpected depth.

Leto searched the faces gathered. "Where is your Janjanbi?"

Althea limped forward bowing her head. She had a bandage on her right ankle and was using a cane.

Leto glared at Althea. "Not you! Where is Maya's daughter, Simone?"

Juni found her leaning against the back wall of the chamber. She took Simone gently by the hand and led her through the crowd.

Leto gave Althea a withering look. "Go back to your painted mistress. Tell her that Raven is no longer in her service."

Althea couldn't believe the way she was being treated. The man was being respected, and she was being thrown to the dogs. She looked over at Sabina for support and pitifully limped a step closer to Leto. She tried to glance up before feeling overpowered. "With respect, Divine Council, the Lady Merlas charged me with this man's safe keeping." Althea used as firm a tone as she dared.

"You've delivered your charge. Raven is re-united with his Janjanbi. Now, away with you." Leto dismissed Althea with a wave of her hand.

A hush fell over the chamber as Althea hobbled out of the chamber, cursing under her breath.

Leto addressed Simone. "Come closer, Child, take your place beside Raven." The old woman took a moment to appreciate the young tandem. She sensed a crack, a tiny fissure in the immutable law of time. Janjanbi were renowned for their inner discipline, and yet this young woman's cheeks were flushed.

Standing next to Mavin threw Simone into confusion. A rush of feelings overwhelmed her. She struggled to regain her self-control. "Divine Council," her voice trembled. "Permission to speak?"

"What is it, child?" Leto asked.

"I swore an oath to protect the Daughter of Avighna."

"And you have brought her to us. Our precious White Crane rests safely in the bosom of Nabhi." Leto looked into the young woman's heart. "Have you forgotten your promise to Karin?"

Simone felt the floor give way. How did Leto know what Karin had asked of her? "Divine Council, I swore an oath to the Merc and the High Council."

"Child, you serve the Triumvirate."

Simone knew the High Council, the Merc, and the Sisters of Nabhi shared power equally.

Leto could sense deep confusion and shame in the young woman. "I'll make it simple for you, Daughter. This man is your responsibility. Do you understand?"

"Yes, Divine Council." Simone bowed low.

Leto examined the young man with the bright eyes. "Now, Raven, what is your question?"

Mavin was caught off guard. Juni had not mentioned anything about a question. He looked at Simone for help, but she remained staring at the floor. Her cheeks were bright red. He wanted desperately to embrace her, and then remembered that the old woman could read his thoughts. He listened to the sound of water spilling into the sinkhole. "How is it the rivers flow into Nabhi and yet it never fills?" He bowed awkwardly and then added, "Divine Council."

Leto smiled. The man had taken his time. He didn't have a question at the ready like so many. "Nabhi never fills because she is bottomless." He was given a question and didn't think of himself. There was something different about this youth. She looked into his mind.

"Is Nabhi from the time of water?" Mavin asked.

"Just when you've helped your cause with good manners, you speak out of turn," Leto admonished.

"But, I have no cause."

"Of course you have a cause." The old woman laughed, letting herself be swept away by the foolish youth. "Just because you were born a man is no reason to give up hope. Believe me, it's a temporary condition."

Mavin set his two feet apart and looked up at the old woman. "I'm not ashamed of being a man." He was sick of all the prejudice.

"So swiftly your masculine pride comes to the rescue." A youthful giggle escaped her lips. "Your thoughts are open to me, Raven. I see you're surprised. No doubt you heard that I concern myself only with the well-being of plants."

Mavin tried to make his mind a blank like when grandfather TwoBeers was giving him the business.

"You think I'm being unjust?" Leto softened her tone. "I've been both a man and a woman countless lifetimes. I speak from experience when I say being a woman is superior in every way. Work through your anger in this lifetime and with luck you'll be born a woman in your next."

"Thank you, Divine Council." He tried not to sound angry, but it had the opposite effect.

"You've been in the cave of the rainbow before." Leto changed the subject.

When Mavin saw the rainbow ball in the mist, it reminded him of an old Zuni legend.

"You remember dancing in the cave of the rainbow with the maidens of the corn." Leto was enjoying herself.

The old seer's words knocked the wind out of him. "You know the maidens of the corn?"

"The four maidens are from the House of Stars." It amused her to see him fighting her every word. "Come sit beside me, Raven."

Mavin did his best to mask his fear as he sat on the cushion beside the frail old woman.

She leaned over and whispered. "I have something important to tell you. You may tell your Janjanbi, but no one else. Do you understand?'

"Yes, Divine Council."

"The seeds you carried from the frozen north are in Kashphera, but I see that you've already guessed as much."

"So, there's still a chance." Mavin was filled with hope.

"Only your Janjanbi is to know the truth."

"My Janjanbi," he said aloud, looking at Simone a few feet away and out of reach as ever.

"The time of the Great Houses is coming to an end. The Triumvirate is splitting like a black bitter seed," Leto whispered.

A murmur swept through the gathering. The Daughter of Avighna was carried into the chamber on a bamboo litter. She was lying on her side deathly ill. It had been two days since she had taken part in the ritual. The soma had nearly ended her life.

Mavin barely recognized the priestess.

Everyone began speaking at once.

"Silence." Sabina held up her hand.

The priestess lifted her head and pointed to the man sitting beside Leto. "Sotāpanna," she whispered.

Sabina went to the young woman's side and felt her forehead. It was burning hot. "Easy, my child. Is this the man in your vision?"

"Yes." the priestess whispered.

"Why is he Sotāpanna?" Sabina asked.

Mavin felt the walls closing in. This is where superstition led, a beautiful maiden pointing an accusing finger. *Will they burn me at the stake for having outward genitalia?* he wondered.

"He entered the river from below," the White Crane said through cracked lips.

"Thank you, Child. Now you must rest." Sabina had heard enough. She had foreseen that the man's arrival would bring chaos. "It is time for evening prayers. We will speak of this in the morning."

Juni showed Mavin and Simone to their quarters. There was no separate place for Mavin to sleep. As far as anyone could remember, a man had never spent the night at Nabhi.

Mavin was grateful to finally be alone with her. He wanted to embrace her and tell her how much he had missed her. "Why do you keep looking at me that way?" he asked. "I thought you'd be happy to see me."

"Trouble follows you like a shadow." She shook her head.

"What did the Crane Priestess mean? What is Sotāpanna?"

"Sotāpanna means to enter the stream. It literally means, stream entrance. It is the highest way to begin the Way of Balance. The stream entrance is accessible only by those who have lived many lifetimes."

"That doesn't help much. What does any of it have to do with me?"

White Crane had seen Mavin in her vision, coming from the Underworld, and entering the stream from below. It was true. Simone knew it was true. She had been with him. "Mavin," her voice cracked. "They want you to drink the Soma."

"What is Soma?"

"It's a mixture of som, a leafless twig mixed with a poisonous mushroom."

"What kind of poisonous mushroom?" he asked.

"It is the death angel. It has white gills and red spots."

"Amanita muscaria. That's not good."

"You must refuse."

"Careful, Simone. I might think you care." He searched her eyes. "Remember the last thing Malina said to me? It didn't make any sense at the time. She said, 'When I see the blue eye, I must eat the mushroom.' How did Malina even know about Soma or the blue pool?"

"This isn't a joke, Mavin. The Soma will kill you. Or strip you of your wits."

"You do care."

"I didn't carry you halfway across the world to watch you throw your life away."

"The way I remember it, I was the one who pulled you out of the ice cold water." He could see she was getting upset. "Look, I'm not wild about the idea." If eating an amanita mushroom was anything like grandfather's peyote, he knew he would have no control over what he said or did. The prime directive would be toast. He would blurt out everything. She was right. It wasn't a joke. The knowledge in his head could change the natural order of the world or worse.

# Soma

We accept it because we have seen the vision. We know that
we cannot reap the harvest, but we hope that we may so well
prepare the land and so diligently sow the seed that our
successors may gather the ripened grain.
–Liberty Hyde Bailey

Late that night, Mavin was summoned to Leto's private
chamber. He bowed, but glanced up as he approached.
She looked completely blind.

"Yes, Raven. At my age, I can barely see at all."

He dropped his head and did his best to clear his mind. He
didn't care to have her stomping around in his head.

"Come and sit beside me," she said.

"Divine Council, may I ask you something?" He kept his distance.

"You wish to know why they call me Leto of the Forest?"

It was intolerable. He pushed his heels against the basalt
floor. Simone told him it would make it more difficult for Leto to
read his thoughts. "Are you from a forest? Are there actual trees
that you can walk beneath? Is there such a place in this world?"

"I have seen such places in my mind, tall trees reaching into
the heavens touching the clouds, our ancestors safe beneath thick
green boughs."

"So you can see the past?" He wondered if she knew his secret.

Leto was impressed at his ability to mask his thoughts from
her. There was no mistake; the ancestral voices were strong in
him. "I have seen many things, Amitolane." She called him by his

ancient name. "The Daughter of Avighna has had a vision. You are to take part in the Divine Soma."

"I'm honored, Divine Council, but I must respectfully decline." Mavin concentrated on pressing his heels against the floor.

*The little time you have spent with your Janjanbi has already strengthened your spirit.* Leto smiled. "So, Amitolane, you would break your promise to Malina?"

Mavin felt like he had been kicked in the stomach. How could she know about Malina? Did Simone tell her? He rocked back on his heels. "I'm a free man. I don't owe you anything. I'm not bound by your laws or customs." Mavin looked defiantly right into the old woman's eyes.

"You are Amitolane, the rainbow spirit. You have brought this body from the other side of the earth, traveled across time, risen from the underworld to arrive here at this moment. Now your little self cries like a baby." She reached and touched him between the eyes. He dropped like a leaf.

# Yanuluha

In many traditions, the world was sung into being:
Aboriginal Australians believe their ancestors did so.
In Hindu and Buddhist thought, Om was the
seed syllable that created the world.
—JAY GRIFFITHS

Simone rinsed Mavin's forehead with a warm towel. A week was too long to be without food or water. His fever had broken in the middle of the night. She held his cold hands and wondered if he would wake up. Even if he opened his eyes, how much of his mind would remain after meeting the oracle? If he didn't wake up soon, he never would. The knot in her stomach prevented her from eating. Her anger was unable to settle on anyone but herself. Once again, she was unable to protect him.

Mavin opened his eyes. He almost didn't recognize her. "What's wrong, Simone? Are you all right?" He sat up.

His ridiculous question pushed her over the edge. She hid her face in her hands. "Mavin." A deep sigh emptied her chest.

"The last thing I remember was Leto touching me between the eyes."

She turned away and quickly wiped her tears away. "I've been squeezing drops of water into your mouth for seven days."

"Holy shit!" He felt clammy all over.

She laughed, relieved that he was himself.

"I've missed you so much." He reached for her hand.

She got up and hurried out of the room.

The next morning, Simone was summoned to a private audience with Sabina and Leto. She used all of her concentration to mask her anger. They had risked Mavin's life without his consent. She counted her breaths and unclenched her fingers.

"How is Raven feeling?" Leto asked.

"Thank the Goddess, he is recovering." Simone controlled her voice.

"As soon as he is able, we need Raven's help," Leto explained.

"Haven't you—" Simone managed to keep from finishing her thought. "Has not Sri Mavin done enough?" *Surely, you're not going to ask him to drink the Soma again.*

"Calm yourself." Sabina showed her disappointment. She expected more discipline from a Janjanbi. "He is Sotāpanna."

Leto gave a signal and the head scribe approached. "This is Devon," Leto explained. "She will assist you. I need not remind you of how important it is to have Raven's cooperation."

\*   \*   \*   \*

Simone bowed. She hoped they were reading her thoughts. They were screaming to be heard.

Later, Devon explained that seven scribes had taken down every word Raven uttered while in a trance. Without training, it was believed the Sotāpanna would have little or no recollection of his vision, but an unforeseen complication had arisen.

Simone once again abstained from the midday meal. She brought Mavin a tray of melon. He was lying in bed staring at the ceiling. "Sit up and eat a little bit. It will help you regain your strength." She marveled at his resilience. He had survived a direct encounter with the goddess.

Mavin took a bite of the cool melon. "Oh, this is heavenly." He looked at the white rind. "What kind of melon is this?"

"It's a sprite melon."

"It's amazing."

"They tell me you talked non-stop for an entire day." Simone had little trouble believing Devon's account.

Mavin bit his tongue in panic. *I probably blabbed out all my deepest secrets.*

"Raven." She allowed herself a guilty smile. "You've tricked them all."

"How do you mean?" He feigned ignorance. *She knows everything?*

"You'll see."

He tried to read her smile. "Please, Simone tell me now, I need to know."

"It's better if I show you. Finish your melon. I'll be back soon." She disappeared before he could protest.

He was too weak to get up. *What if I mentioned machine guns or airplanes?* He practiced excuses, "I don't know what I was saying, I was on drugs."

Simone returned carrying a leatherbound book. "This is the transcript of your vision. The scribes rendered it into your twenty-six-letter alphabet. Are you able to read it?"

Mavin opened the heavy thick cover and struggled with the first sentence. "This looks like Zuni."

"What does it say?" she asked.

"I don't know. I don't speak Zuni." He went down the page. The phonetic spelling made it even more challenging. "I said all this?"

"I wasn't there, but I was told you rambled for hours, seldom pausing for more than a few moments."

"I recognize a couple of words." *How could I speak for hours in a language I don't know?* he wondered. There was a time growing up when he understood what his mother and grandfather were saying to each other. He let out a relieved laugh. The ancestors had found a way to protect the world. He didn't understand nuclear fission, but he knew about machine guns and gasoline, and how to make dynamite. He knew enough to turn the world upside down or burn everything to the ground.

He studied the transcription all day without a break. After a late meal, he continued into the early hours. Simone fell asleep in the chair beside him. Reading his native language drowned him in memories. He found a repeated phrase, "Black seed of the desert." *What is that?* He remembered the dark shapes painted under the rock overhang when he had been in the desert with his grandfather.

His skin bristled. "Why am I still here?" he asked grandfather TwoBeers, as if he could hear. "There must be a reason." He had believed it was to deliver the seeds from Svalbard. *Maybe the seeds are lost for good. They probably wouldn't have sprouted anyway. What if the real seed is an idea in my head?* He realized in that moment what he needed to do. He dipped the quill in the ink and scratched out the first line of his translation, "Love matters more than hate."

"What did you say?" Simone opened her eyes.

"Nothing. Just talking to myself." From what he knew of her, Simone had no interest in measuring the universe, or changing it. She was all about doing her duty. She regarded free will as a kind of sin. *Were women doing a better job of running the world?* Absolute power still corrupted absolutely.

Growing up in the pueblo, he was surrounded by beliefs that he never accepted as being real. Going off to college, he put his faith in science. Whether right or wrong, he had made the decision to cut the cord binding him to his land and to his people. Now he understood the true cost of science and technology. Once the toolmakers had found a way to end life on the planet, it was a ticking clock.

"Ah! I recognize this bit right here!" Mavin said, with a burst of excitement.

Simone peered over his shoulder, "What does it say?"

"Blame it on the Bossa Nova."

"What does it mean?"

"I've absolutely no idea." He flipped through the pages and found another repeated passage. "I love you."

"What is it, Mavin? What's wrong?" She felt him tense up.

He knew it was true, from the moment he looked into her eyes under the fur hood.

"You're white as a sheet. Are you okay?" she asked.

"It's nothing. I'm still a little sick from the mushroom juice."

Mavin studied the transcription for another week while he recovered in bed. He was able to translate the first words he spoke under the influence of the hallucinogen, "I am Yanuluha. I turn the dry earth. Why have you called me?" The words shook Mavin to his bones. There was no other explanation, the god Yanuluha had spoken through him.

Sabina the Elder had been sitting beside him during his encounter with the goddess, rubbing his forehead with rosemary oil. The scribes recorded her words, "Welcome, Yanuluha. Are you the goddess, dispeller of the night?"

"I am the long black seed. My path is stained red," Yanuluha answered.

"Tell us, oh Sapient One, of the Time of Water," Sabina asked softly.

"Ahaiyuta and Matsailema cross the sun. Amitolane, the rainbow spirit flies across the desert. The long black seed is hollow."

Mavin remembered that Leto had called him Amitolane, just before she touched him between the eyes.

Juni woke Simone in the early hours of the morning. "Get dressed. Leto requests your presence in her chamber."

They walked through the halls barefoot and silent. Juni stood watch at the door.

Simone entered the dimly lit room. The old woman was sitting with her chin against her chest as if asleep.

Leto lifted her head slightly. "Come close, Child."

Simone approached and knelt on both knees.

"Come sit here, Daughter of Maya." Leto patted the cushion beside her. "You are the dutiful one. Maya always spoke highly of you."

Simone perked up. "You knew Maya?"

"Oh yes. Very well." Leto covered her mouth and stifled a laugh. "I made her pull weeds in the meadow for months. She was such a rude little girl."

"You were Maya's teacher?"

"Speak softly, Daughter," Leto whispered. "Before I was given the sight, I studied the Way of Balance with the great master, Shari of Benna. Master Benna was fond of telling me, "You are the laziest pupil I have ever had!" Leto squeezed Simone's hand. A carefree laugh escaped before she could cover her mouth. Leto's eyes shone, as if she had been caught stealing sweets. "When I was young, I was headstrong. I argued with my mentor. I spent an angry day and night adding reason upon reason why I was right, and why my teacher should apologize. I found Shari the next morning cold in bed. She had passed in the night. She died while I was sending her all manner of wicked thoughts. I convinced myself that I had killed her."

Simone swallowed her tears, remembering how angry she was the day the wave struck her village. She blamed herself for Maya's death.

"When I first came to live with Shari, I dropped a beautiful water vase and cracked it." Leto continued. "I flew into a rage. I remember Shari held my hand and comforted me. 'Daughter,' she said. 'We are not punished for our anger. We are punished by our anger.'"

Leto's words crashed into Simone's chest like a towering wave.

It grieved Leto to see the young woman so burdened with guilt. "Turning lead into gold is a mere trick, water into wine, child's play. Learning how to transform our anger and destructive emotions into love, that's our real work on earth. You've accomplished so much, my child. Maya would be so proud of you. Now, it's time for you to do one more thing."

Being summoned in the middle of the night, Simone thought it must be something of great importance. "If it is within my power." Simone straightened her spine, ready to tackle whatever task was set before her.

"If mercy is within your power." Leto took both of Simone's hands and held them tight. "First, you must accept that you're not responsible for Maya's death. Nor are you responsible for the death of Karin and your friends. It's time to forgive yourself, for you've done only your best. That is all we can ask of ourselves."

Simone dropped her head and sobbed uncontrollably.

"Sweet mother of us all," Leto whispered. She gently caressed Simone's forehead. "You carried the seeds and the weight of your fallen companions on your back from the top of the world. Now it's time to set them down. Now it's time to be kind to yourself. What would Maya say? Compassion begins with how we treat ourselves. Guilt is a wicked currency that buys only sorrow. You are not wicked. I promise you that once you're no longer using all your energy to torment yourself, you will begin to know your heart. Then you'll be something greater than a Janjanbi."

"What do you mean?" Simone looked up.

Leto knew it would make no sense to tell her that she would simply become herself. "Be kind. Forgive yourself."

Simone wanted to get up and run, but there was no escape from the storm.

"Soon." Leto squeezed Simone's hands. "I will pass from this realm. Then it will be up to you. There will be many obstacles in your path."

# The Absence of Light

I believe in the cosmos. All of us are linked to the cosmos.
Look at the sun: if there is no sun, then we cannot exist.
So nature is my god. To me, nature is sacred; trees are my
temples and forests are my cathedrals.
—MIKHAIL GORBACHEV

When Simone and Mavin set out from Nabhi, the Elders were convinced it was to follow Mavin's vision. He didn't bother telling them what he really had in mind. He trusted Simone to find the desert mound they had passed the previous year on their way south. Without the seeds from Svalbard, it was vital that they find a variety of ancestral wheat to cross with the grain currently being grown. He was confident, with Jai's help, that a disease-free strain could be developed.

Before he left Nabhi, Mavin explained Mendel's experiment with peas. However, discussing reproduction with the Sisters proved to be unproductive, even when considering the relatively simple mating habits of garden peas. The concept of heredity and genes turned out to be insurmountable.

They headed northwest across the bare expanse of the cauldron. The fresh air cleared the fog from Mavin's mind. Ingesting the Soma had broken down barriers in his mind, but it had come at great cost. The simplicity of waking up in the morning and having nothing more to think about than putting one foot in front of the other was far more healing than he could have imagined. It reminded him of his treks with Professor Sinclair. "Don't get too far ahead of yourself," the old man would say. "Happiness is all a matter of adjusting one's expectations."

Having known a rich and bountiful green world, it was difficult for Mavin to accept how much of the planet was now desert. Of the limited plant species he encountered, nearly all had thorns or some form of protection. Water was scarce and birds and animals would seek out moisture wherever it could be found. The absence of a high canopy of trees must have contributed to the change towards a more arid environment.

Professor Sinclair had explained that before Columbus, ninety percent of North America was covered in majestic woods. Without trees, was it any wonder the world had become a desert? The sand in his shoes reminded Mavin to be grateful that his ancestors had long ago adapted to the absence of water.

After her meeting with Leto, Simone felt increasingly untethered. Her promise to be kind to herself had opened a wound. She had never wanted anything for herself, or so she thought. She tried focusing her mind, counting her breaths. No matter what direction her thoughts ran, sadness lay in wait. Leto said she was not responsible for the deaths of her loved ones.

Her guilt melted into a dark sea of grief. She knew indulging in blame was selfish. When she was a girl training to meditate, Maya asked, "What is your mind, before you have a thought?" Simone knew the question had to do with intention. "Every thought that arises out of our mind has a seed," Maya explained.

At the end of the second week, they entered a canyon of intricate lava formations. Mavin began doing double takes, his mind giving the stone formations human and animal form. He wondered if it was aftereffects from the soma, like flashbacks. His anxiety level was steadily increasing. He skirted a giant black bear that loomed ahead, only to pass uncomfortably near the open jaws of a black serpent. His hallucinations became more vivid as the evening shadows thickened.

The wind and sand over the centuries had carved an amazing amount of detail into the giant natural sculptures. As it grew darker, Mavin pleaded with Simone to keep walking. He had no wish to spend the night surrounded by the giant creatures.

From the moment they entered the lava canyon, Simone sensed Mavin's discomfort. She watched him looking over his shoulder and scurrying past the rocks, as if they were moving.

Mavin was relieved when they climbed up a series of crevices to a barren plateau. They slept in the open with no protection from the wind. Mavin didn't care.

For the next week they crossed over a hardpan of chalky white rock. The snow-white desert pavement was grooved by the wind, giving it the illusion of being windswept banks of snow.

"I smell sulfur." Simone pointed upwind.

"I think it's this white dirt." Mavin rubbed some of the caulk between his fingers and smelled it.

"We need to head upwind."

"That's back the way we came," he complained.

"We came from that way." She pointed southwest. "Not to worry, we're not returning to the lava canyon." His legs were getting stronger, but the encounter with the oracle had left a permanent mark. He tossed and cried out in his sleep ever since they had passed through the canyon of Lava. The towering black shapes had awakened something in him.

He followed her into the wind, reluctantly admitting that he may have temporarily lost his sense of direction.

The sulfur smell grew increasingly stronger. By late afternoon, Simone led them to a waterhole. The murky water was warm and smelled of rotten eggs, but it quenched their thirst. They made camp and soaked in the warm pool under the stars.

An hour before dawn, they filled their water bags and headed northwest.

On the second new moon of their journey from Nabhi, they descended a rocky pass into a dry copper-colored basin. Thigh-high drifts of sand grew into high dunes, slowing their progress. Mavin noticed his fingers were puffy and swollen. He tried to ignore them, but his fat fingers itched and no amount of scratching helped.

They were skirting the base of a high barchan dune when Simone felt a sudden gust of wind. "Behind us, Mavin! A sand-storm is coming. We need to find cover."

"What cover?" He looked around. Nothing but dunes lay ahead for as far as the eye could see.

"This will keep out most of the sand." Simone wrapped a scarf around his mouth and then tied a thin band of silk over his eyes. "Can you see?" she asked.

"A little."

She tied a leather cord around Mavin's belt and looped it around her right wrist. Then she wrapped her face with her own scarf. "Keep moving, or we'll be buried alive."

A few minutes later, Mavin could feel pinpricks stinging the back of his neck. The driving sand stung every inch of exposed flesh. He gasped for air and soon became disoriented. The shadowy figure on the other end of the rope pulled him up the steep face of the dune. He sunk up to his knees, crawling on all fours, swimming in sand, sucking the gritty air through the wool scarf. After an hour of climbing, he felt like he had a molten anvil strapped on his back. The thousands of tiny pinpricks soon made him completely numb.

Simone tugged on the cord and yelled. She knew he couldn't hear her over the howling wind. She grabbed him under his arm and kept climbing. When they finally reached the crest, the wind at their backs pushed them forward. They rolled down the back of the dune and found a pocket out of the wind. "We'll wait here," she shouted. "Pick up your feet, Mavin. Stay awake! We mustn't get buried."

He nodded his head, though he doubted she could see him. His throat was too dry to swallow or speak. He felt something hard against his back. He clawed at the clogged wool scarf, gasping for breath.

Mavin dreamt he was buried alive. He woke with a start and tried to pick up his feet, but was unable to move his legs. It was eerily quiet. He ripped the scarf off his head and dug at the sand that buried him to his waist. His throat felt raw. A hint of dawn added to a piece of the new moon that was setting in the west. Simone lay half-awake, her back against a rock. He could hear her breathing in the quiet.

The backs of his hands were blistered as if sunburned. He couldn't close his fist, his fingers were like packed franks. The first rays of dawn glimmered off of the black rock behind Simone. He stood up and felt its cool surface.

Simone was awakened by Mavin's convulsions. He fell on his knees and began dry heaving. "Mavin? What is it?" He was trembling. She wondered if he was having another vision. She felt his forehead. He was cold. "What's wrong? You're scaring me, Mavin."

He pointed to the black rock that had sheltered them from the storm. It was the protruding conning tower of a submarine lying on its side. The diving plane fin stood up like a black sail. The dark hull of the sub stretched out for a hundred feet until it's stern disappeared under the sand. A dozen missile silo doors were open or completely missing.

"What is it?" Simone felt the cold black metal. "It looks very much like Sedna."

"It's a machine, a kind of boat." He searched for a way to explain. "Have you heard of Noah?"

"Of course, she built an ark and saved all the animals on earth from the great flood." Yes, there must have been a flood. How else could this black ship have come to be in the desert?

Mavin overlooked Noah being a woman for the moment. "This boat, this thing—is the opposite of Noah's Ark."

She gave him a puzzled look. "Who could have built such a machine?" She walked the length of the vessel and peered into the first of the round openings.

"Don't go in there, Simone."

"You're the crazy one."

"Thanks."

"Is this the black seed of the desert from your vision?" she asked.

"All I know is, it's evil." He didn't recognize the shape of the hull. He didn't think the design was American or Russian. He remembered weapons-grade plutonium wasn't radioactive, but wondered about the half-life of the fuel rods in the reactor. Was there a working computer onboard? His mind raced. "Can you see anything?" Against his better judgment, he joined her and stuck his head in the missile silo. The round missile ports were more than seven feet high.

*Is this the smoking gun? Proof.* All the silos appeared to be empty. The sub's entire payload was gone. *Mankind ended the world. Was there any room for doubt?*

He stepped into the darkness of the doomsday machine. It wasn't the absence of light that closed his throat. He didn't sense the presence of evil or good. His senses didn't tell him anything, except that he was standing in pure darkness, a darkness that encased his muscles and bones, an experience of the purely pro-fane. He felt pressure in his skull. He was descending deeper and deeper, taking on water.

Simone held onto his arm and steadied him.

His eyes adjusted. With her help, he managed to take a few steps towards the bow before becoming dizzy. He looked behind them. The open silo doors lit the stern. It looked like a tunnel into hell. The hull was completely empty but for a deep layer of sand. "It's hollow," his voice echoed down the massive tube.

For as long as he could remember, he wanted to go aboard his father's submarine. As a child, he dreamed of Captain Nemo's *Nautilus*. Mavin's head began to throb. The pressure between his temples became unbearable. Bulkheads creaked before being crushed by fathoms of pressure. It was too late to blow the ballast tanks. He doubled over, vomiting acid into his raw throat. His stomach was empty. He was empty. Acid burned his insides hollow. *Maybe it's radiation poisoning,* he thought. "Let's get out of here." He tripped over a piece of pipe. He pulled it out of the sand.

"What's that?" Simone asked.

He beat the pipe against the metal hull knocking out the sand packed inside. "I think it's from Captain Nemo's pipe organ," he explained.

"Who?"

They stepped out of the darkness into the clear morning. "Prince Dakkar became Nemo, Captain of the *Nautilus*. Nemo was the name he gave himself after he watched his whole family being slaughtered. He wanted to disappear. Nemo is Latin for nobody."

"Sit down, Mavin, you're speaking gibberish."

Mavin braced himself against the black hull.

"Sit and rest." Simone didn't care for the far away look in his eye or the white-knuckle grip he had on the length of pipe.

Mavin searched his mind for any possible explanation. How could a submarine be in the middle of a desert? Sea level must have risen worldwide; a massive warming melted the ice caps leading to a biblical flood. This helped to explain the amount of silt over the black charred layer that Simone called the black hair. How could the boat be completely empty? It must have been scuttled, stripped of everything. It was the only reasonable explanation. Maybe the missiles were not fired after all? It gave him hope for the human race. Occam's razor held that the simplest explanation was often the correct one. He didn't know the simple explanation, so he held on to what gave him the most hope.

They walked west across the sand. Mavin carried the length of pipe in his hand all day. His shins were bloody from the spiny grass that grew in thick clumps over the dunes. He thought about Luther Burbank's spineless cactus. The plant breeder was said to have talked to his cactus plants. "You don't need your thorns, I will protect you," he promised. Burbank eventually developed a thornless variety.

After the second week of watching Mavin carrying the pipe, Simone finally asked, "When are you going to throw that thing away?"

"Maybe I'll make a flute out of it or something." He racked his mind trying to think of a use for it. He remembered in Colin Turnbull's book, *The Forest People*, the African pygmies would tie a string to a length of pipe, fashioning what they called a Molimo Trumpet. They would hurl the hollow pipe over their heads to summon the gods. *Why in the world would anyone want to do such a thing?* he wondered.

They made camp. Mavin stabbed the pipe in the sand and gathered a handful of stones, placing them in a ring. He rubbed his hands together and pretended he was warming them by the fire.

Simone smiled and joined him; not bothering to point out that there was no wood to be found.

"This place reminds me of Professor Sinclair. We often camped in the deep desert. He brought too much of everything. You would have hated it," he joked.

"How so?"

"For starters, we always had plenty to eat and drink, these ridiculous cheeses. Gorgonzola!" He laughed. "Sinclair made the porters carry stacks of books into the middle of nowhere. He would read me Vigil's *Aeneid* at night around the fire, 'O Muse, recount to me the causes.' The Golden Bough was my favorite."

"Let me guess... it's the story about a man," she ventured.

"There are women in the story as well," he said defensively. "A seven-hundred-year-old Cumaean Sibyl named—"

"What's a sibyl?"

"Sibyl is a woman with the gift of prophecy. Sound familiar? She helps the hero, Aeneas, to pluck a branch of gold that he needs to find his father in the underworld. Aeneas uses the magic bough to enter the Elysian Fields."

"Are theses fields a blessed place?"

Mavin mimicked Sinclair reading from the heavy leather tome, "In no fix'd place the happy souls reside. In groves we live, and lie on mossy beds. By crystal streams, that murmur thro' the meads: but pass yon easy hill, and thence descend; the path conducts you to your journey's end."

Simone gazed up at the stars and drifted into a dream.

# Seeking Far

What did the tree learn from the earth
to be able to talk with the sky?
—Pablo Neruda

"We're leaving the Boundary! It's not safe. We need to turn back," Simone raised her voice over the roar of the wind. The hollow mountain could be seen through the afternoon haze just to the north of them. She wasn't anxious to run into whoever it was that made the wide track of footprints the last time they crossed this flat more than a year ago.

"It can't be much farther." Mavin could hear TwoBeer's silent laugh follow his prediction. What was it about the desert and ghosts? Did they prefer the dry heat? The never-ceasing wind and sand had erased almost every trace of the dry riverbed. He used the length of pipe to point out an unnatural looking dune to Simone. "I think this may have been a diversion dam."

She looked at the bleached white sand and shook her head. She was worried about him. He had been acting strangely ever since they had seen the black metal Sedna.

"Look, there. Can you see?" he insisted.

"I see parched earth."

"This was a canal. This whole area was once irrigated."

Simone looked at the pattern of irregular shaped dunes that stretched out in all directions. The way the morning shadows fell, it was as if the wind had sculpted a thousand eyebrows out of sand. "We need to head back into the Boundary, Mavin." She was tempted to grab him by the elbow and drag him. In the two months since he had encountered the oracle, the changes in his personality percolated to the surface. His obsession with the piece of silver pipe was disconcerting, but leaving the Boundary was a complete breakdown in judgment. Now he was seeing phantom riverbeds.

An immense dark cloud on the horizon rapidly changed shape, stretching, becoming light, and then shrinking into a dense band of ebony. Mavin watched the chaotic patterns in the sky form and scatter, then reform once again. "What's that?"

"It's a cloud of blackbirds."

"Blackbirds?" He thought for a moment. "They must be eating something?" As he stared at the horizon, he could see a faint line of foothills through the desert haze. "We need to get to that higher ground," he insisted.

"We're well beyond the Boundary, it's not safe."

He pressed ahead, ignoring her. *It's hard enough to walk in this heat,* he thought, without having to fight through your resistance every step of the way. No matter how much time he spent with her, they were oil and water. He hated her imaginary boundary, whereas she seemed to relish having lines and corridors to follow. *Do you see imaginary arrows painted beneath your feet?*

When they reached the foothills, Mavin led them up a dry ravine. He plopped down and leaned against a flat rock, grateful for the stillness after being whipped by the wind for weeks on end.

Simone scanned the top of the ridge for movement.

Mavin absentmindedly reached over and pulled a pyramid-shaped top from a stem of grass. He examined the tiny seeds and held them up to her and smiled. "The ancient Romans called this grain, *far.*"

"Okay." She had not seen him smile in weeks.

"It's better than okay. This is wild emmer! We found it, Simone." He had faith that the wild grain would cross-pollinate with the strains of wheat currently grown. With hard work, and a little bit of luck, a drought resistant strain could be developed that would be immune to disease. The famine would be over.

Simone held her finger to her mouth and whispered. "Quiet, Mavin."

A big man crested the hill and called down to them. "Bideshi! You are in Jara lands."

Mavin bent down, stripping the tops off the grass around him and filled his pockets.

"Keep still, Bideshi!" the big man yelled. A dozen bearded men charged down the hill with drawn swords and surrounded them. "Do you submit?" the big man asked, clearly hoping for a fight.

"We submit," Simone said calmly. She drew her blade and tossed it on the grass.

Mavin followed her lead and tossed his knife beside hers.

Had they not been in the Boundary, she would have taken the fight to them. As it was, they were trespassing and had no rights.

"You will accompany us to the Hall of Paine," the big man said without asking their names or giving his own. "You," he tapped on Mavin's shoulder. "Walk behind me. You," he pointed to Simone. "Follow behind." He smiled, hoping she would give him an excuse to gut her.

She understood that she was to walk several paces behind to show her subservience.

They climbed through sage and bitterbrush in silence through the heat of the afternoon. The fading rays of the sun burned through the valley haze, smothering the high snow-covered peaks in red. Their narrow track wrapped a razor ridge. On the opposite slope, a herd of deer stood still in the tall grass and watched them pass.

Simone listened to the birdcalls echoing down the canyon. "Your lookouts should learn the sedge warbler's song. Cardinals are already in their nests by this time of the evening," she said loud enough for all her captors to hear.

Their leader turned and spat in her direction, expressing what he thought of her opinion.

Mavin searched the bare hillside in the fading light and saw neither bird nor man. His legs shook when they topped another long set of switchbacks. He sat on his hunches and sucked air. As they crested a rocky saddle the view stopped Mavin in his tracks.

"Tjörn Lake," their big guide said with pride. The sapphire water shone like an oval mirror reflecting the snow-covered peaks behind it.

A high stack of rocks to the east stood like minarets in the twilight. They walked along the shore of the lake. Bearded men looked up from their fires, whistled, and called out insults.

On the far end of the lake, they crossed a wide clearing to an ornately carved gate. Mavin followed the men into a vast courtyard where a single guard challenged them, acting out an elaborate series of intimidating gestures. Their big guide mirrored the guard's movements adding guttural flourishes. He waited for Mavin and then realized the stranger had no manners. When they crossed the courtyard, the big man cracked Mavin on the back. "Bow, Bideshi. You are about to enter the Hall of Paine."

Mavin didn't like the sound of that. He bowed before stepping across the threshold. When Simone tried to follow, the burly guard blocked her way. She opened her palms and gently pushed. The guard slammed back against the wall and crumbled to the floor.

Mavin glanced over his shoulder and smiled.

A spontaneous roar broke out at the sight of a woman entering the hall. Men at their tables lunged, but none could lay a finger on her.

At the high table, five men in black bear robes sat eating. They paid no heed to the fracas. The smell of the sweaty men trying to subdue Simone was more a threat than their fighting style. The smoke from the cooking fires was her only reprieve from the stench. She strode up to the high table undaunted. A dark-skinned man seated in the place of honor held up his hand. The men attempting to subdue Simone backed away.

Mavin recognized his knife on the table. The hatred in the dark man's eye buckled Mavin's knees.

"I am Paine." The big man's thunderous voice boomed off the rafters. He looked Simone over. "Janjanbi spy, what are you doing in Jara?"

"I am Janjanbi. But I am not a spy," Simone said, defiantly.

"We came to look for seeds," Mavin added.

The big man stood and crashed his fist down on the table. The hall went silent. "Encroachment is a high crime, punishable by death."

Mavin reached in his pocket and held up a handful of seeds. "This ancient grain is called emmer."

"What is your name, Bideshi?" Paine asked.

"I am Mavin Cedarstrom and this is Simone Kita."

"I accuse you of high crimes against the Jara. You are about to be slowly roasted over a pit of hot coals. Do you understand, Bideshi?"

"Yes." Mavin swallowed the lump in his throat.

"In your defense, you offer me weed seed?"

"Yes, that's right." Mavin was too terrified to attempt a full explanation.

Groans echoed through the hall. Paine walked around the table staring at the beardless stranger. "Who cares a black shit about grass?"

"Baa, baa!" Someone in the back of the hall bleated like a sheep. The hall erupted into laughter.

When the hall settled, Paine cupped his hand over his ear. "Ah, all may not be lost, Bideshi. It sounds like you have an ally." Once again the hall resounded with mirth. Paine picked up the blade on the table. "Where did you get this knife?"

"A friend gave it to me."

"A friend?" The big man felt the keen edge of the blade. "Liar!"

"It's the truth." Mavin shuffled his feet.

"What's this friend's name?" Paine pointed the blade at Mavin's heart.

"His name is Hester," Mavin said loud enough for everyone to hear.

"You raise your voice to me?" Paine's lips parted showing his black teeth.

Simone stepped in front of Mavin. "He speaks the truth."

Paine jabbed the tip of the knife between her breasts.

Simone rocked back on her heels, but stood her ground. She felt his hot breath on her face.

A voice called from the back of the hall, "Does this friend of yours smell?"

"Yes!" Simone called out defiantly.

The hall erupted. The tables were pounded in thunderous appreciation. Paine held up his free hand silencing the mass of men.

The voice from the back of the hall grew closer. "And what does this friend of yours do for a living?"

She started to turn her head, but the sharp tip of the blade forced her to remain still. "He is—" It hurt her to say it, "He is a fisherman."

Paine could no longer control himself. He lowered the blade and turned to hide his grin. The hall erupted into chaos.

A clean-shaven man pushed his way through the crowd.

Paine half-heartedly tried to restore order. He asked the clean-shaven man, "Do you know these intruders?"

Hester pressed his nose up against Simone's neck and took an exaggerated sniff. "Aghh! She smells of the south!" He made a face. The crowd bellowed.

Mavin's face lit up when he recognized the man from the river.

The big black man named Melky came up behind Mavin and

gave him a bear hug. "Beardless One, I see you're still eating goat food."

Mavin recognized Jacoby by the rat bite on his scalp. He had almost shot him with an arrow the day they met at the river.

"What happened with your magic beans?" Hester shook Mavin's hand, ignoring Simone for the moment.

"They turned out to be ordinary beans," Mavin admitted.

"Ah! I am sorry. That's why I never take chances with beans. Beans can be like certain people you meet, you can't tell their true nature." Hester glared at Simone. "Life is too short for such risks. This is why I always carry a sack of rocks whenever I cross the northern desert." He looked at the defiant Janjanbi. *Was she afraid her face would crack if she smiled?* "Paine. How do you rule? Are the Bideshi guilty?"

"You've vouched for them, Fisherman." Paine tossed the blade his way. "They're your problem now."

Hester snagged the handle in mid-flight and bowed. "Thank you, O Vociferous One." He turned to Simone. "Sparrow, you look like you could use some air."

The bearded men jeered as the tall woman followed Hester back through the long hall. She looked down at his feet until they were outside. "Where are all the women?" she asked.

"They're home where they belong. Taking care of children, cooking, and cleaning." He saw the disgust on her face. "I save your life and now you look at me like I'm a murderer. You should be thanking me."

"Son of a man," she hissed. "Why didn't you tell me you were Jara?"

"That day on the river? Ha! You were far too busy being a bigot. You hate men."

"That's not true." She pressed and pursed her lips trying for a comfortable position.

"You're a misandrist if there ever was one."

"Says the misogynist." *Why argue with a half-wit?*

"Calm yourself, Sparrow. Don't get your feathers in a bunch."

"I'm a Peregrine. Perhaps it's time I reminded you."

"Ah-ah, careful. Show me the respect I deserve."

It sickened her, but he was within his rights. They were trespassing. She had no choice but to honor her word.

When she looked down at his feet, Hester realized he had taken the game too far. "Wait here, Sparrow, and don't start any fights. I'll fetch your hairless friend. At first light, I'll escort you both back to the Boundary."

She remained, looking at his feet and said nothing until Mavin joined her. They were shown lodging by a young boy. Despite the cold mountain air, they slept on the ground under the stars.

# The Wager

Be like a tree and let the dead leaves drop.
—RUMI

The next morning, Hester and his men accompanied Mavin and Simone back down the mountain. They followed a razor ridge and stopped to rest in a round notch. "We call this place the Crib," Hester said, proudly. They had an unobstructed view of the vast snow-covered peaks behind them. Simone refused to look, keeping her eyes focused on her feet.

Everything she did grated on Hester. *It will feel good to wash my hands of you.* "Where will you go now, Seed Eater?" he asked Mavin.

"Back to the White Crane, I imagine." Mavin hadn't looked that far ahead.

Simone glanced up.

"You didn't mention you were in the service of the White Crane." Hester stood upright. "This changes the circumstances of your visit to Jara."

"The White Crane didn't know we were—" Mavin tried to explain.

"She didn't know you were what?" Hester pressed.

"She knew we might be traveling north, but we only crossed out of the boundary because of the black birds." Mavin couldn't help sounding defensive.

"Blackbirds?" Hester asked, sensing a lie.

"Yes. I knew they had to be eating something, and it turns out I was right." Mavin reached in his pocket for the few remaining emmer seeds. "We need to return to the spot where I gathered this grain."

"Before we go off to find your blackbirds, I feel the need to speak with your White Crane."

"That is forbidden." Simone took a step toward Hester.

"Show respect!" Hester barked.

"I'm sorry." Simone realized after Mavin's slip, she might never be free of Hester again. She looked at her feet and set her mind to accepting her situation.

Mavin's jaw dropped when he heard Simone apologize. "What the hell is going on?"

Hester smiled and winked at Mavin. "Fine, it's settled then. Where might we find your white bird?"

"Mt. Nabhi," Mavin answered.

"The volcano?" Hester couldn't hide his disappointment. He had always wanted to see the high lake country of Kashphera. A smelly sulfur mountain didn't sound very pleasant. "Lead the way, Sparrow. If it will help, pretend that you have a pack of smelly Dog People on your trail."

"Pretend?" she said, sarcastically and darted down the steep trail with every intention of losing them. Mavin would have to fend for himself. She flew down the ridge without looking back. An hour later when she reached the base of the foothills she glanced over her shoulder and smiled. There was no sign of them. She took a drink and set off in a steady run. The fool had told her to go ahead. Now she could make it back to the Nabhi and warn the Daughter of Avighna.

When night fell, she came upon a campfire. She crawled silently, pausing to look and listen.

"You're too late for supper," Hester called from behind her. "We would have saved you something to eat, but we thought you must have gotten lost."

Simone stood up and dusted off. Hester must have known a shorter way down the mountain and purposefully mislead her down the wrong ravine.

"Keep watch tonight, Sparrow, while we get some sleep. Tomorrow, you are once again scout, but stay within earshot. I may need to ask you the way. Have a pleasant evening."

Mavin heard Simone's voice. He was relieved she was back.

Hester walked out of the brush saying something about the Bideshi. Mavin didn't understand. Melky and Jacoby howled with laughter.

"Is Simone with you?" Mavin stood up, expecting her to join them.

"Sit, Raven. Sparrow has first watch and second and third." Hester took great pleasure in rubbing the Janjanbi's face in the dirt, after the way she had humiliated them on the river.

Mavin didn't understand the hold Hester had over her.

"Raven, how do you bear the company of that... woman?" Hester spat in the fire.

"She has saved my life more times than I can count. Once from you."

"True, but still, hardly decent enough reasons. She can't for the life of her mothers, understand why her goddess made men."

Melky grunted in agreement.

"It's so confusing," Jacoby added in a high mocking voice.

Melky joined in with a high falsetto, "Why on earth do I smell like a bowl of flowers?" Melky welcomed the chance to laugh. He was nervous at the prospect of going to Nabhi. He was brought up with bedtime stories about the völur, prophetesses who could travel to the land of the dead. He wasn't happy about the prospect of entering a den of witches.

"It is the season," Hester agreed.

"I don't understand. What's the joke?" Mavin was frustrated.

"Your Janjanbi friend thinks babies come from the White Crane. Ask her, I bet she'll tell you she has two mothers."

"Yes, she does."

"Ha! I thought as much." Hester slapped his thigh. "It's right around the time of the solstice when a smelly man, like say ugly Jacoby here, wakes up in the morning with the worst hangover of his life, and can't remember his own name. He's sore to the touch in his private region and stinks of rose petals."

"I'm sorry, I don't understand," Mavin confessed.

"Seriously, Raven?" Hester wondered if his new friend could really be that naïve. "Does eating bird food make you slow of wit? It's common knowledge that the bitches slip a drug in your tea and then have sex with you. You wake up with your head pounding unable to remember butkis."

Mavin remembered his girlfriend in college, Juanita. She was given a roofie at a club. She woke up knowing she had been raped. The police tested her for Rohypnol, but only found alcohol in her blood. Juanita tried to commit suicide later that fall.

Melky saw the quizzical look on Mavin's face and pounced. "What, Raven? Thinking back on all those mornings you woke up smelling like roses?"

Jacoby was having a laughing fit. "Mercy. Please, no more! I beg you, my sides are splitting."

"I don't believe you." Mavin stood up fighting mad. "Simone would never have anything to do with sleeping with a man, let alone raping one." He didn't understand how two women could physically have children together, but he refused to believe Hester's insinuations.

"I take my hat off to you, Raven. I don't know how you survive her condescension. She would be happier if men didn't exist."

Mavin knew there was some truth in what Hester was saying. "She is impossible. I won't deny that, but you're mistaken."

"You're in denial, Raven." Hester stabbed the fire with a stick before tossing it on the coals.

Mavin liked Hester, but he wasn't going to stand by and let him insult Simone. Hester was like every cowboy he had ever met. "You're full of shit."

"Easy, Raven," Hester cautioned.

"If you're so sure of yourself, care to make a wager?" Mavin wasn't going to back down.

"A wager?" Hester perked up. "I'm listening."

"I'll bet you Simone proves her worth, and saves your ass. What do you say? Are you afraid?" Mavin goaded.

"Say I agree to your wager; what do you have that I could possibly want?" Hester laughed.

Mavin unscrewed the cap on his water bag and passed it around. "This is not like your leaky stopper. This screw cap is watertight. I promise to make a screw cap for any who will take my wager."

"Watertight you say?" Hester twisted the spiral cap and was amazed how it tightened. He held the water bag upside down. Hester held out his hand ready to shake on it.

"Wait." Mavin was confident. "What will you give me when I win?"

"Hair on your chest?" Jacoby offered and laughed.

"I've a better idea."

They listened to Mavin's proposal.

"So, if you win, you want more goat food?" Hester couldn't keep from chuckling.

"That's right, and the Janjanbi becomes my responsibility," Mavin added.

"Why do you get two things and I only get one?" Hester crossed his arms.

Mavin dug in his shoulder bag for the length of pipe. "I'll throw in this stainless steel pipe. It will never rust."

Hester felt the quality of the hollow tube. "I'll tell you what, Raven. If you lose; you swear fealty to me, I get your water bag, and the magic pipe." Hester spit in his hand ready to shake on it.

Mavin swallowed hard and shook. He desperately needed to return to the spot of the previous day to gather more wild emmer. He wished Simone would jump out of the bushes and kick their asses, like the first time they met. It made him crazy that the Jara were too stupid and pigheaded to understand the importance of what he was saying. Wild emmer was naturally resistant to stripe rust and powdery mildew. It could change everything.

Simone couldn't get far enough away. The sound of the men's idiotic laughter echoed in the quiet. It was a waking nightmare. Would they never sleep?

# The Myth of Separation

Handle even a leaf of green in such a way that it manifests
the body of the Buddha. This in turn allows the Buddha
to manifest through the leaf.
—DŌGEN

When they arrived at Nabhi, Hester requested a private audience with the White Crane. Sabina was outraged. She ordered that the wild men be turned away. The White Crane and Leto overruled her decision.

Late that evening, with no explanation, Hester was shown into an antechamber and told to wait. There were no windows or furnishings. A hint of wild honeysuckle hung in the still air.

A beautiful young woman wearing a simple white robe appeared in the doorway. She smiled and took her time studying the clean-shaven man. His brown skin and lean frame were pleasing to the eye.

He had memorized his plan of attack. Now with the moment upon him, the battlefield was nothing like he'd imagined. His adversary was thin-boned and delicate, her manner soft and yielding. The thin silk of her robe accentuated her figure. He guessed her to be just over twenty. Rather than eliciting desire, she radiated a profound innocence.

Clearly, he was expected to speak first. He tried to turn the tables, but the growing silence gnawed at him. She carried no wand or magic staff. She was nothing like the stories of the völur. He knew that he was expected to bow; instead he broke the taboo and looked directly into her eyes. "I am Hester, son of Hester." Still she said nothing. *Maybe she's an old hag, and this is some kind of an enchantment.* "Thank you for agreeing to meet with me."

Her irises were so black, her pupils looked completely open. He swallowed, falling into the darkness.

She wondered if his aggressive eye contact was meant to dominate or was simply a lack of manners? This Jara man had spirit. She was pleased she had broken the rules.

Her silence was unsettling. *Would she ever speak?*

"I've never met a non-believer," she said. Her voice was like ringing crystal.

"So, you can't wait to bring me into the fold?"

"Son of Hester. I would never ask you to change what you believe in your heart."

*She recognized my father,* he thought. *She is more cunning than I anticipated.*

She sensed his frustration. "Is there something that you wish to ask of me, Son of Hester?"

"There is."

"Perhaps you care to discuss how it is we come into this world?"

At least she wasn't shying away from the heart of the matter. She was an arm's length away. *All I need do is strike,* he told himself.

"I sense you harbor a misunderstanding towards the Sisters of Nabhi."

"You sense correctly." The muscles in his jaw tightened. He realized his gift of rhetoric was better suited to an audience. And by audience, he meant a hall full of Jara men. "Misunderstanding? Is that what we're to call it?"

"The myth of separation is powerful."

"What is that supposed to mean?" he asked. It didn't take long for her ritualistic gibberish to rear its head.

"You believe we are separate from one another."

'I am Hester. You are not. You are the leader of a cult. I am not. We are different people, so yes, we are separate."

"I agree. We have differences. This is a great blessing. But you and I are not separate. The Unities make this impossible."

He had no idea who or what 'the unities's were. "Speak plainly or we'll forever be circling the tree."

"You can separate the bee from the flower and their honey, yet they remain linked."

Hester could no longer take her mystical babbling. "I'm here representing the Jara people. No doubt you're aware that your destructive beliefs have spread across the Boundary."

"Which destructive beliefs? That we're from our mother, and our mother came from her mother."

"I love and respect my mother." He took a step closer. "And, I also love and respect my father."

"As well you should." She smiled and tilted her head to the side. She was impressed that despite his anger, he kept himself in check.

"Do you love your father?" He let his arrow fly; confident it would reach its mark.

"I am of two mothers."

"Hah!" A loud guffaw escaped his lips. "You sincerely believe that?"

"I respect your parents, if you're unable to respect mine, then I accept that it's your way." She was led to believe that he was dangerous and unpredictable.

He sensed no malice in her. "It's clear to any adult with the power of reason, that one must have a father. Am I to believe that such an obvious fact of nature has been hidden from you?"

"As I've said, I respect your beliefs," she said calmly.

"So, you don't deny that you have a father?"

"It is not for me to affirm or deny. If you believe in your heart that I was born of a mother and father, so be it. The mother of us all does not demand anything from her children. If you came here expecting to convince the Sisters of Nabhi that paternity is the only way to conceive a child, then you will leave disappointed."

He was anything but disappointed.

"Could it be possible, Hesterson that you're more comfortable debating your Jara brothers?" She smiled. "Here, there is no winning or losing. We are connected. Nothing you can say or do has the power to separate us."

*In one movement I could separate you from the living. What would you say to that? You think you can surrender without giving up anything?* He looked away from her dark eyes and gave into his rage. "You and your twisted cult! You have no idea, do you? I hate you and everything you stand for."

"Do you hate me?" she asked.

"You can play dress up and pretend to be a goddess. Why should I care? Do you know, because of your lust for power my brethren are treated like dogs? Your worshipers treat us like unneeded objects. We are despised and disrespected for no other reason but that we are men. You say we are connected. I'm expected to bow down to your feet. Behind those robes you're just a woman, like any other. Nothing more."

"You're right, Son of Hester." She slid the thin straps from her shoulders and let her silk robe drop to the floor.

The moon had long set when Hester finally emerged from the basalt catacombs.

Jacoby was waiting near the blue hole. "Are you all right? Did they allow you to see the Daughter of Avighna?"

"Yes. I saw her," Hester mumbled.

"What's the matter? What happened? What did she say?"

"Go to bed, Jacoby. We leave at first light." Hester walked to the edge of the deep pool and washed his face. A trace of wild honeysuckle haunted him.

# Return to Kashphera

I thought all the trees were whispering, passing
news and plots along in an unintelligible language...
–J.R.R. TOLKIEN

"We can rest here at the lookout," Simone announced to the entourage.

Sabina the Elder needed a chance to catch her breath in the thin air. It was late fall. They could see their breath in the chill air.

Simone scanned the rocks above them for any movement. The previous month on her first attempt to deliver the White Crane to Kashphera, they had been ambushed. Now, confident they were safe, she turned and pointed across the mist-filled valley. "Cloud's Rest."

The Crane Priestess sat beside Sabina and took in the view. Three lenticular clouds ringed the majestic peak. A recent layer of fresh snow covered the mystical mountain. The wind was still.

Mavin rested by himself and then decided to take advantage of the break to hide the wild emmer seeds he had collected. Given that either the Merc or the High Council were responsible for the Svalbard seeds disappearing, he had no intention of making the same mistake twice. He found a spot just off the path near the outlook and hid the waterproof pouch beneath a flat stone.

Sabina drifted into sleep. The Crane Priestess tucked a wool blanket around her bare neck and stood to stretch her legs. She looked down the path where Hester was carousing with his men.

Hester glanced up and pretended not to notice her looking at him. She bewitched him, and without magic. It made him angry to be so weak. "At least I will finally see Kashphera," he said to himself.

Simone watched the bearded Jara fooling about. She felt protective of the priestess and the Elder Sabina. She went to settle them down before their senseless braying defiled the rare view of the sacred mountain.

Jacoby and Hester were taking turns crowing like roosters. Melky was acting as impartial judge.

Simone gave Hester a disapproving look. "I hate to interrupt such important matters, but what is your plan when we arrive in Kashphera?" she asked.

"Do you think Jacoby sounds anything like a rooster? Be honest," Hester asked in earnest.

"Hmm.... Let me see?" Simone did her best to show the proper concern.

Jacoby cupped his hands around his mouth and crowed. Hester followed with a rhythmic screeching sound, flapping his arms and craning his neck. They both continued crowing louder and louder, waiting for her to show favor.

To Simone's ears, each rendition was worse than the last.

"What say you?" Hester was confident.

"Well?" She tilted her head from side to side. "Hmm? You look like a couple of ridiculous fat men." She scratched her chin. "You smell like a pack of mangy dogs. But you sound ...you sound like a brood of old hens."

The men roared in deep appreciation.

"Well done, Sparrow!" Hester cracked her on the back. "If I didn't know better, I'd say you made a joke."

"So, you have no plan." It was just as she suspected.

Hester marveled at how the Janjanbi could make every word out of her mouth ring with condescension. "Of course we have a plan. We're heroes, after all," he corrected.

She rolled her eyes. Part of her conceded that if Hester and his men had not been with them on their first attempt to reach Kashphera, all would have been lost. The ambush had been carefully planned. Just before the attack, Simone felt something amiss. She signaled Hester and led Leto and the White Crane behind a small embankment, just before the arrows began raining down on them. Hester and his men charged the attackers and soon had them on their heels.

An arrow passed clean through Leto's left shoulder. Simone cleaned and bandaged the wound. Once the old woman was resting comfortably, Simone examined the bloody arrow and confronted Hester. "This arrow is Jara."

Hester ignored her and rolled a dead attacker over on his back. "I've never seen any of these men in my life. And, they fight like women. They're not Jara."

Jacoby had been struck in the forearm by an arrow. Melky used his short knife to make a small cut to either side of the tip and pulled the arrow out. Jacoby wailed and then kicked his friend in the shin to show his appreciation.

She remembered Melky's stupid grin, his face covered in blood. Whoever had planned the attack wanted the Jara to be blamed.

"Please stop crowing!" She lost all patience.

Hester leaned in close. "When the old hag... I mean, ...when the grand seer Sabina the Withered testifies—" His voice was full of contempt as he looked back to where Sabina and her attendants were resting. "Then, heads will roll."

"Heads will roll?" She looked at him with pity. "This is your plan? Why did I ever doubt you?" She pushed her breath out.

'Why are you always such a pain? Should we be worried, Sparrow? After all, are we not heading into the heart of civilization, where dwells only the purest of the pure, and the highest of the high?"

Simone had heard enough of Hester's sarcasm for one day. When they reached Kashphera, the Jara would have to fend for themselves. The important thing was to find the seeds from the top of the world. She joined Mavin near the lookout.

"I've hidden the wild emmer under this rock." Mavin lifted the flat rock to show Simone the waterproof pouch. "How are we going to find out who has the seeds from Svalbard?"

"When we stand before the High Council, I will ask," she said.

"Lady Merlas told me that it would be suicide to question the Triumvirate. You've told me as much."

"If I ask the council directly, then Sabina can demand to know what came of the seeds from the north. First we need to cross the summit. It's time to move." She signaled to the guards and kept a watchful eye on the high ground. She couldn't shake the feeling that something was out of balance.

When they reached the base of the Thousand Steps, a litter was waiting to carry the elderly Sabina. Simone gave Mavin a handful of gingko leaves to chew. She walked behind, watching as he counted the steps. Fortunately, his load was light and he held up much better than the first time they crossed the pass.

When they reached the summit and dropped down into the valley, locals crowded around the track hoping to get a glimpse of the famous travelers. The Daughter of Avighna wore a veil. When the crowd realized she was White Crane, they bowed with their foreheads touching the earth.

A group of attendants was waiting for the priestess on the south shore of the lake. The White Crane bid her farewells to Simone and Mavin. She lifted her veil and bowed briefly to Hester before her attendants escorted her onto her barge.

Sabina looked on, noticing the color in the young priestesses's cheeks.

Hester was sorry the priestess wouldn't be there to watch the High Council eat crow. He was planning to milk his advantage for everything it was worth. The snowy peaks reflecting off the crystal waters of Lake Avighna soothed him. He was impressed by the grandeur of the high valley. He had to admit, it rivaled his own high mountain valley. Avighna was ten times the size of Tjörn Lake.

As they approached the city gates, six members of the Capital Guard met them and escorted them through the dense crowd.

When they reach the basilica, the captain of the guard let Simone and Mavin pass. Hester and his men were asked to place their weapons on a table just inside the entrance. "Your blades will be returned to you," the captain promised.

The rotunda came alive when the Jara men entered. Councilwoman Asra pounded her gavel. "Silence!"

Hester stepped forward and bowed with a mock flourish.

"State your name for the record,' Asra said in a flat tone.

"I am Hester."

"And your mother's name?" Asra asked sharply.

"Hester, son of Hester."

"Hesterson," the councilwoman did her best to hide her disdain. "Are we to understand that you appear before the council today to confess?"

He knew southerners regarded anyone with a father as a bastard. "If by confess you mean, do I intend to take full credit for saving the lives of the White Crane and the old woman of the forest, then yes. Guilty as charged." He chuckled and bowed to the crowd.

His men laughed and shook each other's hands in mock congratulation.

The crowd in the gallery was outraged by the men's behavior.

"Silence!" Asra pounded the gavel. "You're not here to admit that the Jara attacked the holy entourage and murdered Leto?"

Hester snarled. "If this is your idea of a joke, it's gone on long enough." It was true that Raven and the little Sparrow had been treated a bit rough when they visited the Hall of Paine, but this was an entirely different matter.

"Murder is not a laughing matter." The councilwoman's voice was shaking.

"My men and I saved Leto and the White Crane priestess," Hester said defiantly.

"Leto is dead," Asra said.

The crowd in the gallery began raining obscenities down at the men.

Mavin glanced over at Simone. "What the hell is going on?"

"Something's wrong," Simone said.

"No shit!" Mavin was hoping for more than the obvious from her.

The crowd in the galley was quickly turning into a dangerous mob.

Simone watched Sabina, expecting her to step forward. Why was she hesitating? If Hester wasn't careful, things might spiral out of control. Who was she kidding? When was Hester ever careful about what came out of his mouth? Against her better judgment she approached the council and stood beside Hester. "Permission to speak, Councilwoman."

"State your name for the record."

"I am second Lieutenant Simone Kita of the Peregrine Korps." Mavin stood to the other side of Hester.

This quieted the crowd.

"I was at Leto's side when we were attacked by men claiming to be Jara," Simone began. "All would have been lost—" it galled her to say it, "had Hester and his companions not been with us. They fought bravely. The Daughter of Avighna was unharmed, but Leto was wounded in the shoulder by an arrow. When the fighting was over, we buried the dead and carried Leto back to Nabhi on a stretcher. Leto's wound closed and she was recovering well. It was decided that Leto should not travel until she was fully recovered. Sabina volunteered to make the journey here in her stead. When we left Leto, she was in good health. We came directly from Nabhi. I find it difficult to believe that Leto died from her wound. Nor do I understand how the news of her death arrived before us. We came directly from Nabhi. The Lady Sabina can confirm all that I have said." Simone bowed.

Hester looked over at her with a gloating smile.

Simone snapped at him under her breath, "You're not helping." She needed to ask the High Council about the seeds. The chance might not come again. Now, here she was using her only opportunity before the council to intervene on behalf of this insufferable man.

"You're blushing, Sparrow. It's a nice look on you." Hester sucked in his belly and pushed out his chest.

Sabina stepped forward. The rotunda became dead still.

"It's about time," Hester's voice echoed off the high dome.

"I am Sabina the Elder. Remove these Jara dogs at once! I will not soil myself breathing the same air as these murderers for another instant!"

"What?" Hester was about to draw the blade from his boot when Simone put her hand on his wrist.

"Calm yourself, Hester," she pleaded.

"Is this what passes as civilization in the south? I'll take the justice in my own hall any day."

"It pains me to agree." Simone's mind raced. "The truth will come out. Please, Hester, don't try to fight your way out of this."

Councilwoman Asra pointed to the men. "Arrest the Jara!"

A dozen capital guards with short spears surrounded them.

"Officer Kita, surrender your blade until this matter can be looked into further." Asra didn't hold out much hope for the Jan-janbi after watching her perjure herself.

"Wait." Councilwoman Khalsa held up her hand. "Sri Ma-vin, will you testify that you saw these men attack and kill Leto? Speak now and you will be free of the charges."

Hester tried waiting to hear what Mavin would say, but he and his men were forced out of the hall at spear point.

Simone was immediately escorted out of the chamber and to the Peregrine base by two guards, where she was confined to quarters.

# Without Spirit, Without Breath

The axe forgets what the tree remembers.
—African Proverb

Simone paced the length of the barracks. She had no idea where Mavin, or Hester and his men had been taken. She tried to piece together the unfortunate events of the afternoon. Sabina had not been with them during the ambush, and so had no firsthand knowledge of it. It was difficult to know if Sabina was blinded by her hatred of the Jara, or if she was acting out of some dark purpose. Someone had tried to frame the Jara for the attack. *Who wanted the Daughter of Avighna and Leto dead?* She wondered. It was impossible to know if the council was also corrupt, or if Councilwoman Asra was being used.

If it was true that Leto was dead, then she had been murdered. It was said at the dawn of the Third Age, the Daughter of Avighna led the people out of darkness. Once again the White Crane was the only one who could prevent the world from falling back into the darkness. It was just as Maya had said, the old stories do repeat themselves over and over again. "The priestess is in danger," she said to the empty barracks.

She knew that if she asked permission to leave the base, her request would be denied. Testifying on Hester's behalf had called her loyalty into question. If she disobeyed orders, she would be hunted down as a criminal. Her duty was sacred. She sat on her bunk and dropped her head in her hands. "What would Karin do?" She was unable to think clearly. "There's nothing I can do." She clenched her fist and kicked her feet in frustration. Her heel struck the pack under her bunk. She looked inside it and found the Phiran dress that Auntie Sharine and her friends had made for her.

She smiled to the guards at the front gate and signed out. Evidently, they had no orders to detain her. She walked calmly out of the camp and made her way to the lake. She had been confined to quarters and had disobeyed a direct order. She had thrown away her career. A life without honor was a life without spirit, without breath. Now, even death was meaningless. She remembered Leto's words, "Forgive yourself. When you have done this, you will once again be able to hear your heart."

She walked along the western shore of the lake and felt the cool breeze on her skin. A few of the smaller coves were already covered in a thin layer of ice. A fresh layer of snow covered the mountains reflecting off the water. Winter was coming to the highlands. No one would take her to Avighna Island, it was forbidden. The western shore was far too populated to borrow a shikara without being noticed. On the empty stretches of beach, there were only large fishing boats that she couldn't manage on her own. The wind shifted and she caught a scent. She shook her head in disbelief. She turned and walked through a maze of fishing nets. In the waning light, three men appeared and pushed a large fishing boat off the muddy beach.

Hester spun around, drawing his blade from his boot. "Ah, Sparrow!" He was relieved. "If you've come to help us escape, you're late."

"How did you escape?" she asked.

"Like smoke through a keyhole." Hester mimicked walking through walls.

"Where's Mavin?" She searched the shoreline.

"I thought he was with you." Hester slipped his knife back in his boot.

"What do you want with that boat?"

"What do you think?" Hester shook his head. "You heard the treacherous old crone Sabina. There's only one person alive who can tell our side of the story. The priestess."

"Agreed. The White Crane is in danger," she said.

"Time to go, Hess," Melky shouted. He and Jacoby held the boat in the shallows ready to push off.

Hester offered Simone his hand. She ignored him. Unaccustomed to wearing a dress, it took her a moment to settle on the most modest way to climb aboard.

With her long black hair hanging loosely over her shoulders, Hester hardly recognized the fierce warrior who had bested them when they first met. "I thought you hated men. Now I see that you're sweet on me."

She didn't follow his logic. "Surrounded by water, yet none of you deign to wash."

"Had I known you were getting all freshened up just for me?" He sat at the tiller eyeing her long legs.

"Would it have made any difference?" She shot him a withering glance.

"Not really."

Melky and Jacoby were doing more staring than rowing.

"Come on, you bearded wonders. Put your backs into it!" Hester roared. He reminded himself, that even in a dress she was a Janjanbi, not a woman. "Can you jar my memory, Sparrow? What was it you said to the council?"

She ignored him.

Melky used his high falsetto, "All would have been lost, if Hester and his handsome and brave companions not been there to save us."

The men roared in delight.

"Did you swallow a feather, Melky?" Simone asked. "Or did you forget your balls back onshore?"

"It hurts to admit it, Sparrow, but it's great to see you," Hester confessed.

Melky and Jacoby grunted in agreement.

Expecting Avighna Island to be heavily guarded, they beached their stolen boat on the uninhabited side of the island under the cover of darkness.

They approached the temple grounds unchallenged. A light flickered in an upper window of the temple.

"I'll go in first and signal when it's clear," Simone whispered.

Hester thumbed the edge of his knife. "You know what they say, Sparrow. Those who pray together, stay together." He ordered Jacoby and Melky to remain outside the temple and guard their flank. He followed close behind Simone, confident she would sense the presence of any guards before they were spotted. He felt miniature walking through the rows of massive jade columns. The polished marble was slick as ice in his wet leather soles. He wondered how he would be able to fight when he was having a hard time staying on his feet.

Simone stopped. He slid into her, grabbing her from behind. She slapped his hands away. "You're pushing it, Hester."

"It was an accident."

"BS."

"What?"

"Bullshit!" She had learned this handy phrase from Mavin.

They entered an archway and stayed in the shadows. Two guards were stationed at the base of the staircase. There was no way around them.

Simone approached the guards and bowed. "Peace to you."

Both guards were startled and then drew their long swords. Expecting her to give ground, Simone moved between them where they were afraid to strike one other. The guards recovered and bracketed either side of her.

"Lower your swords. I'm a friend." When they lunged for her, she directed her ki towards the guard on her left.

Hester watched as a guard flew backward and slammed against the wall. He ran towards the second guard, but lost his footing and slipped.

The second guard sprang forward. Simone stepped into her opponent and twisted the sword out of her grip.

When Hester looked up, both guards were on the floor unconscious. "Better them than me," he muttered and grabbed a sword. He raced up the stairs where two more guards were waiting.

"Don't harm them, Hester." With a wave of her hand, the guards tumbled backward the wind knocked out of them. Hester took their swords and cautioned them to stay down on the floor.

A large woman blocked the lit doorway.

Simone charged.

"Enough!" The voice of the priestess froze Simone.

The White Crane stepped around her faithful attendant. "Simone?"

Simone knelt and bowed. "We feared for your life."

"Who else is there?" the priestess asked.

Hester stepped out from the shadows.

"You?" The priestess gasped. "You cannot be here. It's forbidden."

"We've been betrayed," Simone explained. "Leto is dead. Sabina swore before the High Council that Hester and his men attacked you and murdered Leto."

"Leto is dead?" The priestess felt a spasm in her chest. Leto was as close to a mother as she had ever known. "Why would Sabina lie? Are you quite certain?"

"Hester and I witnessed her treachery firsthand. Sabina had us arrested. We feared a plot on your life. You are possibly the only person alive who can prevent a war with the Jara."

"War? It's not possible." The priestess shuddered at the thought.

"The Janjanbi speaks the truth." Hester got on his knees and pressed his forehead to the floor.

The priestess was moved to see the prideful oaf on his knees. "Please, get up." She helped Hester to his feet. "I know that I was meant to die in that ambush. When I heard the fighting in the hallway below, I thought it was Miranda coming to finish her work."

"The Merc? You're saying she is behind all of this?" Simone thought she was hardened to anything. All of her life had been in service. She had put all of her trust in the Triumvirate. Sabina the Elder had lied in public, accusing the Jara. Was it possible that the Merc was also corrupt? The golden Triumvirate was rotting on the stem. Simone's arms dangled to her sides, unresponsive to her will.

"Thank you for your faith in me, but my position is ornamental," the priestess explained. "If I were to speak openly against the Triumvirate, they will simply replace me with another younger daughter of Nabhi who they can control." The priestess could see that Simone was not taking the news well. "Simone, are you alright?"

Hester caught hold of Simone's arm just as she collapsed.

"Bring her into my chamber. Sita, bring a basin of cool water and a towel," the Priestess asked her attendant.

Sita looked confused and then hurried away.

Expecting a lavish room filled with golden furniture, Hester was surprised to find only a small wooden bed.

"Set her here, gently," the priestess directed.

"Is there no pillow?" Hester complained. The room was Spartan. "It appears you're being punished for your sins, my lady."

"Do you never tire of your barbs, son of Hester?"

"No. Not really." He felt Simone's forehead. "What's wrong with her?"

"I think she is in shock," The priestess felt Simone's forehead.

"Perhaps she's pregnant," Hester offered.

"Perhaps you're pregnant, son of a man."

"Careful, priestess." Hester laughed. "You're in danger of sounding human."

"What would you know about being human? You've no respect for anything."

"It's true that I don't believe in your snake oil cult. But you're dead wrong. I have respect. I have plenty of respect for this Janjanbi."

Sita returned and set the basin of water beside the bed. She tried to nurse the strange woman, but the wild man wouldn't move out of her way.

"Give it to me. I'll do it." Hester squeezed the cool water from the towel and gently washed Simone's face and neck.

It made Sita uncomfortable to watch the man washing the unconscious woman's bare shoulder and arms.

"She needs food," Hester barked. "She probably hasn't eaten since yesterday."

"Sita, please bring us something to eat."

"And some meat for my men outside," Hester added.

"What happened?" Simone tried to sit up.

"Easy, Sparrow. Rest for a moment. You passed out." Hester leaned over her.

"The astringent odor must have revived me," she quipped.

"If my heart didn't belong to another." Hester flashed his baby blues eyes. "You would be one lucky girl."

"Why didn't I let them take you away when I had the chance?" Simone wondered.

"Because you need my help to rescue your hapless friend."

"Since when do you care about Mavin?"

"Since we made a rather healthy wager. I need him alive and kicking."

Sita brought in a tray of fruit and sweet rice.

"Now, we just need a table." Hester looked around at the bare room and stared at the priestess.

Having a man in her bedchamber was proving to be worse than the priestess had imagined.

"A White Crane is a very understated bird, wouldn't you say, Sparrow?"

"Hester." Simone sat up. "The more nervous you become, the more your mouth runs."

His guilty silence added credibility to her claim. Out of frustration he picked up the tray of food. "I'm going to check on my men."

In the early hours, just before dawn, the priestess said farewell to her faithful attendant of many years. "It will be safer if you don't know where we are going," she hugged the woman who had cared for her since she was a small child. The old woman sobbed uncontrollably.

"Be brave, Sita." The priestess smiled and hurried away before her own tears betrayed her.

Hester and his men waited by the dock. They moored the stolen fishing boat beside the White Crane's barge. Once the two women were aboard, Melky pushed off. They rowed north in the early morning darkness.

Simone tightened the belt on her borrowed pair of trousers and watched the dawn play out on the snow-covered mountains they would have to cross. Sita had packed them food and blankets. As the sun crested the ridge, Simone realized that Sabina's accusations had diverted all attention away from finding out what had happened to the seeds from the top of the world. Maybe that was Sabina's intention all along. Discovering the reasons behind Sabina's betrayal was not the priority. Finding and rescuing Mavin would also have to wait. The priestess had to be protected at all cost. She looked across the water. "Where are you?" She tried to convince herself that he was safe. She held her breath and ignored the pain in her chest.

# The Gift

In some Native languages the term for plants
translates to, "those who take care of us."
—Robin Wall Kimmerer

Hester took another turn breaking trail through the
fresh snow. Jacoby and Melky carried the priestess on
their shoulders. She was swathed in three thick blankets. The irony of their situation was not lost on the Jara. They
believed that the cult of the White Crane held men to be inferior, if not unnecessary. Now, here they were breaking through
waist-high snow, carrying the Daughter of Avighna to safety. The
northern pass had been closed for over a month. A recent storm
had just blown through, creating drifts too deep to challenge.

Before departing, the priestess wrote a letter giving a full account of the ambush and her reasons for fleeing to Nabhi. They
all understood the importance of the letter. If the priestess were
to die, it might be the only thing left to prevent a war between the
Jara and the Triumvirate.

Simone didn't love traveling with the Jara men, but it would
take all of their combined efforts to traverse the northern pass
this late in the year. "If the snow doesn't get any deeper, we'll
make it safely over the summit."

"You said that four hours ago, when the snow was knee high,"
Hester reminded her.

"Perhaps if your legs got as much exercise as your tongue
you'd be having an easier time?" Simone shot back.

"I've lost all feeling in my big toes," Hester continued to bellyache.

"How fortunate, now they match your heart," she answered.

Jacoby chuckled in appreciation, though he could no longer feel his own toes. His pride pushed him to keep pace with the Janjanbi. He both admired and resented her. If Hester said, "It's time to rest." Simone would say, "We must keep moving." Hester would curse and then once again take the lead breaking trail.

Melky struggled the most. He grumbled under his breath, certain that the Janjanbi had led them up the wrong ridge. Simone repaid his constant complaining by putting her arm under his and helping him to stay on his feet. "I can hardly be blamed," she said. "It's not my fault that you're so fat."

"It's all muscle," Melky insisted.

The men laughed. It allowed them to ignore the obvious, that she was doing more than her fair share. When they made the summit, they began traversing the windblown northern slope. The hard crust on the snow held their weight, but one false step meant sliding off the mountain. They tied a rope around each other's waists and dug each toehold into the wind-packed crust.

Jacoby and Hester carried the priestess.

Simone kept to the downhill side of Melky with her shoulder under his arm.

"You're a tough bitch," Melky confessed.

"If only the cold could freeze odors," she replied.

They forged ahead, pausing every few minutes to rest.

When the clouds lifted, they were relieved to see the dry desert stretching out below them.

"We made it," Hester announced, ready to take full credit.

When they descended below the snowline, they gathered wood and made a fire. The priestess continued to sleep.

"Hester, you must deliver the Daughter of Avighna to Nabhi safely," Simone declared. "Guard her with your life. Find out who murdered Leto and deal with them harshly."

"Have you forgotten, Little Sparrow, you're in my service? You're in no position to give orders."

"I have to go back while there's a trail through the snow. Commander Shazia must see the letter."

"Even if you were to manage not to be trapped on the summit and freeze to death, who can you trust? How well do you know this Shazia? The entire Triumvirate could be corrupt."

"If that's true, then it doesn't matter. The chance of stopping a war outweighs any risk."

"All right, Sparrow, you win. But first, drink some tea and eat something. You'll need your strength."

Simone wondered why Hester was being agreeable for once.

When the water boiled, Hester handed her a cup of hot tea. "You know what this means?"

"I'm sure that I don't." She blew on the tea and waited for the big man to come out with it.

"You've entrusted us to deliver the Lady to Nabhi. So, you respect us."

"If you say so." She sipped her tea.

"We are your equals."

Simone kept the cup to her mouth.

"What was that, Sparrow? I didn't hear you." He feigned hard of hearing.

"Respect is a gift we give ourselves." Simone looked into the big man's eyes. "Take my advice, Fisherman: don't wait for it to come from somewhere else."

"So, at last you agree, we are your equals." He needed to hear her say it.

"That's not for me to decide." She knew what they wanted to hear. It surprised her that it wasn't pride in their eyes, but something deep-seated. She had mistaken their brusque behavior as a lack of humility.

"It's not like you to be frightened, Sparrow. Go ahead say it—men are equal to women and you respect us," he pressed.

She finished her tea and held the cup upside down. "I respect you."

"As equals?" He couldn't let it go.

"Yes, I respect all of you as my equal."

Jacoby's eyes swelled with tears. He turned and hid his face. Melky laughed and quietly wept, unable to control his emotions. They had traveled to Kashphera for one purpose, to be shown respect, to walk down the street with their heads held high. They had been forced to retreat without satisfaction.

She felt ridiculous acting as an arbiter for things outside of her control. It troubled her that her opinion should matter? *Do they really believe they are inferior? Why are they crying?* She didn't understand men.

"It's too dangerous for you to go back," Hester pointed out.

Jacoby and Melky grunted in agreement.

"As I've just said, we're equals." She stood up and bowed low to them, hoping that was the end of the discussion. "Good luck to you on the road. May you reach Nabhi safely."

Hester made a signal.

Jacoby and Melky had maneuvered behind Simone. They threw a blanket over her and wrestled her to the ground. She fought hard, but was caught unawares.

Hester wrapped a rope around the blanket just before she was able to break free. He rolled down the top of the blanket so she could breathe. "I'm sorry, Sparrow."

"Let me go!"

"Take it easy. This is for your own good."

"You don't understand."

"But, I do."

"I have to go back!"

"I'm worried about him too, but you need to give Raven a little credit, he can take care of himself."

"You don't understand, he's—" She stopped struggling and broke down.

Hester gently folded the blanket over her face. He could hear her sobbing. "You lazy sons of men!" he yelled at Melky and Jacoby. "Go and find more firewood!" The three gave her a few minutes to gather herself.

It began to rain heavily. The White Crane woke up. When she saw the tied bundle, she thought it was a body. She rushed over and found Simone crying. "What's going on? Are you all right?"

"Untie me."

Hester returned with an armload of firewood and saw Simone staring at him. He dropped his load. Fearful of the Janjanbi's wrath, he took a couple of steps back.

Jacoby and Melky came up the ridge. When they saw the Janjanbi was free, they contemplated making a run for it.

Simone thanked the priestess for untying her, but offered no explanation. "We need to keep moving," she yelled over the falling rain. She looked up at the pass. If the men had not intervened, she would be halfway up the mountain caught in a blizzard.

Hester looked down at her feet when she walked past. Neither said a word.

# The Floating Gardens

We are made for loving. If we don't love,
we will be like plants without water.
—DESMOND TUTU

Farzana knocked and entered Mavin's room without permission. He was a dog that had been dropped off at her kennel.

"Come on in, Farzana," he said in a mocking tone.

"Get out of bed, you lazy son of a man. I've found you work."

He wanted to say, *"How can I get out of bed when you are taking up every cubic inch of space?"* He held his tongue knowing she could pick him up like a rag doll and toss him into the street. "Give me a minute, please." He didn't like her seeing him naked.

She watched him dress. She never missed an opportunity to humiliate him.

He had spent a month as a special guest of the Triumvirate, locked in a cell, deprived of sleep, and interrogated by a hard-nosed commander named, Shazia. She wanted to know where Simone and the Jara were hiding. It gave Mavin strength to know his friends had escaped and were alive. Commander Shazia believed men were mentally deficient. Mavin concentrated on his feet and acted as demure and vacuous as possible. Cmdr. Shazia was either convinced he was telling the truth, or let him go hoping that he would lead her to the Janjanbi traitor. If he knew where Simone was hiding, Shazia's plan would have worked.

Mavin had lost track of how long he had been Farzana's dog. The days were growing longer. Spring was arriving to the high mountain valley a little more each day.

He followed Farzana through the narrow streets while he repeated the same conversation in his head, over again and over again. "Why did Sabina betray us?" he asked Simone, imagining her walking beside him. "No doubt she planned the ambush," she answered. "Why doesn't the White Crane speak out?" he asked. Either it was too dangerous or she was also part of the conspiracy. Without Leto, the Triumvirate was corrupt as the Roman Senate. "So much for women running things better than men," he concluded, knowing it would set her off. She ignored him. "The world is as crazy as it's always been," he mocked her, trying to get under her skin. "The world is under no obligation to make sense," she pointed out calmly.

He caught up to Farzana. "Where are we going?"

"The only thing worse than a man, is an ignorant man who opens his mouth when he was born to be silent." At least she had found a way to get him out of the house during the day.

Mavin learned in the bazaar that the Saffron Way, a group of militants, had sealed off the southern pass below the Thousand Steps. If he were going to escape it would have to be midsummer when the northern pass was open. They reached the shoreline where the houseboats were moored.

Farzana stopped and pointed out a thin older woman standing in a blue shikara.

"Aren't you going to introduce us?" Mavin asked.

Farzana ignored him.

Mavin approached the old woman and bowed.

The old woman gestured for him to climb into the narrow boat.

Mavin hesitated and then stepped into the rocking craft holding on to the gunnels with both hands. "My name is Mavin. I'm happy to meet you."

Using her long paddle as a pole, the old woman pushed off the muddy bottom, sending them out into open water.

He knelt down to keep from falling in. A thin layer of morning mist hung over the calm water. Gliding silently over the lake lifted Mavin's spirits. He was free.

Watching the clumsy man try to turn around without falling in the lake amused the old woman. She shook her head. *What had she gotten herself into?*

A bright orange shikara filled with laughing children passed them on their way to school. Tears welled in Mavin's eyes. The wake from a canoe filled with freshly cut flowers and vegetables heading to market gently rocked them. He took in a deep breath and held it, trying to get a grip on his emotions. He had done his best to accept that Simone and Hester had abandoned him. They must have had their reasons. He didn't expect Simone to break him out of a locked compound, but he spent many cold nights expecting her to rescue him from Farzana. Over the weeks and months, he held onto the hope that Simone and Hester made it out of the valley to safety.

Mavin watched all the activity on the lake as the sun peeked over the snow-covered ridge to the east. His heart had slept through the long winter. The sun warmed his face.

The old woman steered them straight into an island of reeds. He lurched forward and nearly went over the side.

The old woman reached and cut a reed using a small curved knife and then handed the blade to Mavin.

He selected a nearby reed and cut it.

She laughed. "Longer!" She held out her arms. "Long, like the wings of the White Crane. You know, the White Crane?" She could tell the man was a foreigner.

"Yes. I've met her."

She stared at him and then pointed to Avighna Island in the middle of the lake.

"Yes, the Daughter of Avighna. I met her here in Kashphera and a second time in Nabhi."

"You've been to Nabhi?" The old woman's eyes became wide. "Yes."

The old woman knelt and pressed her forehead against the wet bottom of the boat.

"No, Auntie, please get up. What is your name?"

"I am Iris Banu."

"Nice to meet you, Iris. I am Mavin. Mavin Cedarstrom. Thank you for bringing me out on the lake. It's helped me so much, I can't tell you." He couldn't stop the tears welling in his eyes. "I'll work very hard, I promise."

"Soon it will be too hot to work." She pointed at the rising sun and smiled. She reached into her bag for her favorite knife. In no time, they had the shikara stacked high with reeds. Mavin sat on the load with his legs dangling. Iris stood effortlessly on top of the load and slowly paddled across to the far shore. Waves crested over the gunnels and they took on water, slowing them considerably. Iris beached them on another small island near the shore. "Nephew, cut some of those long willow branches."

He was worried about adding any more weight to the swamped boat. He jumped on the sand and realized the reeds were keeping the light craft afloat. He cut the longest willow branches he could find until Auntie was satisfied. He climbed atop the load as Iris pushed off, paddling them slowly along the eastern shore. A thick layer of duckweed covered the shallows. Water bugs skated on the surface. Iris steered them alongside a patch of green.

Mavin recognized melon and bean vines trailing through the grass. He looked at the old woman's proud smile. "Is this your garden, Auntie?"

Iris sat and began twisting the cut reeds together making bundles. Mavin watched, and then began tying his own bundle. She retied his first bundle tighter, showing him how to make a slipknot. Soon, they had a floating raft of reed bundles the length of the shikara. While Mavin tied the last of the reeds together,

Iris bailed water from the bottom of the shikara with a cracked clay bowl. When she finished, she took a flat rock from under her seat and used it to pound a willow branch into the muddy bottom along the edge of their new reed raft. Mavin took the rock, convincing Iris that he could manage. He pounded the willow branches all around the reeds, mooring the reed raft in place.

Iris balanced effortlessly in the empty shikara and used her long paddle to scoop mud from the shallow bottom, stacking it on top of the reeds. Mavin watched, wondering what she was up to. He jumped in the waist-deep water and scooped mud from the bottom with his hands. He suddenly understood. Her garden bed was floating. He wanted to ask her if she was landless. She was obviously poor. He decided to scoop mud and keep his mouth shut.

Mavin woke early and waited on the beach. It pleased Iris to see him waiting in the dark. After two weeks of hard work they created four new floating beds. The dark mud dried and cracked in the sun. Mavin felt the rich soil. It fell apart in his hands and smelled alive. He took pride in shaping mounds for tomatoes and cucumbers. Auntie laughed with delight when he kissed the seeds before planting them.

Without realizing it, he had wallowed the winter away in self-pity. Simone had abandoned him. If she didn't think he was worth the trouble, then he didn't either. Now with the sun on his back and his fingers in the warm soil, he was springing back to life.

Mavin was amazed how fast the vegetables grew. "Auntie, did you learn how to garden like this from your parents?"

"When I was a little girl, we grew saffron crocus. We lived in the higher upper valley. There was a bad summer that ended with a long cold winter. We had to eat most of the crocus corms or starve. The next summer we had only a few corms to plant. My mother sent me away to live with my Aunt Thea. I never heard from my parents again. The next winter the lake was frozen well into summer. Aunt Thea became ill. Before she died, she gave me her shikara."

"Where do you live now?" Mavin felt ashamed for feeling sorry for himself.

"How do you mean?"

"Where is your home?"

She looked puzzled. "I live here."

He realized she lived in her blue shikara. "Yes, of course, Auntie. Please forgive my ignorance." He wondered what she did when the lake froze.

Mavin helped Iris pick sour cherries and wild plums from the scrubby trees that lined the wild eastern bank of the lake. Over time he learned to avoid their spiny thorns. Once their baskets were full, they headed to the outdoor market. Auntie Iris was very proud, but that morning she decided to let him row her beloved shikara. She laughed at how much energy he used, and how slow and meandering their course.

Over the summer, Iris showed him how to pound and press mulberry bark to make lampshades. He learned that rapeseed oil was the cleanest burning for lamps. On slow days they cut willow for sheep fodder. The hundreds of little tin coins they earned in a week were not worth one silver coin.

Mavin told Iris the story of when he was living in the south. One day, the jolly tinsmith Vinita brought him a heavy bag full of silver coins, plopping it down on the table with a tremendous thunk. He acted out the scene.

Iris giggled in delight and asked him to tell the story over and over again while they worked. In the afternoon, when they finished selling the last of their sour plums, Mavin bought a honeycomb for them to share. "Auntie, why is it there is no mold on the rice that grows around the lake?"

"The winter cold kills the bugs and mold. That is why Kash-

phera is the finest place to live on earth." Iris bit into her honeycomb smiling like a little girl who had just lost a front tooth.

Retelling the story of Vinita had reminded him of Jai and his
family. He gave his honeycomb to Iris, unable to enjoy his treat.
"The rest of the world goes to bed hungry, and we are surrounded
by abundance," he said quietly.

That evening, Mavin asked Farzana, "Why don't the Kash-
pherians export food to the south?"

"Everyone knows that southerners are lazy," she tired of
pointing out the obvious. "They don't have winter, so they don't
understand hard work or what it means to plan ahead. They brag
about living in the moment, fornicating, and drinking wine all
day. It's their own fault they're miserably poor. So what do they
do? Like irresponsible children, they blame us for their suffering."

"I didn't see any lazy, wine drinking farmers when I was in the
south." Mavin couldn't believe Farzana's ignorance. Clearly, she
had never been downriver. Unfortunately, many of the upright
citizens of Kashphera shared her narrow-minded views.

"It is an outrage that they've closed the southern pass." Farzana had a great deal to say about Southerners. "It is an act of
betrayal against the very Mercies that bless them with the River
Sky. The leaf cannot shake the root."

"What does that mean?" he asked.

"The Mercies, the snow-covered peaks all around us have the
deepest roots in the world. The farmers who join the Saffron
Way will perish from their offence against nature. The Triumvirate will strip the branches of their leaves."

# The Two Traitors

Here is the dark tree
Denuded now
Of leafage…
But a million stars
—SHIKI

Simone led them into the dark lava tube. Hester followed behind her. The priestess walked between Melky and Jacoby. As soon as Simone dipped under the veil of cascading water at the end of the tunnel, she felt the change. It was an hour before dawn. She dipped back into the dark cavern. "Something is wrong."

Hester glanced back to where Melky and Jacoby were guarding their flank. "We're here now. What would you have us do, turn around?"

"I am a Sister of Nabhi," the priestess said calmly. "No harm will come to us."

"We can trust Juni," Simone said. "I'll find her, and return when I know it's safe."

"Nice try, Sparrow. We stay together." Hester walked through the wall of water. The stars reflected off the black pool. In the dim light, it looked as if his companions appeared from the water itself. Their footsteps were drowned out by the sound of falling water. The hair standing up on the back of his neck told Hester to draw his blade, but it felt wrong to have a weapon in his hand. He looked back at Simone, secretly hoping she would take the lead. He walked down the dark corridor trying his best to act natural. If it was his fate to be killed by a woman, he wasn't going to give her the satisfaction of seeing fear in his eyes.

As they neared the torchlight of the main gallery, they could hear prayers over the sound of the water.

"The Lady of Avighna!" a voice rang out.

They were immediately surrounded.

Althea sat in the alcove dressed in a formal robe. "Welcome home, daughters."

The White Crane priestess and Simone didn't bow.

Hester marched straight up to Althea. "Who are you? And what are you doing sitting in Leto's place?"

"How dare you raise your voice to me?" Althea stood ready to unleash her wrath.

"Answer the question, Althea. Why are you sitting in Leto's place?" Simone stood beside Hester.

"You side with this animal? I am your Elder!" Althea thundered.

Hester seemed as surprised as Althea to receive Simone's support.

Juni and the other Sisters of Nabhi watched, uncertain what to do.

Simone sensed Althea was ready to strike. She would follow her heart, if that meant fighting Althea, so be it.

Hester felt his diaphragm knotting and his throat closing. The old woman must be a Janjanbi.

The White Crane walked calmly between them and looked straight into Althea's eyes.

Althea defiantly returned her gaze.

Juni joined Simone and readied herself for whatever was about to happen.

Althea felt the room turning against her. She could challenge Simone, but she couldn't openly defy the White Crane. She would deal with them later.

"We are waiting for your answer, Althea." The priestess said softly.

Althea put her palms together and changed the timbre of her voice. "Leto died shortly after you left for Kashphera. In Sabina's absence, I was Eldest Sister."

"Leto was in good health when we left," the priestess countered. "I find it difficult to believe she died from her wound."

"We were also surprised and deeply saddened. It must have been an infection. We've been grieving and praying for her night and day." Althea sounded upset.

"I'll give you a choice, Althea," the young priestess said firmly. "Tell us the truth about what happened to Leto or drink the Soma and tell us the truth."

Althea's back straightened. "You question my word?"

"Very well," the White Crane said softly. "Prepare yourself, Althea. Tomorrow you will stare into the sun. The Divine Soma will decide your fate."

"As you wish." Althea bowed and retired to her chamber.

The following morning Althea was nowhere to be found. She slipped away in early hours before dawn. The White Crane priestess banned her from ever returning to Nabhi.

\* \* \* \*

When Hester caught word of what Simone was planning, he stood in the doorway blocking her way. "What do you expect to accomplish by going back to Kashphera alone?" Hester was doing his best not to shout.

"It's time to shake the tree and see what falls out." Simone gave Hester a half-smile.

"And you accused me of not having a plan. Just listen to yourself. The guards will be waiting for you at the top of the Thousand Steps." He remained blocking the door.

"I don't expect you to understand. Go back to Jara, this is no longer any of your concern." Simone tried to push pass him.

"I won't lie. I do miss the company of real people."

"Women are not real people?"

"What I meant is, it will be refreshing to be around people who are what they seem."

"As you say, Fisherman."

Hester smiled remembering their first meeting: "That's it!"

"At long last, have you finally realized what an ass you are?"

"No, Sparrow. I have a plan."

\*   \*   \*   \*

The morning sun glistened off the granite cliffs of the Southern Pass. A sudden downpour turned the Thousand Steps into a roaring cascade. An old woman waited patiently at the bottom until the waters abated. The band of women with saffron arm-bands guarding the steps ignored her. The old woman picked up her load of sticks and hobbled up the long series of steps, her right stiff knee unable to bend. Hunched over from her load, her matted hair covered her dirty face; she slowly limped past the guards loyal to the Triumvirate at the top of the Thousand Steps.

Farzana grabbed her broom to chase the dirty old woman out of her courtyard.

"Where is that son of a man? He cheated me!" The hunched old woman shrieked.

Farzana checked her swing. "That lazy dog lives in Jiang Town. He sleeps in back of the old laundry. Away with you!"

Simone hobbled away, her heart racing. *I'm so close now, Mavin.* She slowed and settled back into character, walking with a pronounced limp.

The poorest of the Jāti lived in Jiang Town. She stepped over the sewage ditch and followed a narrow back alley. The rickety door of the old laundry was propped open with a rock. She wondered how anything could come out of the place clean. The floor was filthy and the smell was not of soap. Thick steam from three large copper kettles filled the room. She sensed something was wrong just as a blunt arrow came out of the mist and hit her on the back of the head.

She woke up on a straw mat in a pitch-dark room. She rolled over and felt the large bump on the back of her head. Her matted hair made it difficult to tell if the wound had bled. She made it to her knees and traced the cold stone wall until she found a metal door with no handle or hinges. She tried to piece together what had happened. Farzana must have been told to report anyone asking after Mavin. After several hours passed, she realized that it could already be daylight. There was no window.

A slot under the door lifted, letting in a sliver of light. A bowl of soup appeared and then the light was gone. She was unsure whether to call out for help. She coughed to clear her throat and the pain in back of her head throbbed, buckling her knees. She felt for the bowl in the dark and sipped the cold soup. It had rice and cabbage at the bottom. She fell asleep again and was jarred out of a dream by the sound of the slot under the door opening.

"Place your hands through the slot. They will be bound," a husky voice commanded.

She had no choice. When the metal shackles were fastened around her wrist, the door opened. The two guards wore masks. This gave her hope. If they were going to kill her, why bother hiding their identity? She was led to a room with two chairs and a table. The smaller of the guards fastened a thick chain to the shackles around her wrists before locking her alone in the room. She pulled, gauging the length of chain. Two high windows let in enough light to hurt her eyes. She sat down and waited.

After what seemed like hours, Col. Bina entered the room. "The Janjanbi traitor returns."

Simone remembered Col. Bina doing everything in her power to prevent her from joining the Korps.

"You have an opportunity," Bina explained. "I can't promise that you won't be hanged, but it will at least postpone the inevitable. Are you interested?" Bina waited a couple of minutes and then stood up. "At least we agree on one thing, traitors deserve to hang."

"I'm not a traitor." Simone glared at Bina.

"A spy and a traitor."

"I'm not a spy."

"You dress up like an old woman and go looking for your accomplice and yet, you're not a spy?" Bina laughed.

"Is Mavin here?"

"If you answer me truthfully, I will let you speak to the man."

"Let me see Mavin, and I'll tell you whatever you wish to know."

"In time, you will tell me everything." Bina opened the door and left without closing it.

Simone was taken back to her cell. The door was closed and she placed her hands through the slot and the shackles were removed. Ten days passed in complete darkness. Once again the slot opened. She was shackled and brought into the small room where she was chained to the wall like a rabid dog.

Three long hours later, Bina arrived. "Have you decided to tell me why you returned to Kashphera?"

Simone looked at her feet.

"When I leave this room, I will not be back."

"What do you wish to know?" Simone placed her shackled hands on the table and looked at her accuser.

"Why are you working with the Saffron Way?"

"I don't know what you're talking about."

"Why did you kill Leto?" Bina leaned closer.

"I protected Leto when we were attacked by men masquerading as Jara."

"Where is the White Crane priestess?"

"She is safe."

"What are the rebels planning?"

"You're not listening." Simone knew it was a risk, but there was a chance that Bina wouldn't come back. She focused.

Bina felt her stomach knot. She tried to call out, but it was too late. Her diaphragm tightened.

"Listen to me, Bina. I could kill you right now, but I'm not the enemy. The trouble is, I don't know if I can trust you. Maybe you're the one responsible for Leto's death. There is a letter that proves I'm speaking the truth."

Bina kicked the table knocking over her chair. She hit the back of her head on the stone floor. Two masked guards rushed in. One grabbed Bina and dragged her to safety. The other guard cracked Simone on her right shoulder with a baton, breaking her collarbone. She curled into a ball on the floor. Two more guards rushed in the room and dragged her back to her cell.

# Bina

I love the fall. I love it because of smells that you speak of;
and also because things are dying, things that you don't have
to take care of anymore, and the grass stops growing.
—Mark Van Doren

"I started out as a second lieutenant and worked my way up the ranks," Col. Bina explained to the hooded figure. "It made me sick to my stomach when they gave you a commission. A foreign Janjanbi in the Korps?" Bina spit on the floor.

Bina had waited six months before deciding to once again risk being alone in the room with the Janjanbi. "All I need do is pull this cord and my guards will rush in here and cut your throat." Although Bina trusted every one of her handpicked guards, it was vital that no one else hear what the Janjanbi spy had to say. She was getting closer to the truth. It took time to penetrate through the layers of subterfuge. "I'm interested in the causes beneath the causes. Do you understand?"

Simone was disoriented from months of interrogation. Her mind wandered. *Causes beneath causes…* She remembered Maya asking, "What is your mind before you have a thought?"

"Who helped you escape?" Bina knew Specialist Kita had walked out the front gate against orders, but how did she get past her guards at the Thousand Steps? She must have accomplices in the service.

"After Sabina lied to the High Council, I knew the White Crane was the only person alive who knew the truth about who attacked us when Leto was injured. I needed to warn the priestess of the danger. I disobeyed my orders and took a boat to Avighna Island."

"You are leaving out the part where you helped the Jara escape," Bina prompted.

"I don't know how Hester and his men escaped. I met them by chance on the way to warn the priestess."

"You are not a very talented liar." Bina had questioned the priestess's servant and knew the Janjanbi and the Jara fugitives had kidnapped the Daughter of Avighna. "How did you enter the Thousand Steps without being seen? Who helped you? Tell me their name."

"We took the pass to the north."

"In winter?" Bina had not considered this. "More of your lies. Tell me the name of the guard that helped you?"

"Everything I'm telling you is the truth."

"Tell me about Nabhi."

"The Sisters of Nabhi is a sacred order of the Triumvirate. I'm not permitted to speak of it."

"Tell me about the letter."

"The White Crane wrote a letter. It gives a full account of the ambush and her reasons for fleeing Avighna. The letter proves that Althea was responsible for Leto's death."

"Where is this letter?" Bina asked.

"When I'm sure that I can trust you, I will tell you."

"There is no such letter." If there were a letter, the Janjanbi would have saved herself months ago. "Who is the leader of the Saffron Way?"

"I can't tell you what I don't know."

"The very summer you traveled downriver, the Saffron Way became active. How do you explain that?"

"I escorted Mavin Cedarstrom to the House of Merlas and returned upriver, without even setting foot on dry land."

Bina had interrogated the foreign man. He was a dullard.

"Mavin Cedarstrom was asked to help germinate the seeds we brought back from the top of the world, but the House of

Merlas was tricked," Simone explained. "Lady Merlas paid a fortune for the same seeds that every farmer grows."

"How do you know all this if you never set foot in Mizurria as you claim?"

"I met Mavin Cedarstrom the following year."

"Where?" When Simone didn't answer, Bina took a guess. "Did you meet him at Nabhi? Is that when you conspired with the Jara to ambush Leto on her way to Kashphera?"

"I've told you. That is not true. The Jara did not attack Leto."

"I have it on good authority that you and the foreigner traveled to Jara country."

"That was an accident. We traveled north in search of a wild grain. Mavin Cedarstrom was convinced that the seed from the wild grain would help end the famine." Simone left out the Divine Soma and Mavin's vision. She was careful to make no mention of the black ship in the desert or the House of Paine. Instead, she described in detail the sand storm, the black birds and finding the wild grain.

Bina listened closely, attempting to fill in the missing gaps in the Janjanbi's story. Bina's network of spies had yet to penetrate the Sisters of Nabhi. Bina didn't trust the seers. The High Council and the Merc were equally adept at obfuscating and bending the truth. Bina believed the only institution uncorrupted by power was the Peregrine Korps. Bina's network had been intercepting communiqués from the Great Houses for years. When Lady Selene passed away ten years previous, the Great Houses voted in their strongest leader. They got more than they bargained for with Lady Miranda. Once in power, Miranda could not be checked. After the Janjanbi, Edessa, foiled an attempt on Miranda's life; the Merc went on the offensive. She played one House against another, eliminating her rivals one by one. Bina knew Miranda was quite capable of switching the seeds that were sold at auction. The Merc didn't care who suffered if it meant she remained in power. If the southern provinces were united, they would pose a very real threat to the Triumvirate.

"Who is the leader of the Saffron Way?" Bina was confident that she was getting close to breaking the will of the Janjanbi.

Simone drifted off into a dream. She recalled scrubbing the school steps as a teenager. She changed the water in her bucket, wondering how to best approach her teacher with her question. If she asked Maya too directly, she would be pulling weeds in the meadow for a month. She waited for the perfect moment, right after the evening meal. "Please, Maya, tell me the story of the second arrow?"

"Explaining the first arrow is easy. It is everything that happens to us."

"Can the first arrow kill you?" Simone asked.

"Do you know anyone who has died?"

Simone felt ashamed of her ignorance.

"The first arrow is everything between birth and death. Do you understand?"

"Yes," Simone answered without thinking.

Maya got up to retire to her chamber.

"Please, tell me of the second arrow." Simone tried not to sound impatient.

"The second arrow flies nearly as swiftly as the first."

"Who shoots the second arrow?" Simone pleaded.

"You are wise to wonder who holds the bow. The answer to your question is perhaps the most important in life."

Simone hated Maya's pauses. She could leave things dangling for weeks, months, sometimes years. "Please, tell me."

"Remind me, child, what is the first arrow?"

"Everything that happens to us in this life."

"So then, what is the second arrow?" Maya pressed Simone for the answer.

Simone tried to think, but panicked under the pressure. "I'm sorry. I don't know."

"The second arrow can be laced with the most poisonous venom or the sweetest nectar. The second arrow can only be unleashed by ourselves."

"I don't understand."

"You will."

Bina ripped off the canvas hood and threw a bucket of water in the Janjanbi's face. "Who is the leader of the Saffron Way?" She started all over again.

At last, Simone understood the second arrow. It was just as Maya had said. She no longer felt pain where the shackles bit into her wrist. She didn't feel tired or afraid. Like the moon falling effortlessly around the earth, she was right where she was supposed to be.

The Janjanbi's face lit up with a smile. Bina called the guards, "Take the traitor back to her cell!"

# Family

Listen... with faint sound, like steps of passing ghosts,
the leaves frost-crisp'd, break free from the trees and fall.
—ADELAIDE CRAPSEY

The seasons flew by and Iris was content. Mavin looked after her like she was his own mother. By the fifth summer, Iris no longer needed to work. She rented out her floating plots and gave food and provided work to the poorest people living on the lake.

Then the winter everyone feared finally arrived. The temperature dropped below freezing. Each night grew colder than the last. The lake froze earlier than anyone could remember.

Mavin found Iris in bed. She had a gentle look on her face, her forehead as cold as the floor on his bare feet. He went outside and shoveled the snow off the blue shikara. He tipped it right side up and swept it clean.

He washed Iris and wrapped her in a fresh blanket. Out her bedroom window, Avighna Island caught the first pink rays of the morning. He carried Iris down the icy steps and carefully laid her in the blue shikara. He thought about loading the boat full of her favorite things and then changed his mind. He placed her long oar under her folded arms. Using her favorite worn knife, he cut dry reeds that stuck out above the snow and placed them gently around her.

The neighbors looked out their windows and realized what had happened.

It took him the rest of the afternoon to drag the boat over the frozen lake to the little cove near Avighna Island, her favorite spot on the lake. He bowed his head and tried to think of a prayer. Despite all the people who had passed away, he had only been to one funeral in his life, his father's. There was no coffin. Everyone waited in the cemetery for a flyover that never came. His mother clutched a flag that had been folded into a triangle, nine embroidered stars showing against the blue. She refused to leave until after the flyover. After sunset, she looked into the darkening sky. "They promised me," she said.

Two Feathers and Latigo carried her, setting her gently on the bench seat of the pick up. They drove to her church, Our Lady the Virgin of Guadalupe. Mavin rode in the back, sucking dust. He remembered sitting in the pew next to his mother, staring at the murals in the candlelight. Dozens of brightly painted kachinas shared the mission walls with the Virgin Mary. Mavin listened to his mother's prayers, mixed with bitter mumblings about the flyover. His grandfathers sat on the tailgate and drank beer until the sun came up. They'd gone to Nam. They knew all about broken promises.

Mavin lit the dry reeds and stood back as the flames leapt up. He watched Iris's spirit rise into the crisp air. He panicked, unable to think of a prayer. He yelled, choking on his tears, "Remember, Auntie. Be reborn a woman!" His knees gave way. He fell, cracking the side of his head hard on the ice. He was back on the ice raft just after Malina disappeared. He was under the mountain, frozen in blue liquid. He closed his eyes pressing his face harder against the ice. It burned hot.

When he opened his eyes, there were hundreds of people, watching the shikara burn. He recognized the faces of people Iris had helped, farmers from the outdoor market, and some who used to say hurtful things. There were shopkeepers in heavy coats and children running around. They all came to pay their respects to the old woman. He rolled over and followed the long trail of smoke that floated high over the frozen lake. "Well, Auntie. So much for you not having a family."

# Saba

I am at home among the trees.
—J.R.R. TOLKIEN

Mavin sold the houseboat and divided the silver coins into small pouches. He hid them in different places on his person, bribing every border guard he met on his way over the southern pass. Once he made it safely over the summit he approached the Thousand Steps with caution. The last traveler he met warned him that tensions were running high along the top of the steps.

A border guard drew her bow and nearly shot him. He held the pouch of silver over his head in surrender.

After accepting the bribe, the guard informed him that there had been recent skirmishes with members of the Saffron Way at the base of the steps. "They will cut you into ribbons by the time you reach the bottom," the guard warned.

Mavin thanked her and picked his way carefully down the crumbling steps, with growing anxiety he neared the bottom. Hesitated on the last step, he held his hands over his head and stepped out into the open.

"Who goes there?" a voice called out.

"Don't shoot, I'm a friend."

Two figures jumped out of the shadows and wrestled him to the ground. They bound his hands and dragged him until he managed to get to his feet.

"Where are you taking me?"

The woman holding the rope jerked it forward, causing him to fall face first.

"I have money," he offered.

This infuriated the woman holding the rope. She kicked him in the stomach, and once again dragged him until he was able to get back on his feet. They continued down the pass in the dark. "Are we nearing the lookout of Cloud's Rest?" Mavin asked. "I've hidden some seeds. It's very important that we find them."

A sharp pull of the rope was his only answer. He would have to escape and come back later for the emmer seeds he had hidden six winters before. Three days later, when they reached the banks of River Sky, a small fishing boat was waiting.

"Get in the boat, son of a man, or we will toss you in," the bigger of the two women said.

Mavin jumped in the boat and remained standing when they shoved off.

"I see you've been in a boat before," the big woman said. "Now, sit down."

"Where are you taking me?"

The woman at the oars stared at Mavin. "Downriver." The desperate look on her face disturbed him.

Mavin sat down and looked at the far bank in the fading light. "The village across the river is called Alrajpur. They know me. They will tell you who I am."

"No one lives in the Alrajpur valley any more," said the woman at the oars.

Mavin remembered the kindness of the poor villagers and fishermen when he made his first journey downriver with Simone. So much had changed. The world had gone mad.

When the first rays of the sun peeked over the Mercies the next morning, the woman at the oars steered them into an eddy and beached them on a wide sand bar. A stout, well-dressed woman in her thirties was waiting. She pushed off and jumped aboard taking a seat on the edge of the bench across from Mavin. "I am

Saba, of the House of Moloch. I will escort you to Mizurria."

"And, if I don't wish to go to Mizurria?" Mavin asked.

"Your wishes are not my concern," Saba replied.

"I've committed no crime. I'm a free man."

"No one is free or innocent in this world, Sri Mavin."

"You know who I am?"

The woman's thin lips went into the shape of a smile. "Every-one knows who you are." She drew a long thin dagger from her sleeve and cut the rope around his wrists. "Much has changed while you were in Kashphera." Saba felt the sharp tip of her dag-ger with her thumb. "There's been a great deal of death."

"I've noticed." Mavin rubbed his wrists and leaned forward, looking straight into Saba's eyes. "The death of respect, humility, and courtesy?"

"Watching your entire family die slowly from malnutrition has a way of changing one's priorities," Saba returned his stare.

"You don't look like you've missed many meals lately." Mavin gathered from her finely made cloak and the disdain that dripped from her every word that Saba was from a privileged background.

"You speak of respect and in the next breath you call me fat?" Saba absentmindedly brushed the dagger across her cheek. She closed her eyes and collected herself. *I would have been more in-sulted, had he mistaken me for a farmer,* she decided. "Even living in Kashphera, I'm sure you've heard the past few years have not been kind to the South, springs with no rain, followed by sum-mer floods, and bitter winters. Whole villages have been forced to move in hopes of finding a way to survive. Fishermen began keeping smaller and smaller fish. Now there are no fish to catch."

"And I'm somehow to blame?" Mavin wondered where all of this was going.

"We are on the brink of a war like the world has never known."

"Bad for business?" Mavin was having a hard time being lec-tured by the merchant class.

"The great Houses have done their best to stay neutral in the conflict." Saba explained. "The House of Merlas chose to become political and were abandoned by the Triumvirate."

Mavin had heard stories of Erica Merlas's head being chopped off on her balcony and thrown into the river. "I worked for Lady Merlas. Is that what this is about? I'm being thrown to the wolves for sprouting seeds?"

Saba slipped the dagger into her sleeve and clapped her hands in mock applause. "Bravo, Sri Mavin. Now, I understand how a foreign Jāti managed to become famous. Save your performance for Shax Moloch."

*Who is Shax Moloch?* he wondered. Was he being blamed for the seeds being switched? He doubted the seeds they brought from Svalbard were still viable. Regardless, there was enough food in Kashphera to export. To stand by and watch people starve was cruel beyond measure. There was plenty of blame to go around. He took a deep breath. "Have you heard of a Janjanbi named Simone Kita?"

Saba sliced her finger across her neck and smiled.

Mavin clenched his fist and thought about lunging for the gloating woman's throat. "If I find out that anything has happened to Simone, you better hope—"

"Save your threats for Shax Moloch."

Mavin didn't care for Saba's cat-that-just-ate-the-mouse smile.

*     *     *     *

The river was running low. As they neared the outskirts of Mizurria, mud flats stretched out on both sides of the river, making it impossible to reach any moorings. Stone mansions along the river began to appear. Armed guards were stationed behind makeshift ramparts at every gate and loading dock they passed. The dull cloudy morning added to the dead sheen on the water. Mavin caught whiffs of sewage in the stagnant air. The great stone steps in the heart of the city were marooned. Women carrying water vessels sunk up to their thighs in black mud trying to reach the water's edge. Of the few shikaras on the water, none were painted or had a shade awning. If there were important personages traveling to and fro, they were dressed in sackcloth.

Mavin was surprised when they made a right turn at the hub of the city. He involuntarily stood up as the woman at the oars steered them under the familiar arch. The boathouse was dank. The fresco, that had been half-submerged on his first visit to the House of Merlas, was a full set of steps above them.

Saba didn't bother to secure the line. "I believe you know the way. Shax Moloch is expecting you." A glutinous laugh escaped Saba's lips.

Anxious to see the last of the odious woman, Mavin jumped onto the landing and bounded up the steps that led to the inner courtyard. The absurdity of racing to meet his death checked his gait. The palace was empty. He was half-tempted to call out. He entered the foyer and thought of the woman in the lavender dress that first led him up the grand stairway. The plaster walls bore the outlines of where the oil paintings once hung. The lavish penthouse was bare. All the grand furnishings were gone. The doorway to the balcony framed a solitary figure dressed in black.

# Shax Moloch

What will the axemen do, when they have
cut their way from sea to sea?
—JAMES FENIMORE COOPER

Mavin's footsteps echoed off the marble as he crossed the bare room. The thick magenta carpet was gone, as was every trace of Erica Merlas. He wondered what it felt like to have your head cut off. *Will I still be conscious when my head hits the water?*

The man in black on the balcony turned.

It took a moment for Mavin's eyes to adjust to the light. He couldn't process what he was seeing.

"Welcome to the House of Moloch."

"Jai? What are you doing here?"

"I came to Mizurria especially to meet you, Sri Mavin."

"I don't understand. Where is Shax Moloch?"

Jai laughed. "He is here."

"You are Shax Moloch?"

"Ha ha! No, Sri Mavin, of course not." Jai beamed a smile.

Mavin grabbed the railing to steady himself. "Please, my friend, tell me everything."

"You remember your partner, the tinsmith, Vinita?" Jai began.

"I remember her well."

"You asked me to take care of your side of the partnership until your return. Do you not remember?"

"I said that to tease you, Jai. I didn't think very much would come of a teapot cap."

Jai looked momentarily confused. "In your absence, Sri Mavin, we hired five apprentices to make your whistling teapot caps,
and then five more to make your spiral cap water bags, and another five to make your wheeled carts. We reinvested the money
from selling the three treasures, and hired five more apprentices,
and then five more. The first year we sold thousands of your inventions. When the House of Merlas became vulnerable, we
bought the Merlas Gardens. The following year Lady Merlas
was unable to cover her debts. We acquired all of her holdings,
including this palace."

"Who is Shax Moloch?"

"You are, Sri Mavin," Jai said gleefully.

Mavin was confused. "You're misinformed. I've been living in
Kashphera for the last six years."

"If the Great Houses knew who Vinita and I were, they
would have cut our throats and taken everything for themselves.
We thought of the most frightening name we could think of—
Shax Moloch. We invented stories how Shax Moloch murdered
anyone who stood in his way," Jai explained.

Mavin took a moment to let what Jai was saying sink in. "How
is your mother, Zia?"

Jai's exuberant smiled disappeared. "She became sick and
died the year you traveled upriver."

"I'm so sorry, my friend. She was a great woman."

"Thank you, Sri Mavin." Jai bit his lower lip and tried to
smile. He dug in his pocket and handed Mavin a copper cap.
"This is the first whistling tea cap that you made for my mother.
She would want you to have it."

"Thank you, Jai." Mavin could see tears welling in the young
man's eyes. He was no older than twenty when they met, now
there was grey in Jai's hair and his face was lined with worry.
"It's good to see you again, my friend. Thank you for buying me
a palace, but—" He looked at the small brass cap and sobbed. "I

don't know what to say." He squeezed the tea cap tight and shook it for emphasis. "This ... this, I will keep."

Jai turned and looked out over the water.

"What happened to Lady Merlas?" Mavin wondered if the story was true.

"Most of the leaders of the Great Houses have fled to Kashphera. As you know, it takes money to bribe your way into and out of the high country. The merchants and the Triumvirate are content to stand by and watch as the people starve."

"It is wicked and cruel." A long silence followed Mavin's statement. "Have you heard of a Janjanbi named Simone Kita?"

"I'm sorry, Sri Mavin. I know of no such person."

Mavin looked out over the water. He refused to believe she was dead. "I heard that Shax Moloch chopped Lady Merlas's head off on this very balcony."

"Fear not, Sri Mavin. That is only a fanciful story we invented to boost the reputation of Shax Moloch."

Mavin remembered Saba drawing her finger across her throat like a dagger and smiling. "Does Saba work for you?"

"Saba was the leader of the House of Azra," Jai explained. "We occasionally hire her to act on our behalf. She is not to be fully trusted."

"Why didn't you come upriver to meet me? Years ago I hid a small handful of wild emmer seeds near the Thousand Steps. It's very important that we return and find those seeds. You have no idea how much trouble Saba and her thugs have caused."

"I'm sorry, Sri Mavin. It's very dangerous to travel upriver."

"I need to get out of here." Mavin's breath raced.

"We are quite secure in the palace. However, if you don't wish to stay, it would be best for us to wait until after dark. Once we are back in Jamurra, we'll be safe."

Just after midnight, Mavin climbed in the back of a shikara and Jai unfastened the lines.

"I'll paddle, Sri Mavin."

"No, please, let me."

Jai was amazed how quick and smooth the shikara glided over the water. "Sri Mavin," Jai whispered. "You master everything you try. Please slow down or you will draw attention to us." Jai laughed. "Never mind. No one will believe that you're not a shikara driver."

"Jai?"

"Yes, Sri Mavin."

"Will there be war?"

"No." The young man sat in the bow and looked into the darkness. "The war has already begun."

# The Saffron Way

The story of a tree is written on every leaf.
—Martin Rubin

When they reached the large wooden gate to the gardens, four women with saffron armbands were standing guard.

"Jai, what are they doing here?"

"Come, Sri Mavin, I want to show you your gardens." Jai's enthusiasm overpowered Mavin's disapproval.

"Why do you keep saying my gardens?" After being beaten and held captive, it was distressing to pass the armed women guarding the gate.

"As I told you last night," Jai explained. "Vinita and I purchased the gardens from the House of Merlas."

Mavin could see dozens of women in saffron armbands going in and out of several large barns. Mavin didn't remember the buildings. "You are a difficult man, Jai."

"Sri Mavin?" Jai's smile faded.

"You are a difficult man, to disagree with."

Jai paused and thought it through. "Oh, thank you, Sri Mavin."

"Before we go any further, Jai. Tell me the truth. Have you been supporting the Saffron Way?"

"Sri Mavin, come and see how we are making your fine inventions."

Mavin clenched his fists. Despite his every precaution, his worst nightmare had come true. "Have you used money from my inventions to harm people?"

"Sri Mavin, you are over-reacting. Jamurra is suffering the worst famine in memory. You saw yourself how the rice and wheat plants die. Most of these people have lost everything. They are the only survivors of their families. They were roaming the countryside, stealing and resorting to violence just to stay alive. We have given them food, work, and a safe place to live."

"Jai. I need a straight answer."

"We make whistling teapots and wheeled carts. Have people died? Yes, tens of thousands. My own family is gone. All dead." Jai was shaking and tears were running down his cheeks. "What would you like me to say? Do you wish me to tell you that I am innocent?"

Mavin felt the burden of the end of the world. It never left him. Was it his fault? It didn't matter. To feel innocent again would be the greatest gift of all. "I'm sorry, Jai. We'll talk about this later. Take me to Vinita. I want to see everything."

"Vinita passed from this world last year."

"I'm so sorry, my friend."

Jai slid open the barn door. Dozens of workers were busy at their stations cutting handles, fashioning wheels, and assembling wooden wheelbarrows. "Vinita wanted to show you all that you have accomplished."

"You, Vinita, and all your workers have created this. I've done nothing."

"You are too modest, Sri Mavin."

# The Point of No Return

What we are doing to the forest of the world is but a mirror
reflection of what we are doing to ourselves and to one another.
—MAHATMA GANDHI

Despite Jai's assurances, Mavin wasn't comfortable being near the women with the saffron armbands. He wasn't sure if it was from the beating he had taken near the Thousand Steps, or the feeling he couldn't shake, that funds from the sales of his inventions were being used for political purposes. After a sleepless night, he was ready to leave.

"Perhaps you would be more comfortable at your palace, Sri Mavin?" Jai suggested.

"I don't mean to sound ungrateful, Jai, but I don't have much use for a palace."

"I understand. Do you need anything?"

It made Mavin crazy to be around the overly helpful young man. "I'm fine, Jai. Please don't fuss. Just do whatever you normally do. I'd like to roam around for the rest of the day and take everything in."

"Are you sure, Sri Mavin?"

"Quite sure."

Mavin was relieved when Jai became engrossed with a worker complaining that the wood being used for the wheel axles was too soft. He took the opportunity to slip out the back entrance. He found a saffron band hanging on a fence post and tied it around his left bicep.

He walked to the river where workers were unloading bundles of wooden slats from a barge. He joined in, keeping to himself. He spent the day working and listening.

By evening he had gleaned that the forces of the Saffron Way had pushed north, all the way to Swan's Ford. The snows were melting late. When the spring runoff was over, they would cross the river on their way to the northern pass to Kashphera. Once the northern pass was sealed, the Triumvirate would eventually fall.

The following morning, Mavin told Jai that he had changed his mind and would like to spend some time at his palace. Jai ordered bedding and food to be loaded in the shikara. "Are you sure you want to row the boat yourself, Sri Mavin?"

"You don't believe I'm capable?"

"Of course not, Sri Mavin. My apologies. I'll come with you?"

"I need some time alone, Jai. Thank you for everything. I'll see you very soon." Mavin was grateful for the sleek shikara. Even loaded with supplies, she felt light as a feather and handled like a dream. The light flow of the wide river made for easy paddling. The following evening, he passed through the city of Mizurria and continued upriver. The next morning, he realized that his Saffron armband rendered him invisible. Within a week, he mastered the nearly imperceptible nod that the river guides and fisherman used.

He was not alone, Simone accompanied him upriver. He spoke with her all day, asking her which roots were edible or what leaves made the best tea. With her help, it was easy to find enough to eat along the riverbanks. The golden sand in the shallows tricked his eyes. He imagined Simone's naked form gliding beneath the surface. He stared into the sun's reflection, expecting her to emerge from under the waves, and flip her long black hair over her shoulders.

He spied an old man fishing from the bank and traded his wool blanket for a fishing net and a hand line. Before dusk, he beached the shikara, pulling the boat into the thick brush to hide. He slept in the boat under the stars and thought of Iris and her blue shikara. "I hope you are well, Auntie, wherever you are."

All he knew was that he needed to reach Swan's Ford. His watery journey somehow reminded him of setting out into the desert with his grandfather as a boy. He asked TwoBeers, "Where are we going?" His grandfather proudly replied, "I have no fucking idea."

Mavin neared the ford with caution. He beached the shikara in a thicket and was immediately surrounded by a group of fighters, all wearing saffron armbands. He asked to see the person in charge, claiming he had news from Shax Moloch. He was wrestled to the ground; a knife jabbed between his shoulder blades.

"Easy with that!" Mavin got to his feet and struggled to stay ahead of the tip of the blade. As evening fell, they walked through the camp of makeshift tents. "Why would I be here if I wasn't a friend?" he asked his guards. Hundreds of campfires on the opposite riverbank reflected off the water. Mavin didn't believe there were so many people left in the world. The host on the other side of the river spread out for miles. He thought about the destructive force bottled in a single hydrogen bomb. Walking along the river he felt the looming battle, the cycle of destruction repeating over, again and again. From where did the destructive energy come?

He remembered the cave paintings depicting all life. The clouds and the yellow lightning bolt. He imagined how terrified the early ancestors must have been by a thunderclap, peering into the heavens in sheer terror. *If only the thing too dark and terrible to give a name was somewhere up there, out of reach.* If only it were so.

An hour later, they reached a heavily guarded tent that sat on a rise overlooking the shallow bend in the river.

The guard pulled the tent flap open and pushed Mavin inside. "We caught this Bideshi spy near the south bend in the river," the guard reported. "He claims to have news from Shax Moloch."

A large figure was hunched over a map with yellow pins stuck in it. Hester turned. "Raven! I don't believe it. You're alive."

"Hester. You're a sight for sore eyes!" Mavin was equally re-lieved and confused.

"It's so good to see you." Hester slapped Mavin on both shoul-ders and patted his smooth cheeks for good measure. "Where the devil have you been all of these years? Still no beard?"

"I've been living in Kashphera."

"It's amazing they let you go. Did you escape prison or did you rat us out?" Hester saw a flash of hatred cross Mavin's face. "Easy, Raven. I'm teasing."

"Where's Simone?" Mavin's tone was hard.

"I haven't seen the little Sparrow in years," Hester said with a little too much gaiety. He poured them both a cup of cold tea. "Years ago, after that bitch Sabina betrayed us, Melky, Jacoby, and I escaped. We ran into Sparrow on the way to rescue the priestess. We fled over the Northern Pass. I still can't feel my big toes. We made it to Nabhi, where a wicked Janjanbi, named Al-thea, was running the show. Simone and the White Crane made quick work of her."

"How do you mean?"

"Sparrow accused Althea of poisoning Leto. The White Crane gave Althea a choice: she could tell the truth or drink the Soma. Althea vanished during the middle of the night. The Crane priestess wrote a letter to the High Council explaining everything that happened, how mercenaries masqueraded as Jara had ambushed Leto. When the plot failed, Althea poisoned Leto."

"What happened to the letter?"

"Sparrow set off alone to Kashphera to deliver the letter to the High Council. I warned her that it was madness."

"You let her go alone?" Mavin lost his temper. "Althea was probably working for Sabina and for all we know, the High Council."

"Easy, Raven, let me explain. The White Priestess suspected the Merc at the time, not that it matters now."

"The hell it doesn't! I can't believe you let Simone return to Kashphera by herself." Mavin felt a knot in his stomach.

"We tried to stop her. Sparrow insisted on going back to clear the Jara of any wrongdoing. But, we all knew the real reason." Hester regretted the words as soon as he said them.

"What do you mean, the real reason?"

Hester couldn't bring himself to say it.

"I never heard a whisper, not even a rumor." Mavin closed his eyes and shook his head. "What could have happened to her?" It had been six long years. He couldn't believe she was dead.

"I'm truly sorry, Mavin. I told her it was madness to go back. You know how she could be." Hester didn't mean to use the past tense.

"So the White Crane priestess never returned to Avighna?"

"As far as I know, she has not left Nabhi. Why?"

"The Triumvirate must have found a young woman who looks very much like the Lady of Avighna. I heard people in the market talk about seeing the White Crane at the equinox festivals."

Hester put his hand on Mavin's shoulder. "For what it's worth, Mavin, you won our wager fair and square. The little Sparrow was impossible, but just as you said, she saved my life and proved her worth time and time again." Hester stared at the map on the table and traced the line over the southern pass. He remembered Sparrow hiding her smile behind the teacup the day she accepted him as her equal. She taught him the strength and the power of humility.

"Six years without a word," Mavin whispered. If she had made it to Kashphera, he would have been easy enough to find at Farzana's. He couldn't believe she was gone.

"You need sleep, my friend. Jacoby will find you an empty cot. We'll talk in the morning." Hester remembered that same look in Simone's eyes when she set off to Kashphera.

"Hester. Are you the leader of the Saffron Way?"

"Ha! Good one, Raven! Thankfully no."

"If you're not the leader of this insanity, then who is?"

"A canny old bird they call the Kukkura."

"The Hen?"

"Yes." Hester clucked, unable to help himself.

"This hardly seems your fight, helping a bunch of farmers." Mavin wanted answers. "I thought you hated southerners?"

"Sparrow gave me a gift that changed everything."

"What gift?" Mavin wondered what Simone had that Hester would want.

"She gave me the gift we give ourselves."

"I want to hear all about it, but first I need to speak with this Kukkura?"

"Not as badly as I do." Hester thumped the map on the table.

"Where is she?"

"She's infamous, but I've yet to clamp eyes on her. She's very secretive."

"This is starting to sound familiar." Mavin began to fit the pieces together.

"What do you mean, Raven?"

"If I didn't know better…. I would say this Kukkura is vintage Jai."

"Jai Rey?"

"You know him? Why am I not surprised?" Mavin's blood began to boil.

Hester's face lit up. "Jai often delivers messages from the Kukkura."

"Of course he does. Something smells of fish."

"You're saying this Kukkura is not all she claims to be?" Hester didn't like where this was going.

"Worse, I'm afraid. The Kukkura is Nemo, No One."

"I'm not following you, Raven. We are about to go to war. Thousands are about to die."

"You have to call off the battle."

"You forget so soon? I'm a man. Even worse, I'm Jara. I know the country across the river and the northern pass. If the Saffron Way didn't need my help, I doubt they would put up with me at all."

"They have a point."

Hester laughed, breaking the tension. "Look, Mavin, unless the Merc herself wades into the middle of the river and falls on her sword in broad daylight—nothing on this earth will stop the inevitable. When the river drops in the next few days, and it's possible to cross the ford, there's going to be a battle unlike this world has ever known. Thousands will die in the first volley of arrows. The river will run red."

Mavin couldn't sleep. He sat by a dying fire and watched the wind fan the coals. His body was bone tired, but his mind reeled. He thought of the three treasures, as Jai called them. How could a whistling tea cap be responsible for the giant host sleeping all around him? Could the fate of the world turn on something so small?

If Jai was the true leader of the Saffron Way, maybe he really did cut off Erica Merlas's head, just like the story? Like young Prince Dakkar, Jai's whole family had died right in front of him. Like Nemo, Jai's pain and suffering twisted him to take revenge. Whatever the truth was, he found it impossible to think of Jai as evil. "If you're indeed responsible for the war, my friend, it's not my place to condemn you."

He looked across the wide river at the hundreds of campfires. If the people of Kashphera were the enemy, he was at a loss as to why. The sky was thick with stars, tiny seeds of light. Mars was near Antares, the brightest star of Scorpius. It was too late to place the blame on Mars, or any celestial gods or goddesses. The instinctual urge to self-eradicate was as much a part of the human soul as the urge to wonder.

# Even A Fool Knows

Everyday, precious, while m'm'ry's leaves are falling…
—JAMES JOYCE

There were no sentries guarding the camp opposite the river. Mavin set out before first light and headed west to the valley where Simone grew up. He wasn't convinced she was dead. There was still a slim chance she was locked away in a cell somewhere in Kashphera. He wouldn't put anything past the Merc.

He walked through the heat of the midday sun, sinking further into dread. He was ashamed for feeling sorry for himself, but he couldn't shake the despair. His feet were heavy. Despite his efforts to keep the past a secret, his worst fears were becoming reality. It would have been better if he had died under the mountain. *Why carry on?*

Saudhra was much further than he remembered. He was out of practice walking all day without food or water. "Pay attention to your feet," he heard her say. "I wish you had taught me the Way of Balance," he told her. A gust of wind blew sand in his eyes. "I should have told you," he said to the wind. He convinced himself that it would have driven her away. Now he would never know. He felt her beside him and reached for her hand, interlocking his fingers with hers. "I love you," he said without turning to look.

"Get up, asshole," TwoBeers interrupted.

Mavin's mind went blank. He desperately tried to recall what he was saying before the interruption.

"Get up!"

"Go away, old man!" Mavin was angry at not being able to recall his thoughts. "Why are you always interfering?"

"I thought you were going to do something with your life, grandson, now look at you."

"I'm not a child. You can't talk to me this way."

"If you want to lie there and become a pile of dried bones, I can't stop you."

"What are you babbling on about?" Mavin lifted his arm off the hot ground to shoo away the ghost. He was lying flat on his stomach. He spit the dirt out of his mouth. It coated his tongue. He rolled over on his back and shielded his eyes from the sun.

"Go ahead and say something, wise-ass," TwoBeers taunted.

Mavin got to his knees and managed to stand on shaky legs. He stumbled forward, holding his hands against his ears to block out the voices in his head. "You know what they say? Don't judge a man by his relatives."

"Ha ha!" TwoBeers shook with laughter. "I'm gonna use that next time I see Latigo."

"I was just telling Simone something. What was it?" It scared him that he had fallen down and nearly died without being aware of it. He slapped himself across the face and stumbled forward. "It's perfect," Mavin said to the spirit of his grandfather. "Here I am, walking away from the fight, like the coward I am." He felt a moment of panic, terrified that he would be the only person left alive in the world. *Anything but that!* "Why didn't you let me sleep? Go away and leave me alone!"

"You walked away from your land and your people," the old man said in disgust. "But sooner or later, Grandson, you're going to have to be a man and come face to face with yourself."

A thick fog rolled over the hills deepening Mavin's delirium. He wandered into a gully and lost all sense of direction. "Is this the way to Saudhra?"

"Why do you want to go there?" TwoBeers asked.

"Just tell me, is this the way?"

"You're right where you are supposed to be. Even a fool knows that much about their life."

Mavin had heard enough; he lunged at the ghost. His arms tangled in the soft boughs of a tree. He looked up. The tree disappeared high into the mist. "It can't be!" There was another tall tree beside it, and another. The whole meadow was chock-full of young redwoods. He remembered that a sequoia grew forty feet high in less than a decade. The new green growth on the edge of the limbs was soft as a baby's little fingers. He ran wildly through the maze of trees. "They sprouted!" He remembered the old legend Simone had told him. The trees vowed to each other that they would never again grow higher than man's shoulders to punish men for their wickedness. He ran screaming through the fog, "You sprouted!" He stumbled and rolled on the wet grass.

The silhouette of a tall woman came out of the mist. "Simone? Is that you?" As she drew closer, Mavin recognized the crimson robes. "The Merc!" he gasped. His heart pounded in his ears. He had walked right into a trap. He wanted to get up and run, but his legs were paralyzed with fear.

As the figure in red drew near, he saw the glint of a blade in her hand. His body shook. She raised her knife and was upon him. He closed his eyes and felt sweet relief.

She drew back her hood and knelt down to be sure. "Mavin?"

He felt her sweet breath and opened his eyes. "You're not dead."

She looked in his eyes and without thinking, kissed him.

"I thought you were the Merc," he confessed.

They held each other for a long time. She gave him a drink of water and stroked his hair. "No, I'm not dead, but I am the Merc." She unbuttoned her red robe and spread it out over the wet grass. She stood naked in the fog, trembling. "I understand you're the one responsible for these trees." She gestured around at the green forest and then pointed an accusing finger. "What have you to say for yourself?"

"You must believe me, I had help."

"Silence! Enough of your tall tree tales. It's high time you were held accountable for your actions."

When they fell together, the weight of the world lifted. For the first time, Mavin wasn't between worlds. Wave after wave of pleasure gave way to imperatives beyond desire. Time didn't move, it was the still point, everything else motion. Steam rose from their bodies and mingled through the soft boughs.

Simone awoke and pressed her cheek against his shoulder, smelling his skin before gently lifting his arm.

Mavin felt her stir. "We're going to have a baby," he announced. "A girl."

"Oh, is that so?" A high giggle escaped her red lips. "And what will we call our daughter?"

"Iris."

"Why Iris? An old girlfriend?" she teased.

"No. One of my mothers," he said proudly.

His reply startled her. She knew she was not the same person he had met under the mountain. Now it was clear, she wasn't the only one who had changed. "Iris is a wonderful name." She squeezed his hand and let go. Time was of the essence. She buttoned up her robe.

"Are you really the Merc?" He caressed her hair.

"When Colonel Bina finally read the letter written by the White Crane, she became my staunch ally. Bina let me out of prison and supported my efforts to restore balance to the Triumvirate."

"What do you mean, when Bina finally read the letter? Where have you been all these years?"

"I'll explain everything later, Mavin."

"What about the seeds we brought back from Svalbard? Do you know where they are?"

"Yes. They're safe in Kashphera. I promise very soon we will plant them and they will grow, like your tall trees."

He suddenly panicked. "You know that the Saffron Way is not your enemy?"

"Yes, I know. Don't worry." She leaned down and kissed him. "I'm sorry, Mavin there isn't time to explain. I have to go."

"I'm coming with you. We have to get back to Swan's Ford before the river drops."

"I'm tracking a very dangerous man. He is the key to stopping the war. You need to trust me, Mavin. Promise me you'll stay in our grove of trees until I return."

"What man? What's his name?"

"Shax Moloch." She didn't understand the look on Mavin's face. "What is it? Is something funny?" She knelt down and looked in his eyes. "You know something. Tell me."

"I'll tell you, Simone, but you have to promise to wait until I'm finished before you—"

"Tell me!"

"I'll tell you, but first promise to—"

She rolled him on his back, pinning her knees on his arms. "Tell me, Mavin! This is serious."

"Hey, that hurts." He couldn't stop laughing.

"Tell me!"

"I'm Shax Moloch."

Catching her off guard, he pressed his advantage. "Now it's time the world learned your true identity. Little Fatty!"

# About the Author

Mark Daniel Seiler is a writer, poet, and musician who lives on the island of Kaua`i. His debut novel, *Sighing Woman Tea* was a winner at the Pacific Rim Book Festival 2015 and was nominated for the *Kirkus* Prize. Mark's second novel, *River's Child* was recently awarded the Landmark Prize for fiction. He is currently working on a murder mystery set in Hawaii. Mark worked alongside Masters from Japan and Taiwan to build the Hall of Compassion in the Lawai Valley. He describes himself as a life-long learner, who got a very late start.

Visit Mark at www.sighingwomanteas.com

# OWL HOUSE BOOKS

## SCI-FI · FANTASY · MYSTERY · THRILLER

### RETURNING TO OUR STORYTELLING ROOTS

Owl House Books is an imprint of Homebound Publications specializing in genre fiction (science fiction, fantasy, mystery, and thriller.) Myth and mystery have haunted and shaped us since the dawn of language, giving wing and fleshy form to the archetypes of our imagination. As our past was spent around the fire listening to myths and the sounds of the night, so were our childhoods spent getting lost in the tangled branches of fables. Through our titles, we hope to return to these storytelling roots.

**WWW.OWLHOUSEBOOKS.COM**

CPSIA information can be obtained
at www.ICGtesting.com
Printed in the USA
LVOW03s1058220318
570743LV00001B/7/P